The King Behind the King

by
Warwick Deeping

Double9
BOOKS

The King Behind the King
by Warwick Deeping

ISBN: 978-93-62761-39-2

Published by

DOUBLE 9 BOOKS

2/13-B, Ansari Road
Daryaganj, New Delhi – 110002
info@double9books.com
www.double9books.com
Tel. 011-40042856

ABOUT THE AUTHOR

George Warwick Deeping, an English novelist and short story writer, was best known for his work Sorrell and Son (1925). Warwick Deeping was born in Southend-on-Sea, Essex, to a family of physicians and attended Merchant Taylors' School. He went to Trinity College, Cambridge, to study medicine and science, then to Middlesex Hospital to complete his medical education. During World War I, he served in the Royal Army Medical Corps. Deeping later left his position as a physician to become a full-time writer. He married Phyllis Maude Merrill and spent the rest of his life at "Eastlands" on Brooklands Road, Weybridge, Surrey. He was a best-selling author in the 1920s and 1930s, with seven of his novels reaching the bestseller list. Deeping was a prolific short story writer whose work published in British journals such as Cassell's, The Storyteller, and The Strand. He also wrote fiction for various US periodicals, including The Saturday Evening Post and Adventure. All of the short stories and serialized novels in American publications were reprints of works originally published in Britain. More than 200 of his original short tales and essays, which appeared in various British fiction journals, were never published in book form during his lifetime.

CONTENTS

CHAPTER I

Fulk of the Forest had taken the way towards Witch's Cross, with the full moon shining like a silver buckler behind him, to find himself standing at gaze among the yews of the Black Gill.

Straight before him stretched a black aisle pillared and arched with huge yews. The aisle ended, like the choir of a church, in a great woodland window where the full moon hung, one yellow rim touching a flurry of clouds. Fulk had drawn aside against the trunk of a tree, lean, alert, shadowy, conscious of something stirring away yonder in the glooms.

As he stood there watching, and straining his ears in the windless silence of the April night, he saw a figure move suddenly into the opening of this woodland window and remain there, outlined against the moon. The figure was wrapped in a loose cloak, and the peak and jagged edge of a hood showed up sharply. Moreover, a curved black line beside it betrayed the line of a strung bow.

Fulk's sinews were as taut as lute cords. Here was a blessed chance sent after many nights of grim watching and waiting for certain elusive rascals who had been slaying my Lord of Lancaster's deer. He began to move like a cat, slowly, sinuously, with a queer trailing action of the legs, slipping from tree to tree. The yews had dropped no dead wood; the turf was soft and sleek, and Fulk moved as silently as an owl flitting down a hedgerow.

The figure with the bow stood above him on a low bank where the yews ended and the fern and gorse began. It was motionless save for a slight turning of the head from side to side, and wholly intent upon scanning the heath beyond. Fulk drew a deep breath, gathered himself, and sprang.

The figure whipped round with a sharp cry. A wave of Fulk's arm knocked aside the stabbing point of the horn end of the bow. The two black shapes grappled, one striving to break away, the other to hold its quarry. Someone's foot slipped in a rabbit hole, and the two came down the bank in a tangle into the dense shade under the yews.

A cloud came over the moon, and out yonder a fat hart had risen and was galloping over the heath. Fulk, on top in the tussle, had a grip of a wrist whose hand had darted for a girdle knife. The figure under him ceased to struggle.

"Caught, you lousel!"

The voice that answered him had a fine edge of anger.

"Let me go, you clown. Have you no more wit than— —"

Fulk sprang back and up.

"What!"

"Fool, let me but get my knife."

"Blood of St. Thomas—a woman!"

CHAPTER II

A woman it was, and a very angry one at that: breathless, a little frightened, yet whole-heartedly defiant. She sat up, feeling her throat that had felt the grip of Fulk's fingers, and looking about her in the darkness for the bow she had dropped in the scuffle.

Fulk had his foot on it, and since it would bear witness against her at the swainmote, and might be dangerous if left too near an angry woman's hand, he picked it up and broke it across his knee. Moreover, he was as angry as she was, but with the cold, dry anger of a man who could not wholly escape from feeling a fool. It was so dark under the yews that he could see next to nothing of the creature that he had captured, nor could he tell whether she was young or old, mean or gentle.

She half lay against the bank, making a little moaning sound, one hand clutching the hilt of the knife at her girdle. Her eyes were two great black circles, her lips thin with scorn and pain. Fulk stood and waited, wondering who the devil the woman might be and whether he had handled her very roughly.

She did not speak for awhile, but lay there like a snake in the grass, ready to strike at him with the naked steel. Neither of them moved. The moon came from behind a cloud, and a stroke of light slashed the woman's figure and glimmered on the blade of the knife.

Fulk saw it, and for the moment it stabbed a half contemptuous pity into him.

"You can put away that bodkin. How was I to know?" he shrugged laconically. "Seven deer lost in three weeks. The forest's full of rogues and trailbastons, and folk who go out with bows by moonlight——"

She put the knife back into its sheath, and shook her hood back from her shoulders.

"Your fingers bit like the teeth of a dog. For being a clown and a fool, you can let me go, just where I desire."

Her touch was a little imperious, and it was hawk hovering against hawk.

"It is three miles to the White Lodge. The swainmote court is held after the next new moon."

"My friend, I shall not be there."

"Good lady, I judge you will."

He saw her give an angry flirt of the head.

"By my troth, to be pulled down by a Sussex badger and rolled on the grass! Pah! What manner of clown are you to stand there and talk of the swainmote?"

He grew the colder as she grew the more fierce.

"I am Lord of the Deer."

She laughed and clapped her hands together.

"Listen to the lousel! Lord of the Deer! Lord of the Swine more likely. Now, Sir Legion, old Roger Ferrers is master of this forest, and you——"

He cut her short, chin in air.

"Roger Ferrers has gone with the duke to bargain with the Scots. Fulk Ferrers, the duke's riding forester, lords it here. I am he. Come, let's have no more scuffling—even with words."

She sprang up suddenly.

"The riding forester! Messire Fulk Ferrers! Good, very good! Messire Fulk, I make you a curtsy. Maybe, you can tell the slot of a deer from the hoof-mark of a mule, even if you cannot tell a man from a woman. Messire Fulk, since you are gentle born, I will dare to wish you good-night."

"You can wish me with the devil, madam, but it will be good-morrow in the White Lodge over yonder. Am I a fool?"

"Oh—well, but not a gallant fool! You will let me go?"

"No."

"Yes."

"I said nay to you."

"So have better men before now—and repented of it."

He was challenged, despite his boyish shrewdness, by a laughing audacity in the woman's voice. Her meek mood was no more than spilt milk. She walked beside him with a swinging motion and an air of provocative insolence, and though her face was a mere grey blur he could imagine a curling of the lips and a gleaming of the eyes.

"I have said nay. Let it stand. As a matter of gossip I'll ask you why I should let you go?"

"Only a fool would ask that!"

"Dub me a fool."

"Because I am a woman—and I ask it."

He laughed ironically, not looking at her but away over the heath.

"Put that in your girdle with your knife. A woman is no more than a man to me when I cherish the deer."

She swung closer, and her voice changed to a mischievous, pleading whisper.

"Ah, but Messire Fulk, listen a moment."

"You may find the verderers more easily cozened when the swainmote meets."

"Good sir, how young you are!"

"Younger than an old fool, perhaps."

"Be careful. It is the young fools who boast."

She became ominously mute and docile of a sudden, and, turning from him, walked out slowly from under the shadow of the yews. Fulk went with her, step for step. She paused where the heathland began, and even as she paused the moon began to disappear behind a black drift of clouds.

"Wretch—traitor moon! Look!"

Fulk looked at the sky when she had meant him to look at her.

"What's amiss with the moon?"

She gave him a significant side-glance, lids half closed, eyes glimmering.

"It is so dark again. Ah, Messire Fulk, you may not see me until to-morrow."

"There is light enough for me to see you safe to the White Lodge."

"Only the shadow of me. Look, now, am I young or old? Oh, come, be gallant!"

He stalked along beside her, lean, powerful, agile, old for his age, which was two-and-twenty, very sure of himself, and more than a little mistrustful of women. A vast silence possessed the night, save for the occasional rustling of the wind in the withered fern. The horizon was the edge of an upturned silver bowl powdered with faint stars. Scattered clouds drifted. Down in the bottoms white mists had gathered, and the woods looked black and cold, and grim. Westwards, about a furlong away, the Ghost Oak stood out on the ridge of a hill, showing like the antlered head of some huge hart.

If he had any curiosity as to his companion's age, looks, name, and degree, Fulk hid that curiosity very creditably. Her voice was neither the voice of an old woman nor of a mere strolling wench, and he noticed that she was slim, and that she held herself like a young girl who had never laboured nor carried burdens nor borne a child. But his hardihood did not flatter her by betraying any consciousness of the eternal mystery of the creature that walked at his side.

She gave a shrug of piqued resignation.

"How monstrous solemn for one so young! Good Master Fulk, you take life and yourself and the deer most seriously. Now, supposing you catechise me. Who am I? Whence have I come? Whither shall I go? Or am I a mere she-ass to be led at the end of a rope?"

His face remained a profile to her.

"Who are you?"

"Ah—we advance! I am neither an abbess nor a great lady, nor a dragonfly nor a windhover. I am something of everything. I can shoot with the bow, dance, sing, play the lute, stab a man for insolence, tell lies, laugh, run like a boy. Guess!"

"I am not good at guessing. Tell the plain truth, or wait till the morning."

She looked at him, and then at the sky where the edge of the moon was swimming clear of a cloud. She smiled to herself, and then touched Fulk's elbow.

"See, the moon is coming out. You can see the shine in my eyes."

Pausing abruptly, she put her hood well back, and stood as though determined to provoke him into taking her challenge. Fulk swung round as the moon cleared the cloud, and saw her white face claiming him as a regarder. Her hair, black as charcoal, was fastened up in a net of some silvery stuff that shone like gossamer on a hedgerow. It was a face of ivory—clear, keen, with eyes that glimmered under straight, black eyebrows. The mouth was long, mobile, audacious. The nose, slightly curved at the bridge, had proud, fine-spirited nostrils. It was a face that could be fierce, contemptuous, yet passionately eager, heroic, wicked, adorable by turns. She held herself as though she could hold the whole world at her service, and had never found herself in a mood to be mastered by any man.

Fulk stared—beyond his expectations. Something flashed a subtle provocation before him, menacingly, temptingly. The chin in air was railing and audacious. The dark eyes glittered at his grave face.

"Am I young or old?"

"I can see no wrinkles by this light."

"Fair to behold and beholden to no man. I have made fools of them by the score—yes, I! Isoult of the Rose. I go where I please and when I please, and no man has my heart. I am desired—and I desire not. I ask, and am obeyed. Go to, now; you will grant me my desire?"

"To go where you please?"

"Even so."

He looked at her steadily, as though holding his manhood to the flame of her audacious comeliness.

"It is to be where—I please."

"So you say."

"And so I mean."

Her eyes pressed his as one sword presses on another.

"So! The boy is not to be cozened?"

"I have been very patient."

"Patient! Honey and wine—patient! Jack Frost in doublet and hose!"

She laughed, scanned his face with some quickening of her audacity, and drew her hood forward again, consenting to realise that he would abide by his words. Her resignation was frank and confident, the resignation of a fearless spirit whose blood flowed too hotly for little malicious and peevish impulses to live in it. She had a shrewd instinct for the worth of a man's word, seeing that life and her own heart had taught her the saying, "There is no man whom I cannot fool."

"Let us see the White Lodge, Messire Fulk. I am growing hungry."

She caught the rapid side-glance he gave her as they moved on together over the heath. Her sudden surrender had made him suspicious, so that he held his head high and nosed the air like a stag to get wind of an ambuscado.

"I play fair," she said; "the game is yours—to-night."

His eyes were sweeping the heath.

"There may be more than one jay in the wood."

"There was but one to-night; but to-morrow, or the next day——"

She broke off with suggestive abruptness, and walked on at his side with a casual complaisance, holding her head high, and watching him at her leisure. She marked the set of his shoulders, and the way he carried his head, as though he lived a hawk's life, looking ever into the distance, alert, part of the wild. He swung along with sweeping strides, the action of a man who could run like a deer, not the busy strut of the townsman. Now and again his profile was sharply outlined for her—a straight, stark profile with firm lips and a thrustful chin.

Presently she began to murmur a song, and the murmur grew into idle, irresponsible singing. She sang in an inward, dreamy voice, the notes flowing out smoothly like water from a marble conduit. It was a rich voice, capable of a delicious flux of sound, subtle, promising many emotions. Fulk kept his guard, though she sang as though it was as natural for her to sing as to breathe. This voice of hers might bring him adventures, brisk blows, and a sore head.

"Sing," said he; "sing as you please. But if you sing any rascal within reach of this short sword of mine he'll not bless your music."

"I sing to please myself, good sir. Listen:

"The bed cover was of purple cloth,

All powdered with golden lilies.

The maid's hair was the colour of gold

And violets and roses were strewn around.

The windows were of finest glass,

Painted with red hearts and silver crowns,

And the scent of her chamber was as the scent of May.

"Good words, Master Fulk—hey?"

"Why sing about maids with golden hair? And roses and violets don't bloom together. Make a song about a hawk, or a bow, or a sword."

"Some day, if it please you, I will sing of the sword, and perhaps of a broomstick. Raw apples should not grumble at sugar."

Below them in a little valley between oak woods the White Lodge showed up under the moon. It was a great, low house of black beams and white plaster, thatched so thickly with heather that the shaggy eaves were two feet thick. The White Lodge lay in the lap of a narrow meadow, with stables, barns, and outbuildings clustered behind it, their steep roofs, black ridged, looking like the roofs of a little town. The oak woods made a dark shelter about the silver sheen of the meadowland. By the orchard a stew pond blinked at the moon. Stout palisades of rough timber shut in the house, outbuildings, courtyard, and garden.

Isoult of the Rose stood at gaze.

"I see the cage," said she. "Tell me, will you let the bird go—or cage it?"

"The caged thrush sings on a sunny morning."

"But a wild bird mopes."

"Perhaps some of our old worthies will open the door."

As they went on down into the valley the moon popped once more behind a cloud, and Isoult's face seemed to grow dark and brooding. She moved beside Fulk of the Forest, mute, solemn, distraught, her eyes looking into the distance where the great downs lay like faint shadows against the sky. A mood of mystery held her, the sadness of foreseeing dolour and pain and blood and the snarling mouths of furious men.

Three old yew trees grew by the gate in the meadow fence, and Isoult paused there and gripped Fulk's arm. Her white face looked into his, and he could see a gleaming inward light shining from her eyes.

"Consider, consider, I charge you. I shall bring you woe."

He smiled in her eyes.

"A witch's trick; an old woman's warning!"

"If you and I were old I might have no pity. I give you your choice."

"You chose for me when you came a-hunting," he said laconically. "I am the friend of the deer."

CHAPTER III

With the air of one who shakes off all ultimate responsibility with a shrug of the shoulders, she followed Fulk through the gate in the palisade.

"Oh, my good bachelor," she said to herself, "you are likely to have your throat cut because of this, and someone will thrust a torch into yonder thatch. The dice cannot serve both players at one throw."

The White Lodge loomed up over them, its long front frowning with black beams. The shaggy eaves threw a band of dense shadow, and the upper storey overhung the lower, being carried out on oak brackets and great carved corner posts. A path of rough stones sunk in the ground led to the porch, with the oak door studded with iron nails and hung on hand-wrought strap-hinges. There were beds of herbs, a grass plot, and a few rose bushes in front of the house; also a sundial set on a stone pillar.

Fulk knocked loudly with the pommel of his short sword. He and Isoult stood together in the gloom of the porch, so close that they could have touched each other; yet neither spoke, but listened to the sound of each other's breathing. A tacit sense of antagonism possessed them. The man mistrusted the woman; the woman thought the man an obstinate fool.

They heard someone stirring within. There was an iron grille in the door, and the little shutter that closed it was shot back. A man's voice bellowed a challenge as though he were bawling at a disobedient hound:

"Who's there?"

The voice seemed to make a draught in the porch, and the high wooden palisade echoed it back.

"Open to us, John."

The bars were withdrawn, and the door opened.

"A catch, master, surely!"

"Nothing to boast of. Get a light."

The fellow made way for them, and went to light a torch at the embers that still glowed on the round hearth in the centre of the hall. He yawned hugely and scratched his head, the torch, as it flared up, throwing on the wall a large and shadowy travesty of a round head and a jogging elbow. Fulk rebarred the door, and the woman Isoult went to warm herself before the glowing ashes.

The forester turned, yawning in her face; but astonishment proved stronger than the incipient yawn.

"Strike me bloody—a woman!"

He held the torch high, and put his face near to hers. His breath, and the sodden hardness of his eyes told her that he was too fond of the mead horn.

"Hey, you hen-harrier! Master, it be a woman."

Fulk turned on him fiercely.

"Kennel up, you fool of a sot! Put the torch in a bracket. Now, go and fetch us a jug of cider and some bread and honey. Hurry!"

The man blinked and went off yawning, but Fulk called him back before he reached the door leading towards the kitchen quarters.

"Dame Ferrers is abed?"

"These three hours, master."

"Good. Bring the cider, bread and honey, and then go and set up the truckle bed in the store-room, and get clean straw."

They were left alone together. Fulk pointed her to a stool by the fire.

"My mother and her wench are abed. They shall look to you to-morrow."

She nodded, and said nothing, but stole a glance at him from under her hood. The smoky flare of the solitary torch was even more baffling than the moonlight, and Fulk was standing, half turned to the light, and examining the two halves of the bow he had taken from her, his face hard, inscrutable, and murky.

"This bow was not made in these parts."

"It may tell you more than I can."

John the forester returned with a jug of cider, and bread and honey on a hollywood platter. Fulk bade him set the food and drink before Isoult. The fellow, none too sober, stumbled against the hearth curb, and spilt half the cider.

Fulk struck him across the shoulders with half of the broken bow.

"Sot! Vanish—get out of my sight!"

When the man had gone he turned to Isoult, frowning:

"A man who cannot rule his body is no better than a beast. Eat."

She took bread, and spread the honey with her girdle knife, nothing but the point of her chin showing under the shadow of her hood.

"Lording," she said, "you are very masterful. Do you rule your men as you rule your dogs?"

"It serves. A cur is a villein; a hound a gentleman."

She took the jug and drank.

"So! We are all dogs, if not of the same litter. And some of us are hated. What do the people sing now:

"When Adam delved and Eve span,

Where was then the gentleman?"

He looked down at her, as from a height.

"A fool's ditty. Will you ask me to prove that a hart royal is no better than a rooting hog? A scullion's forbears were scullions: that's the sense of't."

She held out the loaf to him.

"Will you not eat?"

"I eat but twice a day."

"Proud, even over a platter. Oh, my good bachelor, you will not be long-lived!"

When she had eaten, Fulk took a rushlight, lit it at the torch, and stood waiting. Isoult rose and followed him to the door of the store-room that opened out of a passage leading from the hall. He gave her the rushlight, and their fingers touched.

"Cold hand, Messire Fulk, hot heart."

He said nothing, but waited for her to enter, and then locked the door after her and took the key.

Fulk slept in the hall that night on a deer-skin spread upon a bed of bracken, and so little had the feminine temper of the adventure stirred him that he slept till five of the clock, when he was wakened by John the forester opening the shutters.

"A touch of frost, master, but a fine morning. Peter of the Purlieus has been watching the Pippinford rides. He was to meet me at Stonegate two hours after sunrise."

Fulk was still sleepy.

"Yes, get along. Take a couple of hounds and your quarterstaff, and blow three notes if you see aught that is strange."

The forester started out, and Fulk dozed off again till he woke to the sound of someone singing. For the moment he had almost forgotten the woman in yonder, and to judge by her matins she was in a mood with the birds.

He sat up just as the solar door opened, and a grey figure appeared at the top of the wooden stairway leading down into the hall. The figure had paused, as though listening, its eyes fixed upon Fulk seated on the deer-skin where the morning sunlight poured in upon the floor.

"Fulk!"

"Mother!"

Margaret Ferrers came down slowly into the hall. She was clad all in grey, her head wrapped in a starched white wimple, a cold figure with cold eyes. Her face was as passionless as the face of one lying dead in a shroud, nostrils and lips thin and compressed, the skin bloodless and opaque. This woman had the air of having left her soul behind her somewhere in the past, but this morning her eyes were alert and mistrustful, her face as sharp and pinched as on a bitter winter morning. Isoult was still singing, and with such abandonment that the words could be heard in the hall:

"I put me on a new shift the morning I was wed.

My gown it was of cloth of gold, my hose of Flemish red."

Margaret Ferrers asked no questions. She stood, waiting, like the ghost in the tale forbidden by pride to speak until spoken to. Fulk sprang up, the impetuous youth in him missing the look in his mother's eyes.

"Listen to the caged bird singing. I caught it last night under the Witch Cross yews."

"A woman?"

"Stalking a hart by moonlight, with a bow in her hand. I locked her in the store-room for the night."

Margaret Ferrers still considered him with her mistrustful eyes.

"A woman!"

"Who calls herself Isoult of the Rose. Jade or lady, she goes before the verderers at the next swainmote. We shall have to lodge her here."

His mother was wondering whether she should believe him. They came to all men, these adventures, and yet he carried it off like a boy who had brought home a snared rabbit.

"Who is she? Whence does she come?"

"I know no more than Father Adam. Some gay dame, perhaps, tired of her bower, and come adventuring. She tried to fool me."

Margaret Ferrers listened to the singing voice.

"Some light wench," she thought; but to her son she said, "Give me the key, Fulk. I may find out more than a man could."

He gave her the key without demur, and leaving her to visit Isoult of the Rose, he passed out into the courtyard and washed in the great stone trough under the pump.

Dame Margaret approached the matter with all the uncharitableness of a woman who once in her life had stood in bitter need of the world's charity. Her face seemed to grow thinner and sharper from the moment that she set eyes upon Isoult. The claws of a woman's jealous instinct tore all fripperies aside, and laid bare the sinful body that good women imagine they see under richly coloured clothes.

Isoult was no less instantly upon her guard. She looked slantwise at Dame Margaret, holding her head high, and seeing in the grey and blighting figure mistrust, arrogance, and scorn.

"The day's blessing on you, madame."

Isoult chose to speak in the French tongue, mincingly yet railingly, with a gleam far back in her dark eyes. She spoke Breton French, and spoke it fluently, and with a little mischievous lilt that had the sparkle of fine wine. This solemn flapping heron was to be stooped at and struck with the talons, for Margaret Ferrers' eyes had thrown out the one word that is unforgivable and not to be forgotten.

"I am in love with this fair chamber. It is good to smell the spicery, and the herbs, and the salted meat. Madame, it is through no wish of mine that messire, your son, has inflicted me upon you. But he was so obstinate in holding what he had taken!"

Margaret Ferrers looked her up and down with glances that slashed the gay clothes to ribbons. She had nothing pleasant to say to Isoult, and being the woman she was she said all that was unpleasant.

"Let us understand each other. Some of us go in our proper colours. My house is not an intake, though it must serve as a jail. Have you anything you wish to say?"

Isoult's eyes glittered.

"Madame, nothing, save that grey twilight follows a red sunset. Let us not waste words on each other. I am not what you believe; you may not have been what you seem."

She saw the elder woman's face redden, her nostrils dilate, her mouth grow pinched and thin.

"Enough. I will leave you to my kitchen wench. She will bring you your food, and you can vent your sauciness on her; she will know how to answer properly to suit the colour of your gown."

The dame tried to outstare Isoult, but her eyelids flickered, nor did the flush die out of her face till she had relocked the door upon this strolling jade.

In the hall she found Fulk throwing some brushwood on the hot ashes of the night's fire. An instant flash of Margaret Ferrers' eyes showed her jealous, doubting temper. She strove to become mistress of herself again— the cold woman whose heart had chastened itself through many years of dread and suspense and perilous pride.

Fulk looked round sharply, challenging her:

"Well, mother?"

She made an effort to put the heat of malice out of her mouth, and in the main she succeeded.

"I have little that needs saying. Trust a woman to see through a woman. We must feed the jade till the swainmote meets."

"Who is she?"

"I neither know nor care."

"Whence has she come?"

"I did not ask her. Such wenches come from nowhere and go nowhere, till the Father of Lies takes his own."

The son looked thoughtful.

"You are no wiser than when you went in?"

"Yes, wiser; wise enough."

He seemed to consider the matter as though all the authority were his.

"Give me the key, mother. I must read this rebus."

Her face softened. Some instinct made her afraid, and yet urged her to dissemble her fear, for she was loath to let her son go into Isoult's chamber.

"Do not vex your head about the jade, Fulk. I will see to it."

He said quietly:

"Mother, the key."

Her eyelids flickered as she looked at him with a troubled recognition of something that challenged her inmost conscience, for she saw, more suddenly than ever before, a likeness both in body and mind that was princely and almost terrible. His yea and nay were serenely imperious; he soared at a royal height and stooped to take his desire.

Margaret Ferrers gave him the key and stood stiff and mute, listening to his footsteps as he went along the passage leading to Isoult's room.

The place had a narrow window that was barred with iron, but the morning sun poured in through it, and Isoult herself stood in the sunlight. She had let down her hair, and was combing it with an ivory comb.

Fulk paused in the doorway like a man who has stumbled on a milk-white hind couched in a secret thicket. Nor was the woman blind. She had thrown her green cloak and her sky-blue cote-hardie on a stool, the cote-hardie all embroidered with silver suns and stars, with green tippets at the elbows and buttons of blue enamel down the front. Fulk found her in her shift and kirtle, the latter of holly green, fitting close to the figure, and showing off the curves of hip and bosom. She wore a girdle of red leather with a gypsire hanging from it. Her shoes were of red leather, her hose of grass-green silk.

Fulk paused by the door, a little dazzled by the blackness of the woman's hair, the whiteness of her throat, and all the rich colours of her garments. A strange hunting dress, and a strange huntress! Moreover, there was a world of raillery and laughter deep in her eyes. She had seemed pale by moonlight, but this morning her lips were very red and she was a creature of colour, of white curves, and of haunting health.

"Good-day to you, Messire Fulk."

She looked at him steadily, provokingly, and went on combing her hair. And standing there, one hand on the door-post, he essayed to catechise her, only to be met with a kind of railing silence. It was a new notion to him that a woman should set out to treat him as though he were a clown and a fool.

"Take your chance or lose it. I am in no temper to be kept like a hawk on a perch."

She ran the comb through her hair deliberately and at her leisure.

"If I had anything to say, Messire Fulk, I should have said it long ago. One thing: do not send your mother to me; we shall quarrel, and I have a devil's tongue. Now, I will not hinder you— —"

She turned her back and appeared busied with gathering up her hair ready for the silver net.

"You have nothing to say?"

She gave him one glance over her shoulder.

"No, Messire Fulk, nothing."

He went out with a stiff face, conscious that he had fared no better than his mother.

CHAPTER IV

There were deeps in the forest where a hundred men could hide and never be stumbled on for weeks together. Thieves and outlaws who knew the ways could travel north, south, east, and west, and never be seen by woodward or forester. Moreover, these trailbastons and broken men left the deer alone, for they themselves were part of the wild and the forest was their harbour, and if no deer were slain they themselves were less likely to be hunted.

Now there were forest lodges and foresters at Pippinford, Hindleape, Broadstone, and Comedean, as well as at the White Lodge of the Master Forester; but none of these men of the greenwood and the heather had any knowledge of the queer gentry who were lodged among the hollies of Blackbottom Gill. The holly wood was itself hidden in a great wood of oaks and beeches, and the Polecat, who knew every ride and every path, and the spots, too, where there were no paths, had served as guide to these strangers. The Polecat had lived all his life in the forests, thieving, cheating, robbing when a safe chance offered. He could "burr" like a goat-sucker and scream like a jay, tell the age of a deer from its slot and its dung, and judge just how high the pheasants would be roosting on a certain night. The Polecat had hunted in all the forests in Hampshire, Sussex, and Surrey, and he would slip from one to the other if it happened that the nose of the Law had smelt spilt blood.

In Blackbottom Gill five figures were grouped before a fire in the thick of the gloom of the hollies. The fire had been built in a recess grubbed out of the side of a bank, and a screen of boughs built round it, so that its light should not be seen. And since it was night the smoke did not concern them. They smothered the fire before dawn.

Father Merlin sat on a wallet stuffed with grass, his grey cowl over his head, the girdle of his grey habit unbuttoned. He had taken off his sandals and was stretching out his brown feet to the fire. Over against him, on a pile of dead bracken, sat Guy the Stallion, a handsome, tawdry, swashing sworder with a red head and fiery eyes and a fierce little peaked beard. At the other end of the half circle a lean man with a swarthy, gloating face was cleaning his nails with a holly twig, and men called him Jack Straw. In the centre sat John Ball, the mad priest of Kent, staring at the fire, bemused, lips moving silently, eyes seeing visions. Half lying on a sheep-skin and poking the fire with a charred stick, Big Blanche, the singing-woman, listened to Jack Straw and Guy the Stallion disputing over some point of policy.

The soldier spoke in fierce, characteristic jerks, as though he were making cuts with a sword.

"Let them begin with a little killing. I know a trick or two to make men's blood boil. Let them warm to it, and in a month there will be no gentles left in the land to trouble us. I am a man of the sword, and what I know of war is as much as Du Guesclin or Knowles could carry."

Jack Straw, the East Anglian, thrust out a contemptuous lip.

"Keep your sword in its scabbard. One word from Brother John here is worth a thousand such swords."

"Bah, wait till the work begins. Look at him! Will he keep the hinds from blood and wine?"

Father Merlin showed his big teeth, his harsh face gaunt and long in the shadows. The swashbuckler amused him and piqued the laughter of a subtle scorn.

"Let no man quarrel with the soul of St. Francis," said he. "What say we but that the meek shall inherit the earth?"

They turned their eyes by some common instinct upon Father John, staring raptly at the fire, his lips moving silently, his face strangely radiant. His spirit was away in some fantastic earthly heaven while his body remained among the black hollies of the forest. Even red-headed Guy was sobered by a something that was above and beyond his lustful vigour and his bombast.

"Father John treads the clouds."

"Perhaps St. Thomas of Canterbury is up yonder. When we have pulled Simon of Sudbury out of his archbishop's shoes we might do worse than clap them on Father John's feet."

The Franciscan smiled like a horse champing a bit, drawing back his lips and showing his teeth.

"What God wills—God wills."

"And what the devil wills— —"

"The swashbuckler knows best."

Big Blanche sat and gazed at John Ball's rapt and dreaming face. He seemed not to hear the voices of those about him, and his face was the face of a man drunk with visions.

She pointed to him.

"He has touched neither food nor drink since daybreak. Some day his soul will fly away like a piece of thistledown, and we shall have no one to preach to us."

"Pluck his sleeve, Jack."

"Descend, brother, descend. See here, something warm for the belly."

John Ball started, and stared at those around him as though he had been wakened out of a deep sleep. Big Blanche wriggled across on her knees, and held out the mead bottle. He took it mechanically, and nodded to her with an air of vacant benignity.

"Drink, brother."

Jack Straw was still using the holly twig, and the swashbuckler grew facetious.

"Take my dagger, Jack. We are getting ready to be great lords and gentles all by the cleaning of our nails!"

John Ball's eyes fixed themselves on his neighbour's hands. He began to speak in a slow and inward voice.

"Our brother cleanseth his nails. It is a symbol, surely. All the world shall have clean fingers."

"And no pickings! My cock, father, I must pick up something on the point of my sword!"

The priest of Kent looked up and around at the black boughs and tops of the hollies. His face was the white face of a saint in an altar picture of the passions. His neighbours were so many allegorical figures—Cunning, Ambition, Lust, Bombast—and yet mere men with strong teeth and muscular hands and eyes that looked hungry. This dreamer of Kent whose mouth could fill with fire had a soul whose simplicity made these shrewd and carnal men marvel.

"Has Isoult of the Rose returned?"

"No, father."

"The Polecat is out; we shall have news."

John Ball spread his hands to the blaze.

"The voice of an angel, a bright angel on the white clouds at dawn. Shall it not sing the children into Paradise?"

Big Blanche's face grew sullen and lowering. She glanced up suddenly and caught Guy the Stallion watching her mockingly, laughing at the jealousy that she could not hide. She flounced round and turned her back.

"What will you make of Isoult, father?"

John Ball was blind to such a thing as raillery.

"Isoult shall stand in the gateway of our new city and sing. I will put golden words into her mouth. And because of her beauty — —"

The woman by the fire twitched her shoulders.

"Golden words in the mouth of such a — —"

Father Merlin's figure straightened suddenly, and his hooked nose protruded like the beak of a bird from under the shadow of his hood.

"'Ssst!"

"What is it?"

"Listen."

They remained motionless, rigid, so many stark black figures seen against the glow of the fire. The night was very still and windless, and the hollies seemed weighed down by the heavy, midnight silence. From somewhere came a rustling sound as of dead leaves blown along the forest's floor. Father Merlin's head moved slowly from side to side on its long and sinewy throat; the swashbuckler's hand went to the hilt of his sword.

They heard a jay scream, and Blanche drew in a deep breath and laughed.

"The Polecat!"

"That was his cry."

"Come down into the light, good friend, and welcome."

A little man with a face like a wild cat's appeared from nowhere, and threw himself down beside Big Blanche. His eyes were red and small and wonderfully restless, and his hair looked like a mass of little black snakes writhing all in a tangle. For the moment he said nothing, but reaching out with both hands, grabbed a bottle of mead with one and half a loaf with the other. The animal was thirsty and hungry, and they suffered him to have his will.

Jack Straw was the first to question him.

"What news, Polecat, out of the wood?"

The man still masticated, and answered as he ate.

"The duke's foresters have taken Isoult."

"What! John of Gaunt's green bullies?"

"I always said the wench was too venturesome."

"What have they done?"

"Lugged her to the White Lodge. It was young Fulk, the riding forester, who took her. I might have stabbed him in the dark, but the young wolf was too wary."

Father Merlin grinned and bit his nails. John Ball stared at the fire and said nothing. It was Guy the Stallion who jumped up, swaggered, tightened his belt, and looked at his comrades' faces.

"Nothing to say, good brothers? See here, the sword has its tongue. I'll have Isoult out of the White Lodge, by cock, before they can say a Pater!"

Big Blanche twisted round of a sudden, and snapped at him like an angry dog.

"Sit down, fool. Let the jade——"

"Fool! Shut that jealous mouth of yours. You—to be jealous of Isoult, the hen of the falcon!"

The woman sprang up, furious, chattering, beside herself, a knife in her fist.

"Let the jade rot, I say. You are my man and I'm your woman. By the blood of the——!"

Father Merlin rose up and put himself between them. He was a big man, and had a voice that could thunder.

"Peace, you fools. Swashbuckler, sit you down and cool that hot pot of a head of yours. As for you, Dame Blanche——"

She snarled at him insolently, her large white face like a lewd mask.

"I have a tongue, mind you. I have a tongue!"

Merlin went close to her, and she alone saw his eyes.

"Peace, or you may have no tongue to boast of."

The insolence went out of her, and she cringed and slunk away.

"I meant nothing, good father; but that fool there is my man, and I'll not see him filched from me."

"Peace!"

John Ball had sat through the squabble with the look of a man whose soul was elsewhere. He turned his head slowly and stared at Father Merlin.

"My brother, what shall be done?"

The Franciscan sneered.

"Leave it to me, Brother John. I will go out to-morrow—to hear confessions."

CHAPTER V

Father Merlin set out betimes on a fine spring morning, a hunch of bread in his wallet and his beads hanging down over his grey frock.

Father Merlin walked with his head thrown back, and his beak of a nose with its hungry nostrils sniffing the freshness of the morning; for the forest was in a joyous mood and the birds were singing in every bush and tree. The friar's grey habit brushed the dew from the grass and heather. Rabbits scampered to cover. The primroses were dwindling, but the wild hyacinths were blue in the woods, and the blackthorn hung white against the sky. The soft bloom of a misty morning lay over the forest, deepening towards the grey chalk hills by the southern sea, and filling the valleys with a film of silver smoke. Life cried out lustily with the voice of desire. Green buds were bursting; the great hills seemed swollen with the mystery of birth; the birds were coming from the lands of the sun, and the wryneck complained in the oak boughs, and from the deep woods a cuckoo called. "Joy, joy, joy," sang the blackbirds. Woodlarks hovered and thrilled, dust motes of melody dancing in the sunlight.

Half a furlong ahead of Father Merlin went a little hobbling figure in rags, prodding the earth with the point of a staff, for the Polecat had trudged ahead to show the grey friar the way. Merlin's eyes watched this forerunner of his with cynical complacency. Such creatures were very useful when a man of God could send them down to hell and then tweak them back again at the end of an absolution. Father Merlin was no clumsy, tumultuous bully; his voice had many modulations; he could be as quiet as death and as persevering as a badger.

Now about the time that Merlin passed by the Ghost Oak, Fulk Ferrers stood outside Isoult's door with a cup of water and a platter of bread and meat. He had taken them out of the cook-maid's hands and left her gaping and looking at Dame Ferrers.

Fulk unlocked the door, pushed it open with his foot, and had no need to tell himself that he had not thought to find the woman at her prayers. She was kneeling by the window, the sunlight falling upon the curve of a white neck and the silver net that covered her hair. She did not stir or look round at him, but kept her eyes shut and her hands folded over her bosom.

Fulk crossed the room softly, set the cup and plate on a stool, drew back, and waited by the door. It may have been in his mind that Isoult of the Rose did not know who had deigned to serve her, and that to a woman who prayed with her eyes closed one footstep was very like another.

She remained motionless, and Fulk waited, watching her, meaning to be gone, and yet not going. This woman was a creature of surprises, a creature more wild and subtle than any hart he had ever tracked and hunted in the forest.

"Good-morning, Messire Fulk."

He stared, for she had neither moved nor opened her eyes, for he had been watching her.

"It seems that you see with your ears!" he said.

"Yes, and with my nostrils and my fingers."

"Even while you say your prayers!"

"I was praying for you, Messire Fulk, therefore I knew you, though my eyes were closed."

She turned and gave him the full challenge of her opened eyes—eyes in which there was neither laughter nor raillery, but rather a prophetic pity. The Polecat had been to her window during the night, and the Polecat's claws were to be dreaded because of those magicians whom the Polecat served.

Fulk hovered there like a hawk, not seeing anything upon which his reason could pounce.

"Madame Isoult, wherefore do you pray for me?"

"Because of your great need."

"Think you I need your prayers?"

"Far more than I need yours."

He was puzzled, both by the singing softness of her voice, and by the intent way in which she regarded him.

"I have no knowledge of needing a woman's prayers."

"No? Yet, good sir, since you will keep me here I must pray for you, even though my prayers may be of no avail."

He came a step forward, looking at her steadfastly.

"Always riddles!"

She returned his look as steadfastly.

"You are young, Messire Fulk, and it is hard that a young man should come to a sudden end."

"You are for making a ghost out of a sheet and a candle!"

Her eyes flashed.

"Not so. But I have a kind of pity for that stiff neck of yours. Not very often have I found such stiffness in a man, and in a young man! But go to, now, I talk to a winter frost. Yet it may so fall out that you shall have cause to thank me."

He stood at gaze, and her face was the crystal into which he looked.

"For your prayers—if they are honest—I thank you," he said. "I will stand on guard against the mischances that a woman's prayers may hint at."

She looked at him meaningly.

"Turn your back to no bush."

"So!"

"A vest of ring mail under a doublet may turn a knife or an arrow."

He stood a moment, and then went out from before her thoughtfully, without uttering a word.

Father Merlin overtook the Polecat where the heathland sloped down towards the White Lodge valley. The beggar stood to one side and made the friar a reverence, his red eyes twinkling under the edge of his hood.

"A blessing, holy father."

Merlin stopped and blessed him as though he had never set eyes on the man before.

"How runs the road, my son?"

"Down yonder, father, stands a goodly house, and Fulk of the Forest dwells therein."

Merlin crossed himself.

"My son," said he, "there may be that work to be done which I told you of. Follow, but see that no man mistakes you for my follower."

The Polecat pulled his forelock.

"I will be there, but not seen, holy father, like a toad under a stone."

Merlin marched on, but at the White Lodge he found only Dame Margaret and her wench, and John the forester feathering arrows in the porch. Merlin could be as soft and debonair as any king's chaplain, and a cup of wine and a cold pie were brought out for his good cheer. Dame Margaret was at her orfrey work in the parlour, and Merlin was well content to leave her there and to talk with John the forester in the porch. A second cup of hippocras was to be had for the asking, and the grey friar had much to say of the evil temper of the times and of the villainy of those lewd and meddlesome folk who grumbled because the king and the lords and gentles needed money.

Merlin discovered what he wished to discover, whither Fulk of the Forest had gone.

"For," said he, "I never miss speech with a gentleman in whatsoever parts I may be travelling. I follow in the steps of St. Francis, and all living things were St. Francis's children."

He left drunken John much edified and a little redder about the nose, and set out westwards with his cowl drawn down and his beads in his hand.

Beyond the gorse lands by Stoneygate, where the world was all green and gold, he came to the rich meadows by the vachery and sat himself down under a wind-blown thorn. It was not for Merlin's eyes to overlook the cowherd or bibulcus in leather jerkin and leggings standing by the vachery gate and talking to a man on a rough roan horse. The man on the horse was dressed in green, and the liripipes of his hood were blue and white; moreover, he carried a bow, and a horn slung to a blue and white baldric— colours that were the Duke of Lancaster's, even of John of Gaunt.

Merlin heard a bird twittering in the furze, and he guessed it was the Polecat who twittered. Fulk of the Forest was turning his horse from the vachery gate, and the cowherd went in and closed it after him. Merlin sat well back against the trunk of the thorn tree, his head bowed, his beads in his hands, his ears listening for the hoof-falls of the riding forester's horse.

Fulk, mounting the meadow slope, saw the grey friar under the thorn tree telling his beads. He had no great love for the strolling friars, holding them to be deer stealers when the chance served, and self-seeking meddlers who were breeding an insolent pride in the hearts of the lewd commons. For Fulk had an eagle scorn for the villein folk and the lower craftsmen of the town. Such creatures were to be kept under, and not puffed into a vain conceit of themselves by men who had left the dunghill to put on a friar's frock.

Fulk took a good look at the Franciscan, and from under his hood Merlin's eyes were watching the legs of the roan horse. It was part of his plan that he should seem lost in his devotions and blind to the world till Messire Fulk rode up.

"Good-day to you, Master Friar."

Merlin lifted his head with a start of pretended surprise. Fulk had reined in close to the thorn tree, and Merlin looked up at him as he sat there full in the sunlight.

"Good-day, lording."

The astonishment that he had feigned lost itself in an astonishment that was real. Merlin's eyes fell into a stare; his lower lip drooped; the beads dropped into his lap. For the moment he lost all knowledge of himself, and his subtlety was as a snake that has been stunned with a blow.

"Sir, I am but a poor friar."

Fulk looked him over, and thought him a gaping, stammering fool. Merlin was trying to scramble back out of the open amazement into which he had fallen, to steady his wits, to hide what he had betrayed. He blinked, and bit his cheek. But the thing was monstrous. To whom was he speaking— to a stripling called Fulk of the Forest or to Richard the King?

Merlin was shaken. For the moment he hardly knew whether the earth was real under him.

"Sir," he said, to gain time, "my name is Father Merlin, and I travel in these parts for the good of all souls."

He stood up with a humility that hid much turmoil, doubt, and wonder, yet his eyes were fiercely alive under his grey hood—eyes that snatched at every visible detail, and yet pretended to see nothing.

Fulk considered him as a lord considers a beggar.

"You friars are notorious busybodies. Our own priests say you take away their own alms-dish from under their very noses."

Merlin drew a step nearer.

"Lording, we are much abused."

"And it is pleasant to confess to a man whose face one may not see again."

"Lording, you have a sharp tongue. Yet I will take a groat from any gentleman for the glorifying of our great house in London. And from Messire Fulk Ferrers——"

"Well, I am he."

Merlin stood yet closer. His dark eyes seemed to search every line of Fulk's face with a fascinated and greedy eagerness which could not be hid. Fulk took it to be a notorious hunger for money, for no beggars could beg like the preaching friars.

"Maybe you have been in London, Messire Fulk, and have seen the great and noble church of St. Francis, near to Newgate. Kings and great lords and ladies have given us money, and jewels, and plate, and rich stuffs, not for our glory but for the glory of St. Francis and the good of their souls. Doubtless, when you have tarried at my Lord of Lancaster's Palace of the Savoy——"

Fulk took him up.

"I have never been in your city of London, Master Friar."

A bird twittered in the furze, and Merlin threw up his arms of a sudden, and cried in a loud voice: "Peace—peace! All honour to St. Francis, and let all men love one another."

Fulk looked at him as at one gone mad. Merlin waxed explanatory.

"Sir, at times the spirit stirs in me so strongly that I have to leap and cry out. And assuredly it is a marvellous thing that such a bachelor as Fulk Ferrers should never have ridden thirty miles and crossed London Bridge! Yet you are not altogether the loser, for in a city lurks much wickedness."

Fulk's horse began to fidget, and his master was in sympathy with him.

"We forest folk keep our wits and our money about us, Father Merlin, nor have we much of the latter to lose. I wish you a good journey, plenty of alms, and many sinners."

Merlin showed his teeth and grinned.

"*Pax tecum*, my son."

And so they parted.

The Polecat came wriggling out of the furze as soon as Fulk of the Forest had disappeared over the hill. He rubbed one finger along his nose and spat into the grass.

"Father Merlin is merciful to-day."

Merlin turned on him with the savage impatience of a fierce spirit wantonly disturbed in the midst of some marvellous meditation.

"Back into the grass, you snake. And by the Wood of the Cross, do not budge thence till nightfall."

The Polecat wriggled back, and Father Merlin went on his way, staring at the ground. He had walked a mile or more before he threw up both hands with a snapping of the thumbs and fingers and shouted aloud with exultation.

"A bastard, a prince's bastard! How would it serve to steal and use the likeness of a king?"

CHAPTER VI

It was the poll-tax that had set every common man in England snarling like an angry dog. Hitherto no one had listened to the sullen grumbling of the poor, those brown men with brown faces who trudged in the mud and went out to labour in the winter wind and rain. They were part of the soil, and no one heeded them so long as there was corn to be had and fat beasts to be salted for winter. Edward the King and his great lords had made war in France with a screaming of trumpets, a humming of bow-strings, and the clash of ash-staved spears. They had crossed the sea in their rich-coloured stuffs and their shining harness, had ridden their war horses over the fields of France, and brought back honour, noble prisoners, and much plunder. But the wars were no longer glorious, and the taxes mounted up. A gust of anger had passed over the land, and even the boor flinging mud out of a ditch had paused and asked himself, "Why—and wherefore?" There were many who talked and many who threatened, looking sullenly upon the lord as he rode by in a coat of furs, and thinking even more sullenly of those who sat before the fire with wine and spices ready to hand. Privilege everywhere, valiant pride soaring overhead, and the serf in the mud, suddenly and viciously envious! This anger of the common people had not known how to vent itself, how to speak so that the great ones should hear. This was no baron's business, but a dunghill fermentation, and being slow and sodden and savage, was like to be more terrible when thoughts of blood and fire and vengeance fumed up out of this mixen of discontent.

Of all the great lords of the land no man was more hated than the King's uncle, John of Gaunt. It was said that he had the King in the palm of his hand, that the curse of the heavy taxes flowed from him, and that he had no thought or pity for the poor. Men spoke of his Palace of the Savoy as the most wonderful house in England, packed with plate and jewels, rich stuffs, and armour. Scores of rich manors, forests, castles, houses, and chases were held by him, and his power and his opulence were not to be challenged. Moreover, a certain majestic pride, a casual haughtiness in dealing with lesser men, had not brought him the mob's love. He was an eagle who took no account of the hedge-sparrows, holding aloof and looking far afield, for his was a soaring spirit with visions of kingship and honour in far countries. The little men under and about his feet were just little men to be forgotten. Being over-busied with great enterprises, he had no patience to remember the ploughman and the fool.

Not only was the Duke of Lancaster hated, but all those near to him, and even his possessions, shared this savage hatred. The common people lusted to cut the throats of his stewards and foresters, beat out the brains of his knights and men-at-arms, and to burn and destroy his houses and all the rich gear in them. So in the blowing up of the storm there were certain tall trees marked out for destruction; and Fulk of the Forest, riding his rounds and cherishing the deer, did not reflect that he himself would be a stag marked out for the slaughter.

But Father Merlin knew it, and told himself that a chained hart alive might be of more value than mere venison. Much enlightenment had come to him since that meeting by the thorn tree near the vachery, and Merlin had gathered his gossips round the fire in Blackbottom Gill and whispered a strange story. They had drawn close about him, gaping, amazed, yet caught by the shrewd audacity of his imaginings.

There was no moon when the Polecat climbed the White Lodge fence, opened the garden wicket, let Merlin in, and led him to Isoult's window. The house was asleep, but Isoult lay awake, having been warned of Merlin's coming. She had heard a fern-owl whirring in the oak woods, and, rising from her bed, stood at the window, waiting.

Merlin spoke in a whisper:

"Isoult, art there?"

He could see her grey face at the bars, but she could see nothing of his because of his cowl.

"Speak softly, for the young falcon has strong talons and a fierce beak."

"It is of Fulk Ferrers that I have much to say."

"I am listening."

She was on her guard, though not conscious of it, half ready to put aside any treacherous blow aimed at the man who had captured her under the yews; but Merlin had not spoken ten words before she became enthralled by the strange tale that he was telling her. She stared out into the darkness whence this whispering voice came. And when he had ended she drew in her breath sharply, and fell to listening for any sound within the house.

"Merlin," said she, "have a care. What if it be the King?"

"Comfort yourself. I had word. Richard is in the White Tower in London—has been there all these days."

"Is he so like?"

"Like enough to trick any but his own familiars, and though this fellow is some five years older, the young king looks more than a lad. It is a marvel."

Isoult stood thinking.

"Two kings to play with! To use the one, if the other should prove contrary! Yes; but, my friend, this young man, this Fulk of the Forest, is more proud and stiffnecked than any king I ever read of."

Merlin's voice was sly and insinuating.

"And Isoult of the Rose surpasses all women——"

She cut in on him sharply.

"Be careful. I am not to be played with. But I might try my wits."

She stared into the darkness as though trying to see Merlin's face.

"Have you any plan?"

"Listen, Isoult. All the country is stirring, and all the outlawed men are swarming hither. The word is flying from mouth to mouth. Now, we shall come here and break in. This falcon will fight?"

"To the death, or I am no judge of a man's fettle."

"Good. We will have him at our mercy, and then you, Isoult, shall step in and beg his life. A close prisoner he shall be, and I doubt not that he may be persuaded."

"Be not too sure."

"I am not crossed easily."

"Merlin, one word: think not that Isoult is without honour."

He protested with an eager, murmuring voice.

"No, no; it is but a lure to the lad's spirit. Born out of wedlock, a love child, a king before a king! He is the son of his father's loins. We'll challenge him to the adventure."

"There is the woman, his mother. That is another marvel that one who is now as cold and stiff as a corpse——"

"She may serve or she may not. It does not signify: the man's the master. If only he be persuadable. And you, Isoult, may do much."

Her voice betrayed impatience.

"Let the adventure go on, but do not think of me as hell fire. We shall see how the stag runs. And now, good-night."

She heard the sound of his breathing die away, and knew that the window was empty. Like a ghost he had come and like a ghost he stole away, leaving Isoult distraught and restless.

It was in the half light of a May dawn that Peter of Pippinford came running to the White Lodge with his head all bloody and a short sword in his hand. He had been ranging his ward, and had come back to find his lodge on fire and four ragged rogues waiting for him behind the woodstack. One of them had given Peter a bloody poll with the thick end of a holly cudgel, and Peter had cut off one man's hand, slashed another across the face, and then had saved himself by the grace of his long legs. He set up a furious hallooing outside the White Lodge gate, and Fulk went out to let him in.

Fulk listened to his news with a face that was very quiet and very grim. He had been warned two days ago by one of the purlieu men that the common people were breaking down fences and emptying fish ponds, and that the whole country had gone mad. A tax-gatherer had been beaten to death in one of the villages. The gentry were flying to Lewes and Pevensey, leaving their houses and larders to be plundered by their boors.

"We must get the women out of the way. I will ride over to the vachery and bring Barnabas's people in. Get your head tied up, Peter, and then help John to make ready the great wagon."

Fulk had a word with his mother, Margaret Ferrers standing at her chamber door in her night gear, looking like a corpse in a shroud. Cold woman that she was, she fell to pleading with him, but he put her prayers aside.

"Run away from the lousels? Not I! The men shall take you and Isoult and the women to Lewes, and then come back to me. We will make these scullions skip."

He mounted his roan horse, galloped bareback to the vachery, and ordered the cowherd to the White Lodge with his women and children.

"Turn the cows out and let them fend for themselves, Barnabas. The wagon starts for Lewes in an hour."

When he returned to the White Lodge Fulk found that two other foresters had come in and were helping Peter of Pippinford yoke eight oxen to the wagon, and load some of the household gear into it. Fulk chose Peter to be the leader, and charged them to return when they had lodged the women within the walls of Lewes town. He chose John to bide with him, because John was a coward, and the best men were wanted in the wagon; and John looked sulkily at Fulk, having no stomach for the White Lodge when such rough gentry were hunting men as well as deer.

Fulk passed into the house, went to Isoult's room, and stood in the doorway, beckoning.

"Come."

She was ready, dressed in all her rich colours, her hair in its silver net, her knife and gypsire at her girdle. She looked at Fulk with intent and questioning eyes, considering something in her heart.

"Is it the swainmote?"

"No. The boors have gone mad and are running wild. I am sending the womenfolk to Lewes town for shelter, and you will go with them."

"And you?"

"A deer master does not run away from swine."

Isoult did not move.

"Messire Fulk, if I choose to stay here——"

"On my faith, the choice is not with you. Put on your cloak and hood."

She eyed him half defiantly, yet as one who loved to be defied.

"I'll make you carry me. It may be that you hold a hostage and know it not!"

He went a step nearer.

"What! Are you with these nameless fools?"

"Did I say so?"

"Come, have done; time's precious."

Her loftiness topped his impatience.

"I choose to stay. You brought me here, and if it must be that I should go, you must put me out even as you brought me in."

They stood, measuring each other, Isoult's red mouth smiling provocation. Fulk fell to frowning because some strange emotion stirred in him, a fierce young wonder that had stumbled of a sudden upon this woman's comeliness. Her audacity seemed to beat its wings and to soar against his pride, and her eyes had all the luring gloom of the woods.

"Come; I have no desire to be rough, Isoult."

"Ah, but a man's roughness— —"

Isoult, looking beyond Fulk, saw Margaret Ferrers standing in the doorway.

"Fulk, do we wait for this woman?"

He stood back with a sweep of the arm.

"Come, let us waste no more words."

Dame Margaret's mouth sneered, but her eyes were afraid of Isoult's. She stood there menacingly, as though longing to utter the one word— "harlot."

Isoult's chin went up.

"Dame Ferrers, this woman waits for nobody. I go at my own pleasure."

She passed out, her arm touching Fulk's sleeve, her eyes throwing a quick side-glance into his.

"Stiffnecked as ever. You must take your choice."

Fulk followed her, looking at the red shoes under the edge of the green dress; and as a man notices things at times, simply because he cannot help but notice them, he was struck by the way the woman walked—confidently, proudly, as though beholden to no one. His glance lifted to the white curve of her neck as she passed out of the porch into the sunlight. She, too, could be stiffnecked, he thought, though her throat looked so white and smooth and mysterious.

Tom of Hindleape was standing beside the oxen. The other men were in the wagon with their bows ready, the women and children sitting on the floor. Fulk helped his mother in, and then stood to help Isoult, holding his knee and hand as a man helps a woman into the saddle.

She gave him a whisper:

"Hold the White Lodge and wait for the grey friar."

As the wagon moved off he found her watching him with eyes that were dark and enigmatical.

CHAPTER VII

About sunset Fulk went up to Standard Hill and looked out over the forest. Spread below him, with all the great oaks burgeoning into bronze, was a shimmering sea of gold meeting a sky of amber, and from it rose the singing of a thousand birds. About the group of firs on Standard Hill the slanting sunlight struck upon the young green growth of the heather, and made it shine like the dust of emeralds scattered broadcast over the earth. The yews of Nutley hung like a thundercloud across a band of scarlet, and the distant hills were all soft greys and purples. The western sky was like the mysterious eyes of a woman flushed with love.

Fulk could see nothing stirring on the heathlands, and he turned back to the White Lodge in the valley. The day had passed quietly, and he judged that the wagon had reached Lewes town in safety, and that on the morrow Peter of Pippinford and his men would be back at the White Lodge. A frail smoke spiral went up from the louvre of the hall, and the whole valley was very still save for the singing of the birds in the oak woods on either side of the meadow. The grassland itself was a sheet of gold, and the old thorns by the great ditch were white with flower, and wondrous fragrant.

Fulk passed just within the porch to watch an owl gliding along the edge of the wood; but it so happened that he saw more than an owl. A man in a brown smock came cautiously from behind the trunk of an oak, and stood looking towards the White Lodge, shading his eyes with his hand.

Fulk, motionless in the shadowy porch, called softly to the forester whom he had left on guard in the hall.

"John, bring me my bow."

No one answered him, and he gave an impatient jerk of the head.

"Fool, are you there?"

There was a long silence—a silence that seemed to hint at a suppressed chuckle. Fulk turned and went in, searched the hall, the kitchen quarters, the store-room and upper chambers, but found no John. The fellow had sneaked off, and fled into the forest.

Fulk took his bow and a couple of arrows from the table and passed out again into the porch. The man in brown had disappeared from the edge of the oak wood, and in his place stood a figure in a grey frock and hood, the figure of a grey friar, still as a stone figure in a niche over a church door.

Fulk fingered his chin.

"So you are there, my friend. God's mercy, but I have been bidden to wait for you, and I will wait with a naked sword. Let us see whether any ditch-mender will dare to put a foot over this threshold."

Passing swiftly from place to place, he closed and fastened every door and shutter, but left the porch door open. Brown dusk was falling, and the rafters of the hall were lost in gloom. Fulk kicked up the fire, threw on half a faggot and some logs, and the flare of the flames as they blazed up were reflected in his eyes. A ringed coat and an open basinet hung on a peg above the dais, with a plain black shield and a sword in a blue scabbard. Fulk stood listening a moment before taking down the hauberk. He slipped it on, donned the basinet, and began to fasten the laces to the rings of the chain gorget.

The fire had blazed up brightly, and, taking the shield and sword, Fulk drew a stool near to the hearth and sat down to watch and wait. He unsheathed the sword and laid it across his knees. There was no sound that he could hear other than the crackling of the burning wood or the scattering of sparks as a log fell. He saw a rat come out of a hole in the wainscoting and go gliding along the wall.

His eyes were fated to serve him sooner than his ears, for he had left the heavy oak door wide open, and in the dark streak between the hinge post and the edge of the door he saw something that glistened. It was the white of a man's eye peering through the crack, and looking straight at him as he sat beside the fire.

Fulk's muscles tightened.

"Hallo, my friend! I see you."

His voice was sharp and ringing as the stroke of a dagger upon steel. The glistening eye melted back into the shadows, and he heard whispering voices and a scuffling of feet. There were some twenty men in the courtyard, bunched together like hounds who have come to the mouth of a bear's cave.

One figure took another by the scruff of the neck and thrust it forward, and persuaded it towards the porch at the point of a sword. Fulk heard a man snarl like a dog. Then a mop head came furtively round the edge of the door, red eyes blinking anxiously, as though ready to dodge a blow.

The head jerked back again, and Fulk heard the murmur of voices grow louder. One voice topped the others, and the rest grew silent.

"Leave it to me, sirs; I know how to handle a vicious colt."

Fulk took the measure of the man who stalked insolently into the hall. It was the figure of a strapping bully, swaggering, tawdry, dramatic, clad in a scarlet cote-hardie covered with tarnished embroidery, hauberk, and basinet very rusty, and the blade of his sword, which he carried naked upon his shoulder, jagged like a saw. The red points of his forked beard stuck out like tusks, for he had a habit of throwing his head well back, and looking at people with an aggressive and staring insolence.

Fulk scanned him from head to heel; his nostrils dilating a little, his mouth twitching with scorn. He bided there silently like a hound of the blood waiting to hear a strange cur snarl at him.

Guy the Stallion gave him a swaggering salute with his sword.

"Master Fulk Ferrers, greeting. I have twenty men at my back, and none of us love John of Gaunt and his creatures. I charge you to throw down that sword of yours, and stand up like a good lad."

Fulk's stare was like the thrust of a spear. The doorway was full of hairy faces, of brown smocks and fists that held flails, scythe-blades on poles, clubs, bows, bill-hooks—a boor's armoury.

Fulk showed them an ironical courtesy, a storm sign in a young man of his temper.

"Sir Hacksword, I am much beholden to you. That blade of yours looks as though it had seen wonderful adventures. Step in, knights and gentles all; the honour is mine to be visited by so fair a company."

His scorn struck them like a north wind, and made the swashbuckler's forked beard thrust itself out more fiercely.

"This sword was hammering the French when you were a mere toddler. Have a care lest I come to use the flat of it."

Fulk rose up and walked over towards the man in red, keeping his eyes on Guy the Stallion's eyes, and holding his sword on his shoulder.

"Out—out, you dogs!"

He pointed with his sword towards the crowd of boors in the doorway.

"Out!"

"By cock, you young ruffler, I can take blows better than words."

He had his blow, a flat buffet across the face given slantwise with a lightning sweep of the sword-blade. He staggered, jerking up his arms, his nostrils reddening with blood. There was a crowding in of the smocked figures through the doorway, but Guy the Stallion bellowed them back.

"All hell shall stir for this! Let no man meddle."

He sprang towards Fulk with huge and flamboyant sweeps of the sword.

"Guard, you adder; I'll teach you sword-play."

And so the fight began.

Fulk had drawn back into a corner of the hall where he could hold the ground before him without being taken on the flanks. Guy the Stallion came at him with a swaggering rage, and for the moment the boors held back to watch the tussle, such a smiting together of swords not being seen on every day of the week.

Fulk was as calm as a frosty morning, his face looking serenely through all the whirl and pother of the swashbuckler's blows. Roger Ferrers had been a great man at his weapons, and Fulk had swung a sword with Roger before he was four feet high. He let this swaggerer slash as he pleased, guarding himself and smiling into the Stallion's eyes.

"Strike, my friend, strike harder. You would do better with a bulrush."

Of a sudden his whole front changed. His chin rose higher, his lips and nostrils grew thin, and his eyes ceased smiling. Blows leapt at Guy like flames, licking him on every side and driving him back. The fight ended with his stumbling and shooting forward under Fulk's sword, where he lay like a red beetle, very flat and still.

The men of the door set up a howl of rage, for this tawdry and swaggering bird had made them believe in his crowing. They came pushing in, bunched together, scythe-blades and bills poking forward, lusting to smite, yet afraid of that uncompromising sword. Fulk stood with head thrown back, nostrils dilated, eyes mocking them with a flare of scorn.

"Come, my lords and nobles, come nearer."

His fierce pride of birth, and his lean valour, awed them, though they cursed him and handled their weapons.

"Fetch in the chopping-block, Harry."

"We'll have his head off before cock-crow."

"Knock the whelp's legs from under him with a pole."

They edged forward in a half circle, encouraging each other, and pointing to the swashbuckler who still lay flat on his face. And since all their eyes were towards Fulk of the Forest, they did not see Isoult of the Rose and Father Merlin standing in the doorway.

It was Isoult's voice that whipped the boors back. They parted and let her through, since she carried a knife, and stabbed at those who faltered.

"Out, fools, out of the way."

Her voice might have been the sound of the Last Trump so far as Guy the Stallion was concerned, for he picked himself up, drew a sleeve across his face, and attempted an unsteady swagger. A crack in his rusty basinet showed where Fulk's sword had bitten him.

"Isoult, the cub is mine for the taking. He tricked me the once——"

He flourished his sword towards Fulk, but Isoult's eyes swept him aside.

"Fool, go and wash the blood out of your boasting beard."

"S'death! I'll set hell loose!"

"Poor jay, you pecked at a falcon and got smitten. Stand away. I have no patience to listen to your frothing."

He slunk aside with furious red eyes, while Father Merlin waited in the background, showing his teeth and smoothing his chin.

Isoult passed on towards Fulk, and these two stood confronting each other, the man with the point of his sword resting on the floor and his hands crossed on the pommel. No one but Fulk saw Isoult's face, or the cry of "Hail, fellow falcon!" in her eyes.

"Master Fulk Ferrers, I charge you, surrender that sword of yours."

He stared at her mistrustfully, head up, lips set.

"Dame Isoult, I thought you were at Lewes."

"Ah, my friend, I met comrades by the way. Have no fear, Dame Margaret is safe in Lewes town. We let the baggage pass, but tied up your men. And now, since we are too many for you, it is your turn to surrender."

His pride stiffened itself.

"Let them take me—if they dare."

There was the length of the hall between these two and the rest, but Isoult went closer to him, dropping her voice to a whisper:

"Fulk, listen to me. These wretches have tasted blood; your men are dead; we could not help it. You might kill the first three, but the rest would drag you down like dogs, and I'll not suffer it. You cannot fight, because I, Isoult, stand in the way."

His eyes searched hers.

"You! You are with these vermin?"

"I am, and I am not. But I shall stand between you so that you cannot use your sword nor these Jacks their clubs and bills. The grey friar is merciful. You surrender as my prisoner."

He looked at the floor, frowning and biting his lower lip.

"Come, Messire Fulk"—and her voice had a strange new challenge in it—"come; we change parts for awhile, you and I. And I will not bear to see these bullocks trampling you underfoot, for no man's valour can overcome twenty men. I have my pride, and pride knows its own kith and kin."

He raised his eyes suddenly to hers.

"So be it. But when I am swordless——"

"Think you that Father Merlin and I cannot rule these fools?"

"Isoult, you puzzle me."

She held up a hand.

"No questions. Surrender to me—to Isoult of the Rose. I vow that your sword shall be in safe keeping."

CHAPTER VIII

In the forest there was an old stone quarry, and in the wall thereof some hermit of long ago had cut himself a little chamber; but the hermit had died in the time of the Barons' war, and the quarry was full of briers and brambles, broom and bracken. A tall beech wood shut it on every side, so that the place was like a pit into which sunlight fell only at noon and when the sun was high in summer.

In the doorway of this hermit's cell Fulk of the Forest sat on a truss of dead bracken, and stared moodily at the beech trees. His hands and feet were free enough, but the sides of the quarry went up like a castle wall, and Guy the Stallion and twenty men lay night and day among the bushes that half closed the entry. At night a large fire was lit, and he could hear those who kept guard laughing and singing, and telling lewd tales.

This royal falcon, mewed up and fed upon dainties, was in no mood to be patient. He thought of the "fence" month that was so near, of the deer harried and hunted by boors and thieves, of the hinds, big with fawn, driven hither and thither. The personal part of the adventure balked his wit; he could read no meaning into it, nothing perhaps save the whim of a woman. As for Isoult, he felt no gratitude towards her, but brooded like a Samson shorn of his hair. He was tempted to believe that she had used her woman's wiles to steal his sword away; that she was playing off a jest on him, and that some day soon he would catch its meaning.

As he stared at the young beech leaves spreading in bright green glooms above the mouse-coloured trunks, he saw a figure appear in one of the woodland aisles, a figure that was all green and blue. He knew Isoult instantly by the way she walked, and the nearer she came the keener grew his anger against her. If she had but left well alone he would have driven the boors like sheep out of the White Lodge. He had been a fool to let her trick him and take away his sword.

Guy's men started up and louted to her, and Fulk saw her wave them back into the beech wood. As she entered the quarry he saw that she had his sword buckled to her under her green cloak, the leather belt clasping the sky-blue cloth of her cote-hardie She picked her way at her leisure through the brambles, looking at Fulk with eyes that were full of baffling lights and shadows.

Just without the cell's mouth a broom bush was in bloom, its yellow spikes very brilliant against the green of the young beech leaves. There was a rough stone seat at the entry under the broom bush, and Isoult sat herself down there within a bow's length of the man on the bracken.

Fulk kept his eyes from her, and stared at the beech wood as though no woman with black hair and red lips sat there under the yellow broom.

"Messire Fulk, am I to laugh or to weep?"

He seemed in no mind to answer her, and his shut mouth and haughty nostrils made her smile to herself with an air of intimate and adventurous mystery.

"I am to snivel then, and ask your pardon because I saved you from having your neck put on a chopping-block? And men are said to be grateful!"

He answered her, without turning his head.

"This is a fool's business. I can make nothing of it, save that I was a fool to give up my sword."

"You think that?"

"I have said so."

"Then I made you act like a fool?"

"So it seems. For the rest, I can see no sense in anything. And if it is a jest it is the dullest one I ever heard of."

She regarded him with intent and curious eyes, and, unbuckling the sword, laid it across her knees.

"See, here lies your sword. Stretch out your hand and take it, and I'll neither stir nor cry out."

For the first time since she had come to sit under the yellow broom Fulk looked straight into her face.

"More tricks!"

"Fulk of the Forest, I play fair. Take your sword and rush out against these fellows yonder. But, before your hawk's pride flies in the face of Fate, listen."

He did not move, but kept his eyes on hers.

"Well?"

"I offer you this sword of yours to prove that you do not know the temper of Isoult. Take the sword, play the madman if it pleases you; but I warn you it will make you look the greater fool. Those fellows yonder have had their orders, and each man has his bow. I have heard the orders that were given them, to keep clear, and shoot you through those long legs of yours so that you could neither run nor fight."

She took the sword by the scabbard and held the hilt towards him.

"Choose."

He shrugged contemptuously.

"A fool's business. I can make nothing of it, save that these hedgers and ditchers and horse-thieves are the lords of the forest. Why am I so marked a stag?"

"Because you are—what you are."

"More words."

She laid the sword on her knees, and bent towards him, pointing with one forefinger.

"Listen to me, Fulk Ferrers. Have you been on a wild hill in the thick of a thunderstorm, when the sky is like the lid of a black hell and the lightning stabs the earth here, there, and everywhere? Have you not felt like a hare in the grass, a little thing of no account, a wisp of straw in the wind? But perhaps Messire Fulk Ferrers is too stiffnecked and proud to listen while the doom vault cracks over his head!"

Her eyes were intensely black for the moment, her face the face of a witch. Fulk sat rigid, as though he listened to the sound of elf's horns in the forest.

"True; I have felt it," he said.

Her hand dropped to her knee.

"Messire Fulk, you and I are but children on the edge of a strange, storm-swept country. We cannot help ourselves; we are but little people stumbling over the heather. You ask for the why and the wherefore, but it is not for me to answer the riddle for you. What am I but a storm bird blown by wild winds from over the sea? I tell you there is great wrath and dread and violence afoot. You are here because the chance has seized on you as a red shrike seizes a beetle for its larder."

Her face was a new world to him, intense and white, the red lips uttering words that made him think of the moan of a wind through winter trees, or the clang of swords in a charge of horsemen upon some sunset heath. His manhood bridled, and reared like a startled horse. This voice of hers had reached some primitive instinct in him. His mistrust passed of a sudden and gave place to wonder.

"Strange words!"

Her eyes flashed out at him.

"You may go one way—I another. Someone will speak more plainly before many days have gone. Watch—consider. I know not how you may regard it—as a light adventure, a glorious treason. Do not mistrust me. I charge you, do not mistrust me!"

He gave her a quick, ironical smile.

"There is the beech wood yonder, and out of it will come a dragon, and I shall have no sword!"

"No sword could help you."

His stare was long and shrewd.

"It may be that Isoult of the Rose will ride on the dragon's back!"

"If so, I shall be the master," she said, looking at his hands.

Betimes she left him, and whither she went he knew not, save that she passed away into the beech wood, carrying his sword.

The next morning she came again, and her mood was full of laughter and of the joy of living. She had broken off a white may bough and carried it on her shoulder, and as she came through the woods Fulk heard her singing.

He would not suffer himself to believe that he had looked for her coming, or that her red mouth and her mysterious eyes had any message to move him. Yet that his manhood should leap in him when he saw her among the beech trees in her green cloak and blue cote-hardie, and with the white may bough over her shoulder, was a challenge to his pride. She brought some of the exultant rush of the year with her in the way she walked and the way she carried her head.

"I have come five miles."

Life was at high noon in her, with a glow of the eyes and face. Fulk took some of the dry bracken and spread it upon the stone bench, and the casual haughtiness of the deed was a part of the morning's comedy.

"I tell you, Fulk of the Forest, it is good to live. Run through the names of all the wines—malmsey, ypocrasse, basturde, clove, pyment, muscabell. They are nothing to the wind and the sun on the heath."

Her mood itself was a cup of Spanish wine, and Fulk took a draught of it into his blood.

"Whence have you come?"

"That would be telling! Lying awake under the stars in Gascony and listening to the aspens chattering! Messire Fulk, change with me; take my body and give me yours."

"What, to lie in a hermit's cell, and with that braggart for doorkeeper!"

"No, no; to take my arms and mount my horse on a May morning and gallop after adventures. To fight and break spears, and drink with my comrade in arms; to make love to women! Oh! the brave world, the valour and fun, the cry of the trumpets, the snow and the winter sunsets! The wind on the heath has blown itself into my blood!"

Fulk looked at her curiously. She was like no woman of his imaginings— no soft, sleek, sly thing to be kissed for a month and then left to her needle and her prayer desk.

"If I changed with you," he said, "I promise you that you would love the forest and the red deer, and the heath in bloom, and the laugh of the woodpecker, and the smell of the fern."

"Ah, I promise you. The rich earth, and the red sap of our life. The great woods, the rivers that go down to the sea, the armed hosts in their battle harness, the strength and the valour, the galloping horses, the scorn of treachery, the eyes that look straight."

He nodded towards the mouth of the quarry.

"There are eyes over yonder that look round corners and through bushes. The red beard is watching us, his head all swaddled up so that he looks like an old woman in a wimple."

"That fool! He must have his tongue and his nose in everything! I can play with such bumblebees."

She stood up and called the swashbuckler.

"Guy, hallo there—friend Guy!"

The Stallion came out from behind a holly bush, carrying his sword on his shoulder, the red twists of his beard ferocious as ever.

"Bring me Blanche's lute. I saw her over yonder as I came through the wood; and for my touching of her strings she can boast of Isoult as her comrade."

Guy saluted Isoult with his sword, and disappeared into the beech wood, where Blanche was sitting in a shelter of boughs under a tree, mending a hole in her hose, one bare foot thrust out, her hair bundled up anyhow in a torn net. Her lute lay in a red bag beside her, but as to lending it to Isoult that was another matter. Guy had but to grab at the thing for her to scratch at his face and start screaming like a jay.

Isoult laughed.

"Between them they will break the strings, yet I shall get the lute."

The squabble was soon over, Big Blanche's voice oozing away into a futile whimpering that was smothered by the big oaths and blasphemies of her man. She had wriggled away and was cowering against the tree trunk in order to escape from a foot that was none too delicate in the use of its big toe.

"You sing, you big slug! You have a voice like the bung-hole of a barrel!"

He marched off, and coming to Isoult, presented the lute to her with a fine obeisance, his sword cocked over his shoulder. One red eye looked slantwise at Fulk of the Forest.

"Madame Isoult, sing, and we shall forget to be hungry."

"Or to quarrel—or boast!"

She took the lute to her bosom, and struck the strings, waiting for Guy the Stallion to take himself off.

"What shall I sing, good comrade?"

"Just what comes to the bird's throat."

And so she sang to him of Ipomedon, and Gingamor, and the Romaunt of the Rose, and of strange forests and haunted meres, and of the banners of kings red as the sunset. Fulk's heart went out to her because of her singing, and all his mistrust of her melted like wax.

When she had ended he looked long at her as though trying to fathom her soul.

"Isoult, who and what are you? For some day I needs must know."

"Good comrade, I am but a bird from over the sea, and yet I have no ring on my foot."

"I marvel——"

"That I should sing?"

"No. That you should fly with these jays and stormcocks."

She glanced at him slantwise under black lashes.

"Why should I tell you what no man in the land knows?"

"Why, indeed?" he echoed her.

"We are two riddles, you and I," she said, "to be guessed, some time or never. But whether we shall guess each other, God and our need may show."

Meanwhile, Guy the Stallion lay flat on his belly behind a bush, gnawing grass, and watching them with hungry eyes. The beast in him desired Isoult and hated the man beside her. And from a little distance Big Blanche watched her man, her round, white face sullen, and glum, and jealous.

CHAPTER IX

About that time Father Merlin had news brought him. Runners came to the White Lodge in the forest, where Merlin was to be found sitting on a stool by the pond, fishing; or kneeling in the hall before a little wooden cross that he had hung on a peg in one of the oak posts. Every hour he might be found kneeling there, eyes closed, a smile on his harsh face, looking as though he had prayed for the souls of men and saw the Great Ones of Heaven descending instantly to succour the poor.

The runners came from north, east, and west. Each man had much the same message to give to Father Merlin, and he would listen with a rapt look and then return the fellow his blessing.

"Peace to you, my son. Assuredly, God and St. Francis have remembered the poor."

Merlin knew what he knew as he took his walks in the forest, a thin, grey figure in a great, green world. He would pause upon the hills, and look east and west, his hood turned back, his eyes gleaming, his broad nostrils sniffing the air. Father Merlin had been a villein's son, and all the fierce, sneering spirit of the man sprang back with a snarl of hatred from those who ruled by right of birth. A hundred hungers and humiliations lay on him like a hair shirt. He chafed to tear the pomp from the lords' shoulders and to fling it as a cape of freedom over the poor, though the noble's purse might find its way into St. Francis's wallet and his power into St. Francis's hand.

He cried aloud as the west wind came up the slope of the hill, and blew his grey frock about his knotty knees.

"Blow, wind, blow! The poor shall trample Mammon into the mud!"

Much such a cry as Merlin's had gone through all the land, and the men of the fields had heard it and lifted their heads—brown waters running together in flood time from every ditch and stream. The carter had left his horses; the woodman had shouldered his axe and left the oak bark but half stripped for the tanner; the serf had set his scythe upon a pole; the smith had shouldered his hammer; the charcoal burner had forgotten his fire. Everywhere they gathered, these brown men, with a murmur like the rustling of dead leaves when a great host marches to battle along a woodland road in autumn. Their mouths were uttering strange new words, "The Commons and the King!"

A stupor of fear had seized on all those who ruled. The lords and gentry had shut themselves up in their castles and houses, or ridden off out of the way of the wind. Doors were barred, bridges raised, shutters bolted. Reeves, clerks, tax-gatherers, hid themselves in cellars and hay-lofts. Women shivered and lay awake at night. The suddenness of the thing had astonished the gentles as though the brown earth were heaving under their feet. Knights who had fought in the French wars sat sullenly at home, too proud, perhaps, to risk the pride of the sword against the insolence of a smith's hammer or a labourer's flail. The ignoble many had risen against the arrogant few, and the arrogance was with the mob for the moment.

It was a wild May, both in wind and temper. The hawthorn bloom was scattered like snow, and late frosts nipped even the young bracken. The north wind roared out of a hard blue sky, making the green world shiver, and bringing Berserk steel into the painted pleasance of spring. The mood of the hind suited the mood of the weather. The fields were empty, and the men who should have laboured there were running like madmen hither and thither. The cold spell out of the north seemed to have given a rougher edge to the boorish temper, making it remember the mud and rain in the winter fields, the sour food at home in the draughty clay-daubed cottage; while Master Gentleman sat in his stone house before the fire under the great chimney, and drank hot Spanish wines, and had furs to draw about him. The wolf spirit was abroad. These men of the fields were drunk with years of envy, hatred, and sullen anger; they raged through the country-side, plundering cellars and larders, tearing down the banks of fish ponds, breaking mill wheels, cutting down orchard trees, emptying granaries and dovecots, killing deer, and harrying warrens. Pride of birth was taken by the beard, mocked, and treated to the savage horse-play of these men of the soil.

"When Adam delved and Eve span,
Where was then the gentleman?"

They howled these words in the villages, along the roads, and over the heaths and commons. The French Jacquerie seemed to have come again with its gibbering fury, its wild lust and blood spilling; and many a woman trembled for her honour, and many a gentleman dreamt of his bloody head dancing upon a pike.

Father Merlin knew what he knew. The runners came to him carrying news, and one May morning he sought Isoult. She had taken herself to one of the empty forest lodges where two sheep and their lambs fed in the deserted orchard and a cow came to the byre gate to be milked.

It was so cold that Isoult had brought in wood and kindled a fire, and Merlin found her in the dark, black oak hall, sitting on a stool, and staring at the flames. A loose shutter banged to and fro in the wind, and the twittering of the sparrows in the thatch sounded cold and thin.

Merlin's eyes shone out from under the shadow of his cowl. He pulled up a stool, and, spreading his hands to the blaze, spoke of the roughness of the weather.

"And yet our Rose blooms," said he; "and the young man of the quarry, is he as cold as the wind out of the north?"

She did not look at Merlin, but her eyes were dark and set steadily towards some inward thought.

"He is—what he is."

"Does the scent of the rose count for nothing in June? Come now, what have you seen, my daughter?"

She answered him slowly, almost grudgingly.

"The third finger of the left hand is crooked. A blow from a quarter-staff broke it. And over the right eyebrow there is a small brown mole."

"Good. You would know this apple from another?"

She nodded.

Merlin spread his arms dramatically, and then stared in silence at the fire. The eyes under the cowl glistened, and the harsh face with its savage sagacity looked hungry and exultant.

"We have two puppets and two strings! Speak to me, Isoult. Let me hear what you have to tell."

She rested her chin on her fist.

"I have nothing to tell. I will wager that you cannot take the hood from that hawk and make him fly as you please."

"Say you so! But a young man may be persuaded, and you—my daughter——"

"I, too, have the fettle of a falcon."

"Am I a fool? But what have you done? How have you played with him?"

"Merlin, be careful how you tempt me to be angry!"

He looked at her intently, and then, leaning forward, began to speak with a whispering eagerness, his voice sounding like the blowing of a wind through a crack in a shutter. Isoult sat back, rigid, her eyes staring at the fire, her throat stiffening, her lips pressed together. She was very white when he uttered the first words, but a slow surge of blood rose into her face, and her eyes glittered like water touched by the sun at dawn.

Suddenly she started up, and her face flamed.

"Enough! Am I to listen to this?"

Merlin stroked the air with his hands.

"My daughter, I speak advisedly. Is it not a glory to any woman for her to make and unmake kings? And this Fulk is not unworthy. The blood of a great prince runs in him."

She walked to and fro, and then stood and looked down at him with a scorn that she did not dissemble.

"No. I sing no such song for you, Master Merlin. By my troth, I bid you beware."

He waved his hands with the same smoothing motion, and dared to meet her eyes.

"My daughter, you are in too hot a hurry. The King of the Commons will not have to wed a princess out of France or Spain. She who is comely and proud and valiant can sit by such a king. Come now—consider."

"Merlin, I know that tongue of yours."

"Let us leave it to Dame Nature, Isoult. Love leaps in where he pleases."

"I give you neither yea nor nay."

"In that I must find my comfort."

He sat awhile beside the fire, brooding and fingering his chin. Isoult had gone out into the orchard, but when he sought her there she was not to be found. Merlin crossed himself, and turned back towards the White Lodge.

"A woman's anger is not to be trusted," he said to himself, "for oftentimes it rises out of the passion it pretends to scorn. I must feel how that young man's heart beats. Hot blood is very helpful."

Isoult, hidden among some yew trees on the side of the hill above the orchard, watched Merlin's grey frock disappear into the green of the woods. Her face shone white and hard, but in her eyes there was something of wonder, even of fear.

CHAPTER X

Fulk sat in the doorway of the hermit's cell and watched the dusk come down—the slow, subtle dusk of a still May evening. The beech wood had been full of the singing of birds, and on the top of a holly near the quarry's mouth a thrush had poured out all its joy and desire, its grey-brown breast turned towards the sunset. The beech foliage had changed from vivid green to amethyst, the trunks from grey to black, while orange, amber, and saffron were flung abroad across an exultant west. Now, later still, the woods rose in soft, rounded blackness against a deep blue sky, with the crescent of the moon clear as polished steel.

Fulk sat there brooding, his face growing grey in the dusk. The smoke of a fire rose beyond the mouth of the quarry—a grey, sinuous pillar that swayed slightly from side to side or thrust out a ghostly arm when some breath of wind played upon it. Now and again a voice growled sulkily, but since the birds had ceased their singing the silence had become immense, irrefutable, supreme.

Presently there was a crackling of brushwood. The pillar of smoke swelled to a cloud of draughty vapour; dead wood had been thrown on the fire, and the flames licked through it and rose as crimson and yellow tongues against the blackness of the beech wood. A sense of restlessness seemed to come from nowhere and to show itself in the wavering lights and shadows that played under the boughs of the beeches. Fulk saw a solitary figure outlined against the fire, thrusting a pole under the burning brushwood, and looking, with the jagged comb of its hood, like a sinister black devil.

Something moved in the mouth of the quarry, a patch of greyness that disassociated itself from the vague gloom of the brambles and furze. Fulk's chin went up, and his eyes were on the alert. The figure shaped itself into that of a grey friar, and Fulk guessed it to be Father Merlin.

He came gliding in like a ghost. A grey arm went up and gave Fulk a benediction.

"Peace to you, Fulk Ferrers."

Merlin sat himself down on the stone seat outside the cell, with his staff across his knees. His cowl was drawn, and Fulk could not see his face, but merely a patch of blackness where the face should be.

The Franciscan took his beads and muttered three prayers, and Fulk watched him, wondering what Merlin's business might be, and how far he was to be trusted.

"Has the blood grown restless in you, Fulk Ferrers?"

His voice was smooth and persuasive.

"No more than in a hawk on a perch."

"The hawk would fly, eh! Young blood runs hot. I have many things to say to you, Fulk of the Forest."

The darkness was between them, and Merlin's voice came out of it with a cautious, intimate murmur.

"My son, who has not heard of wrongs that should be righted, of things hidden away under the ground when they should be brought into the light of day? Listen to me, son Fulk. A priest comes by many truths, and by strange stories, and sometimes it is difficult for a man to believe his own ears and eyes."

He bent over his staff and stared into Fulk's face, his cowl slipping back a little, so that a gaunt chin poked out and Fulk saw the gleam of his eyes.

"Listen to strange tidings."

Merlin's voice fell to a whisper; and Fulk, looking into the dim face, felt as though some sly and persuasive hand were touching him. Isoult's enigmatic words were in his ears, and his mistrust bristled.

"Speak out, friar, if you have anything to say."

"Assuredly I can paint you a picture such as few young men have ever looked upon."

It may be that Father Merlin had passed an hour in the quarry before Guy the Stallion and his men heard a throttled voice calling for help. They tumbled up from about the fire and went running into the quarry, dodging in and out between the masses of bramble and furze. Guy had taken a burning brand from the fire, and its flare showed them Merlin flat on his back and Fulk of the Forest on top of him.

They fell upon Fulk, dragged him off, and bore him back against the quarry wall. He did not struggle with them, and his passivity was part of his scorn. Merlin turned over on his hands and knees, wheezing and fighting for breath, his lips blue, and his eyes full of tears. He gathered himself up, coughing, and feeling his throat.

Guy swaggered forward.

"Give the word, father, and we'll make an end."

Merlin's hood had fallen back. He turned on Guy with grinning, furious face.

"Fool! Tie the man up, and put a sack over his head. And keep that dagger of yours out of mischief."

A man went off towards the fire, and returned with leather thongs and an old sack. Merlin was still fingering his throat, and his voice was a hoarse whisper.

"Make no mistake over it—tie him up as a spider ties up a fly."

He stood and watched them, and when the thing was done he went very close to Fulk and stared into his face.

"Fool! What of six feet of cold earth under a beech tree? Sleep on the edge of the black hole, my son, and look down into it when the daylight comes—the cold grey light after cock-crow."

Fulk kept his mouth shut and his eyes on Merlin's. His nostrils quivered. There was no slackening of his pride. Merlin sneered at him.

"Put the sack over my lord's head, and lay him down like a baby to sleep on the bracken. Fulk Ferrers, I wish you good dreams, and cool blood in the morning."

It was Isoult, mistrustful of Father Merlin's subtlety, who came through the beech wood just when the grey light of the dawn was making the world look huge and vague and very mysterious. She found the men sleeping about the fire, and Guy the Stallion, who should have been on the watch, sitting doubled up with his head on his arms.

Isoult glided past them and came to the doorway of the cell. It was so dark within that she could see nothing, though she could hear the sound of a man's breathing. She stood there and called softly, putting her hands about her mouth.

"Fulk! Fulk of the Forest!"

He was sleeping lightly, and woke with a start to the presence of an old flour sack over his head and shoulders, and the leather thongs about wrists and ankles. It was very dark in the cell, and his waking mood was as coldly grim and implacable as his proud disgust could make it. He had fallen asleep with the prospect of having his throat cut in the morning, and it was no affair of his if some fool woke him so early.

"Good comrade, are you still dreaming?"

She had stolen in, but could see little but a vague shape lying on the bracken. Fulk bristled at the sound of her voice.

"Isoult?"

"Surely! Speak low. The birds are just beginning, and our friend Guy is asleep."

One piping note had thrilled up from the beeches, and of a sudden a score of other bird voices followed it, making the grey light quiver.

"Is the sun up?"

"Surely a man can see with his own eyes!"

"With a sack tied over his head! Here is something for a woman to laugh at."

She came nearer.

"What! Have they tied you up? I had a feeling that you and Merlin had come to the dagger point. Has he spoken?"

"Spoken? It would have been his last sermon if those fellows yonder had given me three more minutes."

She knelt down beside him and he felt her fingers moving over his face.

"Lie very still."

Isoult took the knife from her girdle, thrust the point through the sacking, slit it crosswise, and turned back the flaps. A haze of grey light was streaming into the cell, but it was not strong enough to show her the set and rigid hostility of his face.

"So Merlin has spoken. Now, good comrade, do you see the light?"

His lips moved stiffly, ironically.

"I see many things—treachery, and lies, and dishonour, and the hands of a woman."

Isoult sat back on her heels, and thrust her knife back into its sheath.

"Ah, so you look askance at me, and my hands are full of treachery!"

He did not look at her, but at the vault of rock above him.

"What God knows the devil discovers. This madman Merlin spoke of shriving me at dawn. He shall find me stiff in the neck."

"This madman would make and unmake kings; he will use you, Messire Fulk, or break you, if he can. Wait, answer me one question. Think you that I am so mean a thing as to play the quean at Merlin's bidding, even though I follow the same cause?"

"With hedgehogs, and rats, and field-mice— —"

"Answer me this question."

Her voice challenged him with an edge of passion, and her eyes looked straight at his.

"What do you believe of me, Fulk Ferrers?"

"Everything—and nothing."

"So! My hands fastened these thongs on you?"

"It may be."

She bent over him with sudden vehement fierceness.

"Fulk Ferrers, look at me."

Isoult's face was so close to his that he could feel her warm breath upon his mouth. The daylight had gathered, and her hair was like a black cloud, her face the moon, and the red of her lips was the dawn. Moreover, her eyes held his as desire challenges desire, or as a sword presses upon a sword.

"Look at me. Am I a cut-throat jade, Merlin's creature? By my maidenhood, I should not be here an I were. Listen. The truth may say that you are a bastard brother to the King, that you are as like as two apples, that you may serve as well as he. I say it may be so, else why should Merlin be so venomously wise? As for you, you say that you have chosen. Good. But I too have a choice to make; the hands you mistrust might unfasten the bonds that bind you!"

He looked up at her with a half-sullen fire in his eyes.

"Call me a bastard, and the mother who bore me a — —. No, by God, I'll not put my lips to it! Let that truth stick in Merlin's throat."

She sat back and gazed at him.

"Oh, stiffnecked, proud, splendid fool! Were I to soar, would you not follow? Such a flight of falcons into the blue together!"

He turned his head aside, for her eyes, her mouth, her voice tormented him.

"Isoult, have done. Whether this be one gross lie or not—I'll not wanton with it, or with these scrapings of the fields. God—if I have a prince's blood in me, I'll play the prince."

She thrust out her hands, eyes alight, her breath coming and going more quickly.

"Ah! That has an echo! I soar to that. I——Listen! Did you hear?"

She turned sharply, and Fulk saw her bosom, throat, and face outlined against the doorway.

"Merlin's voice!"

She started up and passed out into the quarry just as Father Merlin's grey cowl appeared among the furze bushes. He was alone, and his face seemed to narrow when he saw Isoult.

She went to meet him boldly, head held high, and with an imperiousness that attacked and did not wait to be challenged.

"Merlin, you have neither the wit nor the hands of a woman. What! Brought to the footpad's threat of the knife and six feet of earth already? Thank me for being up before dawn."

He eyed her cautiously, and when he spoke his voice was still harsh from Fulk's crumpling of his throat.

"Ah, my bird of the morning!"

"I have uncovered the man's eyes. A woman's face is fairer to look at than the inside of a sack. Wait and see whether there is no magic."

Merlin laughed noiselessly.

"We are less proud this morning?" he said.

CHAPTER XI

The men of Sussex were on the march, and Father Merlin rode on a white mule, with Fulk on a forest pony beside him, and the Sussex men wondered who the priest's prisoner might be, for Fulk was lashed to the beast he rode, and his head was swathed up in white linen. Father Merlin rode softly, smiling upon these children who were to lay all the lords and gentlemen of England in the dust. When the chance served he talked to Fulk, using a scathing, ironical, and tempting tongue, and hinting at adventures that tended towards both heaven and hell.

Isoult of the Rose also went with this great company of the poor, mounted upon a black horse that had been stolen out of somebody's stable. She had put off her gay colours and rode in russet, though the red leather shoes remained. They had given her a pony to carry her lute and her baggage, and Guy the Stallion marched at no great distance like a sergeant-at-arms, with fat Blanche trailing sulkily after him.

Isoult was a silent woman that morning, but her eyes were very watchful and missed little that was to be seen. June had come; the woods were like great green clouds against the blue; the bracken was frothing round the oak stems, and lush grass stood knee-deep in the meadows. Not only was it thundery weather, but a blight seemed on the land, an oppressive stillness, an invisible terror that waited in the hot and stagnant woodland. Other companies of the poor had been on the march before them, and had left the slime of their track behind—a burnt barn here and there, an empty manor-house with the gate broken and the house door hanging askew on its hinges, and once, the body of a man with a black face dangling from a tree. The country-side seemed very empty, save at some tavern or intake where a knot of noisy oafs with bills and cudgels in their hands waited to join the great company of the poor.

Very often Isoult was in the thick of these marching boors, and her nostrils showed the subtle shadow of an incipient scorn. The day was steamy, and the mob smelt and sweated, shouted and swore, spat, jostled, cracked coarse jokes, and drank out of bottles. Its breath was not pleasant. The hairy faces were leering and cruel, and their exultation belched in the face of the morning. All along the track she heard them bawling:

"When Adam delved and Eve span,

Where was then the gentleman?"

"Hinds!" she thought. "Where was all your insolent, sweating dust! I could half wish you at the mercy of a hundred galloping spears!"

Moreover, some of them crowded about her, and hot faces were smeary with a gloating thought of her comeliness. She saw the dull lust in their eyes, and her pride became ice. They were like cattle jostling, leaping, bellowing. Now and again the shrill and screaming laughter of a woman eddied up. There was one huge fellow with a purple birth-mark covering half his face, who strode along carrying a small cask as a drum, and beating it with a hammer. He shouted perpetually with the voice of a cow that has been separated from its calf, "Death to all the lords and gentles!" and when he shouted his mouth looked like a red sore.

Late in the day they were crossing a lonely valley, where a stream ran between willows and aspens. A mill-house, built of timber and white plaster and thatched with straw, stood in the thick of an orchard about a hundred paces above the ford, and Isoult saw a dozen men break away and make for the mill-house. The fore-hoofs of her horse were, in the water when she heard a woman's scream, a scream that was smothered instantly as though a big hand had been clapped over the screamer's mouth.

The men near Isoult laughed.

"Old Bill o' Mead Barrel will be first in, I wager you."

She turned her horse sharply, scattered the men, and rode through the grassland along the edge of the stream, and leaving her horse at the gate by the footbridge, crossed over by the planking that passed close to the mill-wheel. There was a little garden of flowers and herbs in front of the house, and from within came the cries of a woman.

Isoult's voice was merciless.

"Back, you dogs!"

Her right hand was armed, but the men fell away sheepishly from before the steel of her scorn. A woman lay cowering in a corner, and the big fellow with the purple face who had been beating the barrel like a drum was standing over her with a torn piece of cloth in one hand.

Isoult beckoned the woman.

"Come."

She twisted past the big man, and, half crawling, fled to Isoult's knees. And the men let her go, standing mute and balked, avoiding each other's eyes.

Isoult pointed the woman over the bridge.

"Go; take to the woods. Hide while the wild swine are abroad."

She kissed Isoult's hand and fled.

Isoult waited on the footbridge, but the men hung back in the mill-house, for her scorn had sobered them.

Turning to cross the bridge, she found Merlin riding up on his white mule between the willows and aspens. His cowl fell back as he dismounted, and he was showing his teeth like a horse minded to bite.

Isoult called to him.

"Merlin, are your swine to root as they please?"

He made light of it, sneeringly.

"Keep away from the sty, Isoult; your nose is too delicate. Things must happen. I will speak to the fools."

As he passed her on the bridge their eyes crossed like swords.

"Sing to our hooded falcon to-night, my daughter. It may be that I have softened his heart."

She gave Merlin no answer, but, remounting her horse, rode back slowly towards the ford.

A halt was called under the edge of a crimson sunset that overtopped the black plumes of a forest of firs. Isoult left her horse with Guy the Stallion, and walked towards the spot where Merlin's white mule was tethered, and where men were pitching a rough hide tent.

Merlin came out to her and his eyes were enigmatical.

"The lute and the voice and the eyes may serve," he said; "and yet, Isoult, why should I trust you?"

"Because my wrongs were great, and because I should be a worse enemy than friend."

"The falcon is hidden away over yonder. He shall have wine and meat, and a fair woman to sing to him."

"No spying upon us, Merlin. Let me play with him as I please."

She found Fulk in a green dell on the edge of the wood, nearly a furlong from the place where the men of Sussex were camped for the night. He was sitting amid the bracken under a fir tree, ankles and wrists lashed together, his face masked by the linen swathings. Two men with bows over their knees were squatting on the edge of the dell, their faces half hidden by scarlet hoods. Isoult guessed that Merlin had followed her, and, glancing back, she caught sight of his grey figure moving amid the trunks of the firs. He called to the two men on the edge of the dell, and they arose and left Fulk and Isoult alone together.

"Good comrade, I am to sing to the King's brother at Merlin's desire, but not to a man muffled up like a leper."

She put her lute on the ground, and, kneeling behind him, unfastened the linen band that covered his face.

"Wrists and ankles might also be free!"

He answered her without turning his head.

"I am not to be tempted."

She smiled from her vantage point, and, throwing the linen aside, sat down close to him among the bracken. A stone bottle of wine and a clean cloth full of bread and meat had been sent to Fulk by Father Merlin.

"Let us eat and drink, comrade; and then I will sing to you."

He glanced at her as though he took her to be mocking him, and she remembered his helpless hands.

"I must not untie you, or Merlin would be suspicious. The wood is full of eyes. But my hands can serve for both of us."

She fed him and gave him the wine to drink, and though she laughed over it a little, to Fulk it was a fool's business, and he was shy of her eyes and hands. His grim face sought to hold her at arm's length, though the redness of her mouth tormented him.

Dusk was falling, and the fir wood behind them began to grow very black against the sky. The Sussex men were lighting fires in the valley, and making a great uproar like the noise of beasts at feeding time. Isoult's eyes grew restless, and kept watching the darkening wood.

"Fulk, shall I sing?"

"You were sent to sing."

She reached for her lute, which lay between them.

"Merlin is a grey ghost, ready to haunt us. I must sing, for he may be listening."

Her eyes had strangeness, mystery; they were eyes that whispered, and drew him aside into the intimate shadow of her plotting.

"Listen, and live."

She struck a few thin, plaintive notes, and her voice was a mere murmur:

"Pride goes with a valiant heart;

Honour is my desire.

I would not ride with patchwork men

When a kingdom is on fire."

Her fingers leapt suddenly to a crackling and jaunty tune, and she began to sing some ditty that went like a drunken horseman galloping a young horse. It was for Merlin that she sang—Merlin, whose presence she felt away yonder in the near shadows of the fir wood.

From the valley came a roaring of voices shouting the old refrain, and Isoult dashed her own empty ditty aside like a cup of bad wine:

"When Adam delved and Eve span,

Where was then the gentleman?"

"Listen," and her chin went up scornfully. "Listen to the dogs howling! I have heard it all day."

Fulk watched the little black figures jerking round the fires.

"Some day they shall discover the why and the wherefore," he said.

"As for me, has my pride turned against them already? I tell you that one day has been sufficient, with the sweat and the smell of these cattle."

"So fickle—and so soon!"

"Sometimes one sees the truth very suddenly; these unclean beasts were made for the yoke and the goad."

His eyes were ironical.

"And yet, Isoult, you were sent to tempt me."

"It is true. And I was ready to tell you the truth. I—in my turn—have been tempted."

"By Merlin?"

"Yes, and no. I'll not tell you my story. No man yet has earned a right to that. But this much I will breathe to you. I was driven like a bird over the sea, and the hate and wrath in my heart were bitter against all those who called themselves of gentle blood, and whose pride was a mere ruffian's castle. Who succoured and saved me in those evil days? A burner of charcoal, a cook's boy, and a harlot! They were chivalrous when the great ones were lustful and treacherous. So I swore a feud against all men who carried a device upon their shields, all those who wore gilded spurs. Hence, many adventures and a voice that has sung to the poor."

In the dusk under the trees her eyes held his, and from her red mouth the words came with the vehemence of a rhapsody. Fulk felt like the strings of her lute swept by the fingers of that dim hand that now rested among the bracken. The pale vehemence of her beauty called to the man in him with the clashing of cymbals and the wailing of flutes.

He thrust his face nearer to hers, almost fiercely.

"Isoult, have a care; I am no mere boy."

She drew in a deep breath.

"A boy? You, with that fierce mouth and eyes like a hawk's! The naked soul of a woman calls only to the naked soul of a man. I'm not one to plead and wheedle. What did Merlin desire? That I should debauch you into playing the King."

He set his jaw at her, and his hands strained at the thongs.

"I guessed it."

"And I, at first, thought of it as a great adventure, as of two falcons soaring together into the blue. But now I see the shine of your pride, and my pride is bright as yours."

He felt a strange stirring of his blood.

"Well—what then?"

She thrust out her hands.

"No one will persuade you, not even Isoult of the Rose, nor will she stoop to't. Therefore, Merlin will grow savage, and Fulk of the Forest will lose his head."

He smiled at her with a grim and challenging approval.

"You reason well."

"I may reason better. The hands that helped to spread the net may unfasten it again. Look not like that. I make no bargain; my pride is as good as yours."

He spoke in a hard whisper.

"And I ask nothing—nothing of you, Isoult. But if you play this game on Merlin, you'll suffer—where I——"

She moved closer to him, her eyes shining.

"What a stiffnecked boy it is, with a wit as stiff as a sword-blade. Why, the woman in me is three times as wise as the man in you. Merlin—ssst!—I can fool any Merlin!"

His grey face threatened her in the dusk.

"And fool me—also!"

"Easily in some ways, if I would. And yet—I could not."

They stared at each other a moment, breathless, irreconcilable, wondering—two proud birds hovering breast to breast. Desire played like summer lightning. Each saw the other's pale face flash out of the darkness of dreams wreathed with a wreath of flame.

Fulk opened his mouth to speak, but no words came. In the wood they heard a sharp crackling of dead twigs, and the harsh voice of a man muttering out prayers.

"Merlin!"

She sprang up, snatched her lute, and slipped away among the trees.

CHAPTER XII

Isoult saw Merlin loitering for her among the fir trees, and she could imagine the smile on his face—that face with its red, libidinous mouth and hungry, restless eyes. He stood there in a little alley of the wood, a figure like a grey monolith marking the spot where some king had fallen.

Isoult's soul hardened itself against him, and she struck the strings of her lute and murmured the words of a song.

"Trust a priest to cheat at any game."

He shrugged.

"I walked in the wood to keep fools from straying upon you, and when I came close I said my prayers so that you should hear."

His head poked forward on its long neck like the head of a vulture, and he seemed to sniff the air.

"What tidings, Isoult; what tidings?"

"The falcon is tamed."

"What? You have cozened him? May all comely women be praised! I did not believe that the man lived who could say you nay."

She caught the leer in his voice, and guessed how he would be looking at her and licking his red lips. And from that moment she hated Merlin with all the hot pride of her nature.

"Make no boast of it, for I do not."

He laughed gloatingly, and she could have struck him in the face with her knife.

"Are you sure of the fool, Isoult?"

"As sure of him as I am of your piety! No meddling between us; I have more songs to sing."

He said nothing for a moment, but she felt his eyes upon her.

"Isoult, I can teach you no subtlety in singing. You will make sure——?"

Her patience carried her no farther.

"Save your words, and let the night look after its own darkness."

"I'll leave youth with youth."

She heard his beads rattling, and he turned to go.

"Bonds stronger than thongs of leather," he said. "Fasten them upon him, Isoult, and I will give you my blessing."

So strong for the moment was the revulsion of her pride that when Merlin had gone she walked to and fro under the trees, raging against the tangle in which she found herself. The fires in the valley were as so many red eyes watching her in the toils of her dilemma. To have to cheat such a man as Merlin, lie to him, make a jest of her own honour in order to blind his eyes! And why? Because that stiffnecked fool down yonder sat like a Simeon Stylites on the pillar of his pride, and would not slacken one fibre of his obstinacy in order to save his precious head.

She saw the past, the present, and the future all tangled up in a strange medley—the ringlets of a river thrown wide across green fields and orchards, the chattering of aspen leaves, the roses in a garden, the grey tumbling sea, the singing woman who sang to men with her knife ready at her girdle, the fierce thrusting back of lustful fools, the mocking flush of the eyes, the wanderings, dreams, and adventures, the wrestling match with the man who now lay yonder most damnably determined to die.

Well, let him throw his raw scorn in Merlin's face, and suffer for his stiffneckedness. What was it to her? How did it concern her? Men knew that Isoult of the Rose was not to be handled or clutched at with greedy fingers, and that her anger was not a thing to be tempted. And was she to make herself look an outwitted and shameful fool, a soft-hearted ninny tricked by a man's tongue!

She walked to and fro under the trees, and the tangle made her furious.

"By our Lady, let the fool pay for his pride. Why should I meddle?"

The wind of her passion changed just as quickly, and blew her mood to the other side of the fire. She began to curse like a man, and to snap discords from the strings of her lute.

"By the blood in hell, I'll do it; I'll do it!"

She turned and went back towards the edge of the wood like a leaf caught up and blown along by a gust of wind.

Fulk was watching the fires in the valley with the little black figures going to and fro about them. He heard Isoult coming back through the fir wood, and the sound of her footsteps made him harden his heart. He was wrath with himself because he saw everywhere the red mouth, the pale face, and the mysterious eyes.

Isoult sailed down on him over the lip of the dell like a bird with the wind.

"What had Merlin to say?"

"Leave Merlin with the devil!"

She dropped on her knees close to him, tossed the lute aside, and pulled out her girdle knife.

"Hold out your hands."

She spoke and acted like one in a fever of impatience, who could brook neither argument nor delay.

"Hold out your hands, fool! Don't sit and stare! Shall I have to push you and your pride out of death's way? I have lied and played the jade for your sake, and I tell you I am out of temper. I'll cut you out of these thongs, and say good riddance."

Her anger was so headlong that he felt driven to breast it as a swimmer breasts a wave.

"You have been putting Merlin off with lies?"

"That's right—ask every question you can think of! What can we do with such a stubborn fool but tell lies on his account? I said I had persuaded you to play the King. Hold your hands out."

He did not move.

"Oh—well, I can begin elsewhere."

She bent forward and cut the thongs that bound his legs and ankles, severing the leather with vicious jerks of the knife.

"Now—the hands. I want the burden of your pride off my conscience, to be rid of your heroics. They put one in a tangle."

He held out his hands, and she cut them free.

"Done. The falcon will find his wings stiff. Fly ten miles before daybreak. As for me—I may be able to get some sleep."

She sat back on her heels and began to laugh with a casual inconsequence that had a touch of mockery. Fulk was stretching his arms, and moving his wrists and fingers, and all the while a slow and puzzled anger was gathering in him against Isoult. He could make nothing of her moods and passions, and this laughter of hers mocked the desire for her that seemed to have flashed out of nothingness but an hour ago.

"You can set a man free, but you cannot make him walk."

She still laughed softly as though her whole nature mocked him.

"Am I to drive you like a pig to market? Take up your bed and walk, my friend, and thank my mouth for deigning to tell a lie."

He turned on one hand and knee, and stared at her fixedly.

"Have a care how you laugh at me."

"Threats! Oh, my good comrade, run away and leave me in peace. You know not what manner of trouble I have had to be rid of you and your pride, to get your neck out of Merlin's grip. Be grateful for having made me laugh a little."

His hands flashed out and caught her wrists.

"By God's blood, is it all laughter? What will you say to Merlin to-morrow?"

She did not try to free herself, but threw her head back and looked him in the eyes.

"I shall tell him that you made a fool of me and ran away in the night."

"Isoult!"

His grip tightened upon her wrists.

"No, by God! I'll not lend myself to that! Speak the truth. You laugh, that I may not think you too generous, and call me fool—to make it easier for me to go."

Her eyes glimmered at him.

"Well—go. I can deal with Merlin."

"Merlin! What right has that rat to gnaw at your lute strings? Let him go to his own damnation. Merlin—a grey rat—to say you yea or nay!"

She freed one hand and laid it over his mouth.

"Ssst, you wild forester. Speak softly. Who knows what the wood holds?"

The fingers of her hand were like a spell set upon his lips. He looked into her eyes and was dumb.

"Now, are you cautious?"

She took her hand away, yet almost with a caress.

"Isoult, what is this hedge priest to you?"

"Nothing—less than nothing."

"And what are these ditch scrapings and plough-boys?"

"A little more than Merlin."

"Your pride is as good as mine. I'll not go, Isoult, unless — —"

"Unless?"

"Two falcons soar into the blue."

She kept him at arm's length, but her eyes were shining in her dim face.

"Ah, you think well of yourself, Fulk of the Forest. Have you the strength to fly with me? I tell you I am a flame, a storm, a sunset."

"I have wings as strong as yours."

"To fly in the face of the sun?"

"Over the moon—if needs be."

They were like two flames, flaring and leaping against each other. An intoxication seized them, though there was a challenge and a defiance in the rushing together of desire. Their hands gripped hard, yet resisted. Their mouths provoked each other, yet held apart.

"Isoult, I swear troth."

"Wait—wait, madman!"

"Troth until death; I swear it."

She swayed towards him, drew back as suddenly, and started up, dragging him with her.

"Ssst, see—there!"

She pointed towards the wood, and Fulk saw vague movement in the darkness, and heard the rustling of bracken and the crackling of dead wood.

CHAPTER XIII

They were away, running hand in hand, and even their chance of death had an exultant cry in its throat.

A voice snarled in the darkness behind them:

"Shoot—shoot! No mercy!"

Fulk let go of Isoult's hand, and swung behind her so as to cover her from the arrows of Merlin's men, but she hung back and would not suffer him to serve her as shield.

"No, no; I take the same chance as you, my friend. There are oak woods down yonder—they will be our salvation."

"I will show them a woodland trick or two."

Arrows went past them, first one, and then three flying together and whistling like wind through the keyhole. A cross-bow bolt struck the turf close to Isoult's heels, and they heard the harsher twang of the arblast cord.

"That was Merlin's shot. He has poached many a bird."

"Let them shoot. It means they will lose in the running."

They heard Merlin's voice, furious and strident.

"After them. Bring down both, lording and jade."

The stiffness went out of Fulk's legs like wax melting before a fire. He felt monstrously strong, ready to run on air, with never a thought of tiring. Isoult, being a woman of sense, had twitched her skirts up over her girdle, and she ran beside him like a deer.

"My desire, you have good wings."

She laughed, feeling the mounting pride of his manhood in her.

"An I were naked I would dare any man to catch me—save you, perhaps!"

He glanced back with an exultant lift of the chin.

"They shoot like townsmen, and it is all down hill. Skim, swallow, skim!"

"In the oak woods we'll make a maze for them."

"Let me but cut a quarterstaff, and I'll thank any five of them to come within striking distance. Jump, jump—a ditch!"

They leapt it together, and an arrow struck a thorn bush near them on the farther bank.

"The luck is with us!"

"I could sing, but breath is precious! Ah, Master Fierceheart, my pride flies with yours!"

He swerved close in, so that their shoulders touched.

"Isoult, when did it begin with you?"

"Ah—when! And with you?"

"God knows! Someone lit a torch in me—Hullo!"

Fulk had heard the whir of an arrow shot at a venture, and the sound of its striking home. He felt Isoult's fingers contract on his, and heard her utter a sharp cry.

"Isoult, ar't hurt?"

She flagged and faltered, with one hand to her side.

"It's over with me, Fulk; put your arm under my shoulders."

"Dear heart, where has it struck you?"

"Here, where God thieved from Adam."

He heard her breathing through clenched teeth, and she began to weigh heavily upon his arm.

"Fulk, I can go no farther."

"I'll carry you."

"No, no; lay me down, dear madman, and run for it. Our luck is out. I have got my quittance."

He felt the arrow in her side, and the warmth of her blood upon his arm, and a wondering wrath came over him. Her body seemed to melt, to slip away, to surrender all the thrilling tenseness of its muscles.

"Lay me down, my desire—and go."

He laid her down very gently, yet the twisting of the barb made her cry out.

"A curse on the pain."

He knelt by her, but she tried to thrust him away.

"It is my death wound. Up, dear fool; go—I charge you."

"Not I. Give me your knife."

She threw out her arms and caught him about the neck.

"Go. You cannot save me. Go. I ask it, with the blood of my death wound on me. Oh, strong heart—once—the last!"

She drew him down and kissed him fiercely with lips that clung, and then thrust him off.

"Take the knife; I shall never need it!"

"Isoult."

"Now—go!"

"By God—I cannot!"

"My own mad fool, what can you do now? Come back with the sword to-morrow—and take your vengeance."

He sprang up, her knife in his hand, as a man came out of the darkness. Fulk struck him so fiercely that he went down without a cry. Another rushed at him, and had the knife in his throat; but the rest of the pack were closing in.

Fulk heard Isoult call to him.

"The life is out of me, my desire. Run, cheat Merlin, and I'll die happy."

He threw himself down beside her, kissed her mouth, and sprang away from under the feet of Merlin's men. A flurry of arrows went after him in the darkness, but they flew wild and wide, and before they could shoot again Fulk had reached the woods.

How long or whither he ran Fulk of the Forest never knew. Isoult's last cry had flung him forward into blind, physical activity that was fanatical and dazed. He blundered through the underwood and between the trunks of trees, hardly feeling the hazel rods stinging his face. Once he crashed into an oak bole, and went on with his head singing. A voice kept crying in him, "Run, run!" and his limbs and his senses were mere brute beasts that served.

Fulk ran for some three miles before the self suddenly awoke in him like a raw wound uncovered to the air. He faltered in his stride, dropped to a walk, and then stood still, staring at the ground in front of him, as though he had been running in his sleep.

"Isoult!"

He thrust out his hands with a fierce cry, and then covered his face with his forearms. Vision had come to him so vividly and with such bitterness that he rocked as he stood and breathed like a man in pain.

Dead! He could not believe it. Her lips were still alive to his, and her hands still thrilled him. Had it all happened, that passionate conspiring of theirs, that rushing together through the darkness, that mad, exultant love flight? He heard again her cry when the arrow struck her, her fierce pleading with him to leave her, and felt her arms holding him and her lips pressing themselves to his. Mother of God, those lips of hers! They had left him on fire, those lips of hers, and she herself was dead.

A savage compassion swept over him, an impotent and furious love rage that struggled against a sense of utter and incredible emptiness.

"Isoult!"

He bit the flesh of his wrist, and cursed himself. She was dead by now for his sake, this incomparable, strange creature, with all her fierce, wayward pride. Why had he run away and left her to Merlin? She was his, though dead; the hands, the lips, the eyes were his. He should have fought it to a finish with that scum of serfdom, and not left her alone in death. It was monstrous, damnable, fit only for the spittle of a superhuman scorn.

What had he lost? And yesterday his eyes were blind! He saw it all now in a flare of tenderness, her desire to save him, and the stiffneckedness of his own pride. What was he that she should have suffered to save him, that she should have stooped to a lie against her honour, and lost her life at the hands of Merlin and these boors?

Merlin!

His passion turned like a wounded boar, seeing something to strike at, something to slay. By the Cross, he would make amends, come by arms and horse, and join himself to those who were ready to trample this stubble of the fields into the mud. And this knife of Isoult's that he had at his girdle should be kept for Merlin—the grey friar.

CHAPTER XIV

The terror was abroad, such terror as had not possessed the land since the days of the Black Death.

Fulk, tramping it, with an oak cudgel over his shoulder and his face set like a stone towards London Town, saw nothing but empty fields and great woods that seemed to smother the land in silence. He kept to the open country, his forest instinct standing him in good stead, and once only did he go down into a village to beg or seize bread for his belly. He found only women, children, and old men there, for all the labourers were on the road to London. The women fell upon him like a crowd of wild cats, and he was forced to clear himself with ungallant sweeps of his cudgel.

"A gentle, a gentle, by the cock of his chin!"

And since his club kept them at a distance they pelted him out of the village with stones and broken potsherds, and Fulk got no bread that morning.

He was sore within, most devilish sore, and full of the wrath of a strong man in pain. He heard Isoult's voice singing, and the lips that were dead tormented him. His humility towards the thought of her contrasted with his fierce desire to fly at the throat of this Blatant Beast that went bellowing through the countryside.

He was hungry and in need of a horse to carry his wrath more swiftly, and chance served him before the day was out. Coming upon a solitary manor-house, half hidden by woods at the end of a meadow, Fulk adventured thither to find a horse in the stable, food in the larder, but also two hairy men eating and drinking like lords at the high table. The folk had fled to the woods, and the men in the hall were two of the Commons of England, guzzling and laying light fingers on anything that could be stolen.

One was a swineherd, the other a tiler, and being two to one, and Fulk no labourer in looks and dress, they showed a bullying valour, and fell upon him together. All Fulk's fury took its outlet. He left both of them flat on the floor, helped himself to the wine and food, and was cheered by finding some rusty harness and a sword in an oak chest in the cellar. The horse in the stable would have carried the two boors, so Fulk had no qualms over saving him from such a fate. He saddled and bridled the beast, and rode on till the darkness made him call a halt.

Fulk passed the night in a wood, trying to sleep and making no great success of it. The ground was hard under him, and his heart sore within. Not for a moment could he get the dead woman out of his thoughts. She was in the darkness about him, in the rustling of the leaves, in the stars overhead, in the scent of the fern. He turned from side to side, his brain on fire with a restless and compassionate grieving for Isoult of the Rose.

It was on the morning of the second day that Fulk came within sight of the Thames. At dawn he had started over the great chalk-hills with their beech woods hanging in a glimmer of golden light, and had seen the river country, dim and blue under the northern sky. A skull-faced old priest whom he had met riding on an ass along a sheep-track, had pointed him out the way.

"Cross the river west of London, my son," he had said, "for they tell me the southern roads that lead to London Bridge are full of the mob. God have pity on the fools! Peace, and a safe passage to you."

As for peace, it was the very last thing that Fulk desired, but he meant to know how much truth there had been in Merlin's words, and a wholesome curiosity possessed him. Moreover, the lords and the gentry would be gathering about the King; it was at the White Tower that swords were needed, and men to teach the rabble of the fields that there was rhyme and reason in the pride of the sword.

So about seven of the clock Fulk rode down into the river country where the lush green June mocked the lover in him. His eyes saw blood upon the grass, and the shining meadows all white and gold with flowers. Here was a dream country, a lover's land fit for idleness and laughter, yet even the splendid summer stillness of the trees filled him with a measure of scorn. Bare woods, a whistling wind, and a flaming sunset, and brown men to be galloped after over leaves and mud! That was his mood, whereas, here, by the river, he saw herons flapping peacefully over the meadows, and the whole land seemed full of succulent green life, with poplars that pricked the blue, and willows trailing their branches in mysterious and secret waters. Reeds and sedges laughed and rustled, and he caught the thunder of weirs and mill-races. It was dewy, languorous, full of slow and glimmering delight, but for such a peaceful picture Fulk had no use at all.

As he rode through Kingston towards the ford, he saw that nearly all the houses had their doors and windows barred and shuttered. The road was deserted save for a few hens pecking at garbage, and sparrows bathing in the dust. Fulk might have ridden naked past the houses, and no one would have taken offence. The morning sun blazed on the thatched roofs, the black beams and white plaster, but gossip seemed dead, and the tongues of the old women silent.

Fulk rode down to the ford, and reined in abruptly, with his horse's fore feet in the water. Out of a grove of poplars lining the farther road came a jigging of pennons and a glittering of steel, with dust flying like smoke from the hoofs of horses at the trot, and a whirl of colour amid the green. Fulk saw it to be a company of some fifty spears led by a knight on a towering black horse, a knight who rode in full battle harness, save that his head was covered by a red velvet cap. The whole glittering, clangorous, many-coloured mass came to a halt in the roadway, the spears standing straight and close together, the dust still making a mist about them in the sunlight.

Fulk's heart grew big in him, and his eyes shone. Here was the grim splendour of the sword out on a summer morning, and his nostrils quivered as he pushed forward into the stream.

He was a third of the way across when the knight of the red velvet cap kicked his heels into the flanks of his black horse and came splashing into the shallows. He of the red cap had the face of a great captain—haughty, shrewd, iron about the mouth, with blue eyes that looked straight and far, eyes that could strike like a sword. Fulk felt the man's eyes on him as they splashed through the water towards each other; moreover, as they drew nearer he saw something like astonishment gather on the other's face like a dazzle of sunlight on a shield.

They met, and reined in in the midst of the stream, the knight on the black horse bending forward slightly in the saddle. His eyes seemed to wait, and to wonder, and his iron mouth remained shut like a trap.

Fulk saluted him.

"The grace of God to you, sir. I have seen nothing but brown villeins for the last ten days."

The knight still stared and said nothing, sitting stiffly in the saddle.

Suddenly he opened his mouth as though his astonishment could hold back no longer.

"By the tail of the devil, my friend, who are you?"

Fulk was on the alert.

"The Duke of Lancaster's Riding Forester, the son of Roger Ferrers."

Fulk saw the knight's eyebrows come together.

"Roger Ferrers' son!"—and he spoke as though talking to prove to himself that he was awake—"Roger Ferrers' son! Have I eyes in my head or not? Look you, my friend, have you heard the name of Sir Robert Knollys?"

"Surely."

"I am he. Come close in, your knee to mine."

Fulk edged his horse closer, and he of the red cap sat and stared at him, and at every part of him from eyebrows to hands. He traced every line, every trick of the body, and the more he looked the more he seemed to marvel.

"Monstrous! You have steady eyes, young man."

"And an easy conscience!"

"Come, tell me now, Master Ferrers, whither do you ride, and for what purpose?"

"I ride nowhere, and I keep my own counsel."

"Tsst, no fencing with me. I am to be trusted."

"To be honest with you, sir, I have had to run for my life from certain people who were for making me dance like a doll on a wire."

"And how was the doll to be dressed?"

"In a King's robes, and with a crown on its head."

He saw Knollys' eyes flash and harden.

"By the Three Leopards, speak out! How much do you know?"

Fulk told him the tale that Merlin had poured into his ears, and Robert Knollys listened, never moving his eyes from Fulk's face. Their horses stood shoulder to shoulder, with the water washing under their bellies, while the armed men on the northern bank wondered why their captain tarried so long at the ford.

"The ruffian priest! And the woman saved ye, and lost her own life? That was bravely done. But look you, my friend; the truth's writ on you in flesh and blood. You are as like the King as one bean is like another, save—this in your ear—you have something the King lacks. I judge a man by his eyes. How old are you?"

"Turned twenty."

"And old at that. Let me think, let me think."

He laid his right hand on Fulk's shoulder, and, leaning forward, looked into his eyes.

"I loved the Black Prince, and I have lain across the door of his tent at night. In the French wars we were brothers in arms, and, by God! you have his eyes, the set of his head, the very turn of his shoulders. It's damnable, marvellous!"

His grip tightened on Fulk's shoulder.

"The King is but fifteen, and you some five years older, yet you might pass, before a crowd, for the King. That friar had quick wits! What a devil's game, with half the country in a panic and the other half foaming like a dog gone mad. Lancaster in Scotland, Woodstock in Wales, half our best knights sailed or sailing for Spain! Fulk Ferrers, has no man ever whispered this tale to you before?"

Fulk had no need to shirk the other's eyes.

"Never a word. I have lived the forest life."

"Who knows the truth? She—who——! Damnation, it was her splendour to mate with such a man, and no shame."

He turned his head, and stared at the water running past, his hand still on Fulk's shoulder.

"If we had but such a Prince! Bah! what am I saying?"

His eyes flashed up to Fulk's.

"Come now, what's in your heart? Out with it. If you are the son of your father you will be gallant and generous."

"I swear troth to the King. Let men call me a bastard if it pleases them; there is good blood in me."

"Am I to trust you?"

"As you trusted the Prince."

"That carries! But, by my honour, we are in the thick of crooked happenings. A boy King, and the rabble rushing to make a Jumping Jack of him, and he none too stiff in his knees! You see—I trust you. We rode out here to see if any of this scum had crossed the river. I see no other way but to take you back with us."

"I ask nothing better than to follow Robert Knollys."

They had taken each other's measure, and they gripped hands.

"I am to trust Robert Knollys, as he trusts in me."

"Take my oath on it."

"It is given and taken."

The elder man thought a moment.

"Lad, no one yet must see your face."

He turned in the saddle and shouted to a squire who was waiting with his pennon on the northern bank.

"Fitzurse—hey!"

"Sir?"

"Leave my helmet on the grass. Tell my gentlemen to ride back straight to the city. I follow—with a friend."

He and Fulk waited, sitting their horses in the midst of the river, while the company of spears turned and rode off with a churning of dust into the aspen wood. The thunder of the horses' hoofs had nearly died away before Knollys stirred.

"Come."

They splashed through to the northern bank together. A vizored bassinet lay on the grass beside the road, and Knollys pointed to it, and glanced meaningly at Fulk.

"Cover your face, my son. A good hawk will not bate at being hooded."

As they rode towards the city through the fields and orchards, Knollys desired to hear Fulk's adventures and all that he could tell him of the temper of the rebels in the south, and he in turn was frank with Fulk, unbarring his thoughts to him as to a comrade in arms.

"No such thing as this would have happened," said he, "with the sire or the grandsire ruling. There is no master, and the country has lost its wits, every man cowering in a corner and afraid to utter one bold word for fear of a cutthroat."

"Where are the great lords and their people?"

"Man, I know not! The King can count on no more than five hundred spears in London, and the city scum is said to be with the rebels. The country is besotted with apathy and fear. Never in my life have I seen such poltroonery—the men who should be in the saddle turned to a crowd of old women. I am asking myself whether this can be the England that sent our armies to trample upon France."

His haughty and scornful seriousness was not to be questioned, and Fulk felt that the case was desperate when such a man looked gloomy.

"What of the King? Is he in peril?"

"It is those who stand between him and the 'Jacks' who are likely to be in peril. There are wrongs to be righted—who doubts it?—but the shipmaster must rule the ship. The Jacks in France were very near overturning a kingdom."

"I thought to find a great host of the lords and gentles in London."

"A few old pantaloons in the Tower. I promise you I would not stake a groat on half of us having our heads upon our shoulders this time next month."

They passed a group of the common people standing outside an alehouse, and some of them jeered and put out their tongues like children. One fellow ran about on all fours, howled, and lifted up a leg. Another had a dead cat, which he held up by a thong fastened to its neck. He shouted, and jigged the dead cat up and down: "Ha! John of Gaunt dancing on a rope!" Knollys rode by as though they were dirt in the gutter, but his eyes were the eyes of a leopard.

"Honest mud in the wrong place, friend Fulk. Many of these fellows are good lads when not in the wolf pack."

He stared into the distance.

"If death could give us back the father for one week! But with this boy, and a few old women round him! Lancaster would be useless, even were he not parleying with the Scots. The people hate him like poison. Never breathe it that you are John of Gaunt's man, if you are taken."

"There must be good men somewhere."

"Faith, what are a few beacons when the whole country is burning? I tell you it needs a comet in the sky to master these mad peasants. Fate lies with the King."

"If he is the son of his father——"

"If, if! That's where the devil's laugh comes in!"

The dust of Knollys' company of spears drifted eastwards before them, and hung like a haze among the elm trees beside the road. The silver loops of the river came and went, until the towers of Westminster rose from among the orchards, fields, and gardens. A great silence held everywhere, and even as they rode towards Ludgate past the great houses on the river bank and John of Gaunt's palace of the Savoy, the people who loitered thereabout looked mute, and sullen, and watchful. The purple edge of a thundercloud was looming up over the city, deepening every patch of colour in the streets, and making the vanes and steeples shine like gold. The air was close and ominous, like the spirit of the people.

As they passed the Savoy, Knollys cocked a thumb at it.

"See your duke's house. I'd not give a penny for it if those wolves cross the river."

Fulk had a need of silence, for his head was like a skin full of new wine. All was strange, and vast, intricate, and grotesque to him, and the great city itself was like a forest with its spires and towers and gables and narrow winding ways. It was a world of new sights, new sounds, new smells, new colours. He looked at the houses and the people through the bars of the vizor, and felt a strange unrest stirring in him, a yearning to play a mighty part, to strike some blow that should make all these heedless and unfamiliar faces gape and stare. The pride of mastery cried in his blood—the cry of a heritage that yearned in him.

They saw the spears ahead of them winding through Ludgate with the clangour of iron-shod hoofs on the cobbles. A trumpet blared, and people crowded out of courts and alleys to see Knollys' war-dogs ride past. To Fulk these people were like sheep crowding at gaps in a hedge. The trumpet's cry wailed for a something that England lacked, a voice like a trumpet's cry and the mien of a lord.

They came to Knollys' lodging, and by noon Fulk found himself in a little attic under the tiles, with thunder rumbling overhead. The window looked out over roofs and gables through a sheet of drenching rain that glimmered when the lightning flashed. There was food and wine, and a truckle bed in the room, and the door was barred on the inner side.

Knollys had left him there to the thunderstorm and his own thoughts.

"Let the sword lie hid in the sheath," he had said; "trust me, good lad. Perhaps I have dreamed a dream!"

CHAPTER XV

Isoult, seated on a bundle of straw in the bottom of a wagon, saw stretching for more than a mile behind her an undulating mass of marching men, a veritable river of humanity oozing with mud-brown eddies through the green of the June fields. The oxen harnessed to the wagon went at a stolid walk, and the wagon itself, with its creaking wheels, seemed to float on this river of bobbing heads and swinging legs. On a plank laid across the side rails sat John Ball and Merlin the Franciscan, each holding a wooden cross above the dust and the smell and the heat of all these herding peasants. Isoult could watch the faces of those who marched on either side of the wagon—the coarse, weather-stained faces of workers in the fields, all straining forward with fanatical and greedy eyes staring at something a long way off. Pikes, scythe-blades fastened to poles, pitchforks, bows, flails, axes, and old swords were carried on the shoulders of this marching multitude.

For the most part these peasants plodded along in silence, a silence that licked its lips and thought of the morrow. Thousands of feet hammered the road, and an indescribable, harsh roar, blended of many sounds, suggested the rushing of water over a weir. Now and again a man would throw up his head like a dog baying the moon, and howl out some catch-cry.

"Death to all clerks and lordings!" "King Richard and Goodman Jack!"

The single howl would be caught up, and carried in a roar, like a foaming freshet along the surface of this flowing multitude. The sound was stunning, elemental, horrible, the bellowing of some huge monster, the reverberations of whose belly made the whole land tremble.

Isoult, sitting on her straw, with a face that looked straight over the tailboard of the wagon, felt that she had sat all day close to a great water-wheel that rushed round and round and never slackened. The June day was a blur of sweat, and dust, and movement. She had ceased to notice things very vividly. Sometimes a big man on a white horse would ride up to the wagon—a man with a square black beard and teeth that showed between hot, red lips. She knew him to be Wat the Tiler, the master beast of the sweating herd, for the men roared his name whenever his face swam near above the dust of the tramping feet.

More than once he dropped behind, and rode at the tail of the wagon, and Isoult felt his round eyes fixed on her. Hers had met his but once, and the gloating curiosity in them had seemed part of the sour smell of the cattle who kicked up the white dust on the highway. Sometimes Merlin spoke to her, glancing back over a bony shoulder, and his sneering voice was full of an ironical fatherliness.

"Courage, my daughter. In three days you shall sing to King Richard."

She did not trouble to answer him, but let herself be carried along on the tide of all this rage and exultation. A sense of the immensity of all that was happening round her made her feel that she was but a blown leaf being hurried along with thousands of other leaves. What did it matter what happened to her, that she was alive, being kept like a bird in a cage at Merlin's pleasure? She knew in her heart of hearts what all these men desired, and what they purposed, and that her pride would be torn from her even as many a fine cloak would be torn from the shoulders of the rich. Yet somehow she did not care. The savage eagerness of this plodding multitude, the noise, the sweat and dust, the roar of their voices when they cheered, made her feel that she was watching the workings of an inevitable doom. What could stand against this brown flood of men, this whole people that had risen to smother the hated few? She knew that the whole land was moving on London, that these Kent and Sussex men might be but one multitude among many. It was like all the forests of the land plucking themselves up by the roots and rushing to fall on the few woodmen who had ruled with the edge of the axe. Who could stop them? And as for their being fooled by promises, the men who led them were too shrewd and desperate to be tricked by promises.

Of Fulk she thought vaguely with a distant tenderness that looked back at a fragment of the past, and asked nothing of the future. What had become of him? Did he believe her dead? Or had he guessed that she had lied to save him, and pretended that she had come by her death wound when an arrow had done no more than pierce the flesh of her flank? She could not have run with that arrow in her side, and Fulk would have been taken with her had she not acted a lie. What had become of him? What part would he play in this savage overthrow that threatened a kingdom? What could a thousand such men do to stay it? The valour of a prince's bastard seemed to her a mere thread of steel set to bear the blows of a thousand bludgeons.

The day's march ended upon Blackheath, and the peasants of Kent and Sussex camped there to the number of some sixty thousand men. The oxen were unyoked and the wagon left standing on some high ground close to the road, and so placed that Isoult looked northward towards where the great city hung upon the silver thread of the river. The sun was low in the west, and through the haze of a June evening she fancied she could see a distant glimmer of vanes and steeples, a something that looked like a forest touched by the long yellow rays of the setting sun.

Fifty yards away, John Ball, mounted on a barrel, was preaching to the people. The crowd was very silent, and his voice came to her with the sound of bells ringing in the distance. She saw his arms waving exultantly as he flared like a torch burning in a wind. Hundreds of intent, hairy, and fresh-coloured faces looked up at him, open-mouthed, with eyes that glittered. And away yonder lay the great city, dim in the yellow light, like a dream on the uttermost edge of sleep.

Isoult heard a man's laughter, and, turning about, saw a face with a forked red beard look at her over the tailboard of the wagon. It was Guy the Stallion, gorgeous in a red camlet coat with a silver baldric over his shoulder, his bassinet polished till the pits of rust had been rubbed away. He rested his elbows on the tailboard of the wagon, and cleaning his teeth with the point of his tongue, stared at Isoult with an insolent relish that made his red-brown eyes look like points of hot metal.

"Ha, Madame Isoult, it has been a great day, surely!"

She felt all her pent-up scorn flash up at the sight of this absurd boaster's arrogant face.

"A great day indeed for the cattle who go to the shambles."

He opened his mouth wide and cawed like a bird.

"Tell me, fair one, where now is the gentleman? Our great barons have fled out of the kingdom, to make war on Spaniards, since it is safer. We shall march down yonder, and eat up all the King's creatures, all the fat merchants and clerks and moneylenders. John Ball will be our archbishop, Wat our Lord Marshal, Merlin our Chief Councillor."

"And you, Master Chanticleer?"

He spread his shoulders.

"I shall be a great captain. I shall march to and fro, hanging the gentry and storming their castles. I have seen more war than any lord in England. Yes, I shall be a great captain, with ten thousand bows and bills at my back."

The fellow might be contemptible, but it was such as he that led the Blatant Beast by the nose, and it is always possible to learn something, even from a Welshman with a red beard.

"Will it be so easy to eat up all the nobles and their people?"

He was very ready to prove to her how the kingdom would be won.

"See now, how can one knight in full harness fight a hundred ploughmen? Why, they have only to tumble him over, and beat him with hammers like any old pot. I know what I am saying; the lord on the high horse is only good to fight his peers. We have only to hamstring their horses, pull them down like big beetles, and then use the knife. I have seen it done in the French wars. Besides, half the lords are out of the country, and the rest shivering in their skins. The King's but a boy, and most of the Londoners are with us. The whole country's up, and we mean to have the King in our hands and to use him. By cock, what can a few hundred lobsters in steel coats do against so many?"

He pulled his beard, and looked at her with half-closed eyes, convinced that he was a devil of a fellow, and ready to challenge her to pose him with her questions. And for once his swagger had a fierce reality behind it. Even his boasting seemed to fall short of the truth.

"No doubt you will be a great captain," she said; "and, my God, what a country it will be to live in!"

"We honest fellows are as good, and better, than the fops and squirelings."

"Better—oh, far better."

She spoke half in a whisper, and with an irony that went over his head.

"When are we to be in London, great captain?"

"In three days."

"So soon?"

"We want to be in, and to have the glory, and some of the pickings, before the easterlings and the midlanders come up."

"To be sure."

She smiled at him as she might have smiled at some extravagantly bitter jest. He leant over the tailboard, and his eyes leered.

"Isoult, you shall be a great lady."

"I shall be nothing, my friend, just nothing."

"Wait till some of us have our castles and our lands."

"What, some of you mean to be lords in the places of—these gentlemen?"

He gave an inimitable shrug of the shoulders.

"Bah! these sheep! One must let them bleat. But the shepherds know whither they are going."

She rested her chin on her hands and stared at him till he began to blink.

"You are not such a fool, then, lord Guy! You have caught the twist of Merlin's tongue. Oh, these honest firebrands! Always the sheep—always the sheep!"

She saw the sun go down behind the swashbuckler's head, so that it haloed him and the red tusks of his hair that stuck out so jauntily. He frothed for a while and then took himself off, kissing the blade of his sword to her as though he were to carry her favour in the lists.

Isoult smiled bitterly, glimpsing her own helplessness.

"To have to listen to such a jay! Where is the hawk that should tear the heart out of such creatures? Friend Fulk, if you were King—ah, things might happen!"

Dusk fell, and the heath became one great uproar, a kind of huge playing field for all these rough men of the fields. They sang and hooted and hammered on pots and pans, danced, wrestled, rolled over each other, played leap-frog, giving each other huge smacks and buffets.

All their elemental grossness seemed minded to express itself in an orgy of physical delirium. They mocked Nature, and made a jest of her, and the close June night was full of the sound of their horse-play.

Isoult sat and listened, her hood pulled down over her face. These cattle! They whinneyed, squealed, grunted, blew wind between blubbering lips, pranced, butted each other. And in the midst of all this obscene clowning there were three faces that haunted her—Wat the Tiler's, Guy's, and the face of Merlin the Priest. She had seen the same elemental hunger in the eyes of these three men, a lust that watched and waited to seize on the thing that it desired. A sudden loathing of her own body rose in her, a loathing of a thing that might be carrion, to judge by the crows that watched and waited. And mingled with this loathing was all the horror of helplessness that overtakes one in the midst of an evil dream.

CHAPTER XVI

The window was full of the deep blue gloom of a summer night, with stars shining like the feathers of silver arrows shot into a target. A black curtain shut off the window recess from the King's council chamber within, where candles burnt in sconces on the walls.

In this window recess in the south wall of the White Tower two men stood talking in whispers—great lords both of them, the Earls of Salisbury and Warwick. The shorter of the two had opened one of the lattices, and was kneeling with one knee on the padded seat. He rapped with his fingers on the stone sill, and watched the sentinels going to and fro upon the walls, and the river sliding smoothly under the stars. The night was very still—so still that they could hear the stream plashing along the walls by the water-gate. Hardly a sound came from the city, and the very muteness of the night seemed ominous and strange.

A clashing of arms, sudden and sharp, in the courtyard below, and the tramp of feet, told of the changing of the guard. A voice shouted orders. From beyond the curtain came a queer, whimpering sound as of a girl hiding her head in her cloak and weeping.

The man who knelt on the cushions turned sharply, and his lips were drawn back over his teeth.

"Psst—listen to that! Such snivelling when the kingdom's turned upside down!"

"Not too loud!"

"What will happen when he hears the wolves howling under the walls! And Walworth could promise——?"

"But little. Eight thousand burghers skulking in their houses behind closed doors; and thirty thousand ready to shout for the gates to be opened."

Warwick turned fiercely and glanced up into Salisbury's face—a massive, stolid, cautious face, in no hurry to betray emotion.

"What's to be done? Are we to let this herd of swine root up the whole kingdom?"

"Ring their snouts, my friend."

"And who's to do the ringing? That—that—in yonder!"

They turned by some common impulse and stared at the black curtain that hid them from the council chamber.

"The lad has no more heart in him than a hare!"

"He is what he is."

"A snivelling girl! Thunder of heaven, if we could but have the sire back in his stead! Why, look you, if these rebels can but get him into their hands, they'll have no more to do but to pull ugly faces. He will run and hide his face in his mother's bosom, and let them hang every gentleman and friend in the kingdom."

Salisbury nodded his head.

"Weak King—no kingdom. I am wondering how many of us will keep our heads on our shoulders."

"Hallo, who's this?"

Footsteps came towards them. The curtain was plucked aside, jerked back again, and a third man stood with them in the window recess. It was Robert Knollys, with the face of a ship's captain, looking straight into the thick of a storm.

He laid a hand on Salisbury's shoulder, and spoke in a harsh whisper.

"Look in yonder; it is enough to make the heart of a strong man sick."

He drew the curtain slightly to one side, so that they could see into the great council chamber lit by the candles set in sconces upon the walls. Half a dozen knights and gentlemen had withdrawn to the far end of the chamber and were standing there like men discomfited, knowing not whether to stay or to go. At the lower end of the council table sat Simon of Sudbury, clad in a plain violet-coloured cassock with a small gold cross at his breast. He had a richly-bound missal open on the table before him, and he made a pretence of turning the pages. Now and again he raised his eyes from the book with binding of scarlet and gold, and looked at the Princess, who sat in a great carved chair set upon a low daïs in the centre of the chamber.

For this woman's face was a tragedy in itself, struggling to mask pity, shame, anger, and a kind of incredulous scorn. She was dressed in some golden stuff that caught the light of the candles, so that her figure seemed to draw the light to it from every corner of the great room. A cap of silver tissue covered her black hair, and her face had a fine and spirited comeliness that strove not to be humiliated by the thing that lay upon her knees.

For on her knees lay the head of a King—her son. Her hands covered it, hands wearing many rings that sent out from their whiteness sparkles of red and of blue, of green and of purple. Richard was kneeling before her, his hands clasping the arms of the chair—frail, delicate hands, tapering towards the nails. Two thin ankles and feet shod in shoes of gilded leather were thrust out from under the folds of a robe of blue and white silk. His shoulders were twitching, and as they twitched the heels of his gilden shoes smote together.

Knollys dropped the curtain and blotted out the room.

"God help the lad; he should have been born a girl."

They stood close together, morose, grim, baffled.

"How can one put blood into the boy?"

"Ask me some other riddle, my friend! He has been like that ever since Newtown came to him to-day from the mob upon Blackheath. Newtown babbled too much—a pity they did not hang him."

"And we have promised that he shall parley with them to-morrow."

"Yes; and he swears that he will not go."

Warwick struck the wall with his fist.

"Go; he shall go! By God, are we going to be brought to perdition because the lad's a coward! He has come to a man's state. Thunder of heaven! Think of what the sire was at his age, and the grandsire before him. Some tricksy devil must have got into the marriage bed."

Knollys stroked his chin, and his eyes fell into a hard stare.

"Sirs, I have something to say to you."

And to such purpose did he tell his tale that the murmur of their voices continued behind the curtain for more than an hour.

The next dawn was that of Corpus Christi Day, and Richard the King and his lords and gentlemen heard Mass in the Tower chapel. Those who knew what to fear saw that the King's face was like the face of a sickly girl, and that his thighs shook under him as he knelt on his crimson cushion. When Mass was over he returned to his chamber with the Princess, his mother, meaning to robe himself to meet these rebel peasants. They were to send their leaders to the southern bank near Rotherhithe, and the King was to go in his barge and listen to their grievances.

What passed in Richard's chamber no one but his mother knew, for she served as confessor, squire, and page, and the door was closed on them for more than an hour. She gave him strong wine to drink, and used the lash of her scorn, so that there was some colour in his cheeks when he went down with his lords and gentlemen to the water-gate where the barge was waiting. Trumpets blew, and the lad's chin went up as though his manhood crowed an answer to the trumpets. Salisbury, who walked at his side, watched him narrowly, knowing how much hung upon this youngster's wit and courage.

The barge swung out into the river with a steady sweep of the long oars, and headed towards Rotherhithe, with the King's banner flying at the stern. Salisbury, Warwick, and Suffolk, and certain knights and gentlemen were in the barge, and all wore armour under their robes. The rowers were men who could shoot straight if needs be, and bows were ready under the thwarts. Towards London Bridge many boats were lying, full of people in red and green hoods and many coloured doublets, so that they looked like great painted birds upon the water. These London boats stayed by the bridge, none of them putting out to follow the King, for Knollys had rowed up with two sergeant-at-arms and had it proclaimed that no boat should venture past the Tower.

In the King's barge all men were silent, and avoided each other's eyes as though fearing to see what each man felt to be too urgent in his own. Richard sat stiff as a wooden figure in the stern, an earl on either side of him. He wore his crown and robes of state, and the royal sword lay sheathed upon his knees. Warwick, who sat at his right elbow, kept pouring a whisper of words into his ear; but Richard never opened his lips, nor did he seem to hear. His eyes threw out uncertain, flickering glances that wavered from side to side. He watched the blades of the oars churning up foam, and since his lips were dry, he kept moistening them with his tongue.

As they drew towards Rotherhithe, a knight who was standing in the bow of the barge uttered a "Grace of God," and shaded his eyes with his hand.

"My lord, look yonder!"

Salisbury stood up, to see what should have been a green meadow sloping to the river, turned brown by a great swarm of men. Thousands of peasants were crowded along the southern bank, and they were silent with a strange, hungry silence, waiting for the coming of the King.

"By the Virgin, they have sent ten thousand men instead of ten score."

Then, quite suddenly, as though from some crack in the earth, a huge, rolling shout went up from the southern bank. They had seen the King's banner at the stern of the barge, and the whole brown multitude bayed, and jostled, and jumped on each other's shoulders to get a view. The clamour had a ragged and ferocious edge to its exultation. It was like the uproar among caged beasts when the keeper appears with red meat on an iron spit.

The lad wearing the crown sat rigid, and went white to the eyes. The two earls looked at each other over his head, and drew closer to him as though to warm him with the heat of their manhood. He was cold in the sun, and his teeth were chattering.

"Courage, Sire."

"They shout for the joy of seeing you."

Salisbury spoke sharply to the steersman, and the barge ran on, the crowd along the bank unfolding itself like a grotesque tapestry upon a wall. Every sort of face seemed there—hairy, smooth, red, sallow, old, young, round, lean, some like screaming birds, others like neighing horses, all hooting, bellowing, and howling so that each open mouth was a red hole spouting sound. The uproar made the ears sing. Some of the men had stripped off their clothes, and danced with a kind of obscene bravado. Caps were waved, fists shaken at the nobles.

Salisbury, who was standing up, very white and fierce and calm, signed to the rowers to rest on their oars and let the barge glide along about thirty yards from the bank. A storm of cries swept across the water.

"Land—land."

"Come ashore!"

"Death to the lords!"

"Come ashore, King Dick; we honest men would speak with you."

"Wow, wow, wow!"

"Father Adam's come to court."

"Sit you down, big belly. Up with the King."

The two earls sat close to Richard, half holding him with the pressure of their bodies.

"Courage, Sire."

He shut his eyes and broke into a voiceless chatter.

"No nearer, sir, I charge you. I—I am your King. Bid them row farther off."

"They mean you no harm, Sire."

"By the soul of your father, open your eyes, and look at them as you would look at a herd of swine."

"No nearer. Row farther out, I say. I'll not speak to these beasts."

The barge turned, and then began to row to and fro at a fair distance from the bank. For a while the crowd grew quieter, as though it were puzzled, and waiting to see what those in the barge would do.

Then the shouts broke out again.

"Come to land."

"Curse you, lords! They are making a mock of us and of our King!"

"Ho! Hallo! Hallo! Give us our King; we have much to say to him."

Some of them who were naked began to wade into the water. Salisbury glanced at the coward under the crown, spoke to the steersman, and held up a hand for silence.

The crowd suffered him to speak.

"Sirs, you are not fitly clad, nor fitly mannered for the King to speak with you."

He faced them, nostrils inflated, eyes bidding them back to the soil. The barge was edging away, and for a moment the crowd was silent. Then of a sudden it understood.

The roar that went up was the roar of a multitude that is balked of its desire. Fists shot out; men sprang into the river, felt for mud, and threw it, even as they threw curses. Hoots, yells, whistlings followed the splashing oars.

The King's barge returned to the Tower, and the peasants to Blackheath, to tell the thousands who had tarried there how the King and his lords had refused to treat with them, but had held aloof as though they were so many lepers. Wat the Tiler, Merlin, and John Ball had no wish to see the mob in a peaceful temper. If these lords and gentlemen were to be trampled out of existence, it behoved them to keep the Great Beast to its fury, and set it to rend and slay.

The whole host poured from Blackheath, and by noon there were sixty thousand peasants in the suburbs, rushing hither and thither, breaking into religious houses, plundering the taverns, breaking down doors, and smashing fences, following any wild whim that served to lead them. They demolished the Marshalsea and set the prisoners free. Hundreds of uncouth figures came crowding to the closed gates, and howled threats at the guards upon the walls.

"Open the gates! Open the gates!"

The cry became one long, monotonous, unchanging howl.

Walworth the Mayor spoke with them at the bridge gate, standing on the curtain wall between the towers, and looking down upon a sea of upturned faces. The rebels shook their scythes and pikes at him and threatened him with their bows. Some of them had brought up tree trunks and ladders, and shouted that they would break the gates down or storm the walls if the city did not open to them.

Walworth parleyed with the crowd, and rode straight to the Tower, where the Council was sitting without the King. Walworth's news was desperate news, nor could he promise much for the goodwill of the city. The wealthier guilds might muster some eight thousand armed men, counting prentices and servants; Sir Robert Knollys had his six score men-at-arms, quartered about his lodging; Sir Perducas d'Albreth had some fifty more. There were in the Tower with the King his two maternal brothers, the Earls of Salisbury, Suffolk, and Warwick, the Grand Prior of the Templars, Sir Robert de Namur, the Lord of Vertain, Sir Henry de Sanselles, and a number of knights, squires, and yeomen. The Kent and Sussex rebels could count on the great mass of the common people within the city, and the easterlings and the midlanders were on the march. Walworth shrugged his shoulders and spoke of opening the gates.

"I tell you, sirs, there is nothing for it but to keep these gentry in a good temper. The King alone can shepherd them. They will listen to no one else. Yet if they are met bravely and with fair words— —"

The lords looked at each other across the council table. It was as though Walworth mocked them, bidding them send out a white pigeon to coo to all these ravens. There was some quarrelling before the Council broke up, having come to no judgment in the matter; but Salisbury and Knollys drew Walworth aside and spoke with him apart in a window. Warwick and the archbishop joined them, and they debated for a long while in undertones.

It was Salisbury who pressed the issue.

"Walworth speaks the truth. We are in the last ditch, sirs, and something must be risked by desperate men. Let Knollys bring this marvel in."

"But the Princess? Is she the lady to suffer her son— —?"

"Let us all go to her together. She is a woman of sense and spirit. Come, gentlemen; we have no time to lose."

This "woman of sense and spirit" heard them with so much patience that Knollys rode to his lodgings as dusk fell, and climbed the stairs to Fulk's attic. The last edge of a red sunset showed through the window, and Fulk was standing and leaning his arms on the sill. For days he had been cooped up in this upper room, seeing no one but Knollys' old squire and trusted comrade in arms, who brought him food and drink, and stared him in the face as though he were Edward the Black Prince risen from the dead. For hours together Fulk had stood at the window watching the smoke rising, the pigeons on the roofs, and the swifts circling high above the steeples whose vanes glittered in the sunlight. Isoult's beauty was still burning in him, making his restlessness a consuming fire.

He turned sharply as Knollys entered, and his profile showed clear against the sunset. The very cock of his head was for adventure.

Knollys closed the door. He had a green cloak and hood, and a grey scarf over his right arm.

"The King behind the King!"

He gave a short laugh and tossed the things upon the bed.

"It's like the smell of the sea when the ships put off for France. On with the cloak, lad, and wrap the scarf over your face. It will be dark enough in the streets."

Two strides brought Fulk into the middle of the attic.

"I was ready to knock my head against the wall. What news?"

"Leave that for an hour. We must get through while the streets are open. The mob may break in before you can sing an Ave."

Fulk put on the cloak, and covered his face with the scarf, so that nothing but his eyes showed.

"What lodging for to-night?"

"The Tower, lad, the Tower!"

CHAPTER XVII

All through the night those who were awake in the city heard the rebels howling in the suburbs outside the walls. They had ransacked wood lodges and pulled down palings, and made great fires in the streets and open places, so that a yellow glare streamed up into the sky. At low tide some of them had swum the river and waded about on the mud under the water gate of the Tower, hooting and shouting, and jeering at the guards on the walls. At one time there were so many of them in the water that they looked like a swarm of big black rats whom fire had driven out of a merchant's warehouse.

The King's Council, sitting soon after dawn, realised its own helplessness and the danger of rousing a more ugly temper in the mob, for the Tiler and the leaders had threatened to burn the suburbs if the gates of the city were not opened. William Walworth himself rode out to see it done, but the news had spread before him, shouted hither and thither from Aldgate to Black Friars. The meaner folk had put on holiday clothes, and were swarming in the streets, making a motley of many colours, with the women, in clean wimples, and the young wenches with ribbons in their hair. Some of them broke into the churches and rang the bells, so that the whole city was a jangle of exultation. The wealthier folk, the brethren of the richer guilds and companies, kept close in their houses with doors barred and shutters up, all the able men in harness, and with arms ready to hand.

On London Bridge a crowd had gathered to see the bridge gate opened, and the river below was crowded with boats. Walworth and his men had trouble to push through. Horns and trumpets were blown, handbells rung, drums beaten, and from beyond the gate came the answering roar of the peasants. The gates were to be opened, and all these savage, simple souls took it for a surrender, the throwing wide of a new and spacious season, the beginning of the end of long tyrannies and oppressions. No more forced work upon roads and bridges, no more forced hewing of my lord's wood, of ploughing his land and harvesting his corn; no more gross manor rights, no heriots, no fines, no reliefs, no dishonouring of brides; no more takes, no more arbitrary statutes, no more grindings at the lord's mill. All men were to be free to give service for a free wage. All men and women were to wear the clothes they pleased, to go whither they pleased, to serve whom they pleased. The gates were to be opened. The great lords had surrendered!

The people on the bridge cheered Walworth the Mayor, for their hearts were with the men of Kent. The sun shone, the bells jangled. It was like May Day, and a new season was coming in.

A certain soldierly orderliness marked the marching of the peasants over London Bridge, and Walworth, who saw them cross, turned and spoke to the City Fathers who were with him.

"These sheep are not without shepherds. We shall have news to hear before nightfall."

John Ball and Wat the Tiler headed the multitude, riding side by side, the priest carrying a wooden cross, the Tiler a naked sword. Five hundred bowmen in one company followed them, marching in step, their caps set jauntily, their belts stuck full of arrows. A wagon rumbled behind these bow-bearers, drawn along by a crowd of men who shouted and pointed their fingers at things allegorical.

Father Merlin sat in the front of the wagon, holding a steelyard on a staff, and the crowd called him Father Justice. Behind him, on two stools, were Isoult and Guy the Stallion, each clad in scarlet and white, the swashbuckler wearing a pasteboard crown, Isoult a garland of white roses. King Jack and Queen Jill were their pageant names, and it was said that they symbolised the right of the people to rule.

Isoult had no smiles for the crowd, but her partner was in royal fettle. The red tusks of his beard bristled with arrogance, and he turned his head from side to side like a haughty and staring puppet. Now and again he presented his poleaxe, which served as a sceptre, for the crowd to kiss, nodding his head at them and declaiming his titles.

"By cock, I am King Jack—King of the Commons! Let the lords and gentles shrive themselves, for assuredly I shall crack their skulls. I am King Jack, the King of all honest fellows."

They went at a snail's pace over the bridge. The roadway between the houses with their painted signs and plaster work and their carved, overhanging gables, shook with the tramp of feet. The bowmen put their caps on their bows and shouted together, and from the boats on the river came the braying of trumpets and the beating of drums.

Isoult's heart was out of the crowd. She was conscious of scorn, of an utter lack of kinship with these rustics who crowded in their thousands over the bridge. The walls of the White Tower rose against the blue, speaking to the pride in her, a pride that had blood in the mortar between its stones. Yet she owned to a vague curiosity, a desire to foresee the end of all this storm and bluster. Was it possible that her own perverse but discarded dreams were to come true, that she was to behold King Jack crowned and throned on the seats of the mighty? She felt someone nudging her, and found the swashbuckler thrusting at her with the handle of his poleaxe.

"Look alive, wife; grin at them, bob your head. By cock, we are very great people, you and I!"

Certainly his greatness had expanded. His eyes flared, and his beard looked even redder than usual. The allegory had got into his head.

"You are fine enough to serve for both!"

"What, no heart for adventure? We are great people, I say. Listen to the bells, and the drums, and the fine bellowing voices."

"They bellow loud enough, even for your fancy."

"Well, Queen Jill, I shall sit in the King's chair at Westminster. But spur and saddle's the word, when we have done with all this mummery. We'll show these lordings how to handle a spear."

Isoult returned to her own mute inner self, and left this stuffed figure and the crowd on the far edge of her consciousness. She saw things without seeing them, heard sounds without hearing them. Her thoughts were back in the forest with its green and secret ways, in the wild fern, in the singing of birds at dawn, in the smell of the torn blossom, in the strong arms of a man. She was weary of being tossed along on the foam of this mill-race. It would carry her under the wheel, no doubt, and leave her broken in the still waters of the days beyond. She tried to keep in the past and not to think of the future. What did anything matter, unless the strangest of strange things happened?

The day's happenings were to be spread out before her like some pageant or wild miracle play, for the wagon went with the multitude, carried along by it like a barge on a muddy stream. The peasants poured through the city, past Paul's, and through Ludgate towards John of Gaunt's palace of the Savoy. This great and noble house was the first thing to feel the mob's wrath, and since they could not lay hands on the master, they were determined to wreck his house instead.

The wagon was left standing in the street, and Isoult saw all that happened. King Jack had joined the crowd; but Merlin remained in the wagon, holding his emblem of justice. The mob broke down the gates of the Savoy, slew the porters, and threw their bodies out into the street. A torrent of fury poured through into the courtyard till the great palace was as crowded as a beehive, and the uproar within never ceased. Men began to straggle out, carrying in their arms all manner of rich gear, plate, and jewels, and beautiful hangings, tapestries, furniture, armour, glass cups, mazer bowls, salts, clothes, dorsers, chalices, gold candlesticks, caskets, and mosaics. Everything was hurled down in the street beside the wagon where Merlin sat, until there was a pyramid of tangled magnificence lying in the roadway. When they had emptied the palace Merlin stood at his full height and waved long arms.

"Destroy, destroy, let nothing be left!"

They fell upon the pile, crushing the jewels to powder with hammers, battering the cups into shapeless lumps, hacking the gold and silver dishes to pieces, tearing the silks, embroideries, and tapestries to ribbons. A hundred armourers might have been at work in the street, by the clangour of axes and hammers. The air was full of dust and of silken shreds floating iridescent in the sunlight. A red stream came trickling out of the gateway into the street, for the mob had rolled all the wine barrels into the courtyard and staved them in, letting muscadel and pyment and hypocrasse gush over the stones.

Merlin looked at Isoult with his ironical eyes.

"We trample pride into the dust, but we do not steal it. See now, what a watch-fire they are kindling."

Blue ribbons of smoke were uncurling themselves from the windows, and in a few minutes it began to rise in black masses from the turrets and the great lantern of the hall. The mob had set the palace on fire, after hacking the wainscoting to pieces, and piling it up to make a blaze. The river of wine still ran through the gateway, soaking into the mass of gorgeous rubbish that had been trampled like litter in a cow-yard. As the windows reddened, the last of the mob came pouring out, sweating, shouting, exultant. Soon the heat became so great, and the smoke so thick, that Merlin's wagon had to be dragged away, and the greater part of the multitude followed it back into the city.

The Hospital of St. John shared the fate of the palace of the Savoy, being sacked and set on fire. Merlin's wagon rolled through the streets with wild faces round it. They passed John Ball running like a madman through West Cheap, waving a crucifix, and shouting, "Let Nineveh be destroyed!" All the shops were shut; a sudden terror had seized the city; the May Day mood of the morning had gone with the dew. The mob's blood was up, and its head taking in strong drink, for the tavern keepers had to keep open house and dared not ask for payment. The houses of the wealthier citizens looked shut up and deserted, but through cracks in the shutters many an eye peered and men handled their weapons behind barred doors.

Isoult saw Richard Lyon, Wat the Tiler's enemy, murdered in West Cheap. Later she saw Flemings dragged from their houses and butchered before their doors, their bodies hacked in pieces and thrown into the gutters. Very few Flemings escaped that day, for these men of Kent had no pity on them. The Lombards shared the fate of the Flemings. The mob had smelt and tasted blood, and its face became smeared and hideous.

Isoult went through the day, mute, wide-eyed, possessed by a sense of her utter helplessness. She was conscious of anger and scorn, and of a deepening disgust that hardened her face and pinched her nostrils. The dust, the sweat, the butchery, the odour of burnt wood, the flat smell of spent ale, the screams, the shouts, curses, and laughter, the blundering violence, the stupid, ruthless faces. She had a feeling that nothing could stop the mad rush of this multitude, that nothing could master it. The lords and great ones, the castles and richer houses, the whole proud scheme of things would go down before it and be left buried under mud and wreckage.

Merlin was watching her, and her loathing was too great to be dissembled.

"Lord of Foul Beasts, are you proud of the day?"

"No fire without smoke, Isoult. These fellows are as quiet as lambs in their own fields, but the wrath of God is in them."

"The wrath of God may prove stronger than your wisdom."

"Let them but shout and drink, and let a little blood, and they will be the more easily ruled when they are weary."

"This blood lust is useful to you!"

"It shall purge the pride of the oppressor."

"Assuredly it is a marvellous thing that we should be Christians."

Towards evening the mob gathered in the square of St. Catharine's by the Tower, and fixed their quarters there for the night. Here was the very heart of the kingdom, the castle of all castles, and the sight of its walls and towers roused these peasants to the very top of their frenzy. They crowded close to the walls, hooting and howling, and singing songs, boasting of the day's happenings, and promising themselves nobler things on the morrow. In yonder were great lords whom they hated, and Simon of Sudbury, the archbishop, whom many of them had sworn to kill. The King should come out to them and grant all that they desired, or they would break in and take him out of the hands of men who were their enemies.

Merlin's wagon had been drawn into the square of St. Catharine's, and from it John Ball and Wat the Tiler spoke to the crowd. Fulk, lodged in a little upper room above the King's chamber in the White Tower, could stand at the window and look down at the crowd about the wagon. One of the figures in it was that of a woman in a red robe, a mere red line set among the other little figures that stormed and waved their arms like dolls on a puppet stage. Isoult was too far away for Fulk to recognise her, nor did she guess that he was in the Tower.

CHAPTER XVIII

The great lords and gentlemen sat round the table in the Council Chamber in the White Tower, and out of the summer night came the shouts of the peasants. They had lit bonfires in the square of St. Catharine's and were making merry, there being no lack of meat and drink, for they had taken whatever they desired to lay their hands upon. Hundreds of them were drunk before sunset, and the multitude kept up a fuddled uproar, marching to and fro under the walls, hammering on pots and pans, and making every sort of noise that it was possible for tipsy fools to make.

The King was not at the council board. He had gone to his chamber soon after sunset, and ordered all the windows to be closed, for the wild shouts of the mob had terrified him, even as a child is terrified by the howling of wolves on a winter night. Salisbury, Simon of Sudbury, and Walworth the Mayor had gone to his chamber, to find it lit by a blaze of candles, and the King abed with a great purple quilt, embroidered with golden suns, pulled up over his head. He had turned his face away and refused to speak with them, muttering that one of his uncles had conspired to raise the rage of the people against him.

These three councillors had looked at the room with its tapestries of green and red, its eastern carpet, its mirrors, its hutches packed full of jewels and clothes. It was more the room of a woman, soft, sensuous, with bunches of flowers in bowls, and a lute inlaid with mother-of-pearl lying on a scarlet cushion. The smell of it was like the smell of some rich courtesan's chamber.

This lad in the bed was not to be counted on. Salisbury and his companions stood by the door, whispering.

"He is best left where he is."

"Better still in his mother's bed. He is the greatest peril we have to fear."

"If these rebels can but get him into their hands they will make him hop as they please."

"It would be giving them our heads. Now—this bastard!"

They returned to the Council Chamber, where some of the younger men were standing at the windows looking down at the bonfires and listening to the shouts of the crowd. Salisbury drew Knollys aside before the Council gathered about the board.

"Your fellow must serve. They shall change caps to-night. I have planned what to say to these gentlemen."

They came together round the great table, and the King's half-brothers and some of the hot-heads were for a night attack. They talked of arming every man they could muster, opening the gates, and sallying out to attack the mob. The peasants were drunk and fuddled, and could be slaughtered like sheep in the shambles.

Salisbury put their desperate measures aside with the wise air of a sage captain.

"Sirs, we have spoken with the King. He has taken heart of grace, and swears that to-morrow he will speak to these people as their King. Brave words will win more from them than blows."

They were for arguing the point.

"What, treat with these clowns?"

"Let the King go into the midst of them!"

"They'll not stand against gentlemen and men of metal. The whole pack is drunk."

It was Walworth who smothered their adventurous truculence. He had his spies in the crowd. Two of them had been let in at the water-gate, and he had spoken with them after leaving the King's chamber.

"Sir, a few thousand tipplers do not make up the whole mob. Do you think that the men who have raised this storm against us are mere sots and fools? I tell you I know the truth, and how matters lie out yonder. The Tiler and his comrades have thousands of fellows ready in the streets, men who are too savage against us to throw away their chances for a pot of ale. All the pother down yonder is so much froth. Those who are sober are on the watch, and would thank us were we to open the gates and fight with them, one man against ten, and in the dark. I tell you they would ask for no easier way of putting your heads upon their pikes."

The hot-heads were less ready to put on their harness when they had heard what Walworth had to promise them.

The Council broke up, and the two earls, the archbishop, and the Lord Mayor passed straight to the chamber of the Princess, the King's mother.

Though it was past midnight they found her up and dressed, and walking restlessly to and fro between her state bed and the window. She was alone, having just returned from the King's chamber, and her face looked white and hard.

She turned on them sharply, and spoke as though she were in a fierce haste to have some shameful truth confessed.

"Gentlemen, since our case is so desperate, it must be as you please. I have spoken with the King."

They saw her wince and stiffen her neck and body.

"I have spoken with the King. I had thought that I should strike a new courage into him, that he would be shamed, stung to the quick. Well, it is not so. Do what your wisdom desires. I have no more to say."

Salisbury stood forward and bowed his head before her.

"Madame, trust us. The case must be desperate when we use so desperate a disguise. You yourself have suffered at the hands of these common men, and they have grown more savage since they have grown in strength. Let us remember that the King is but a lad."

She turned away from him and went and stood by the window, her eyes hot with tears.

"Do not seek to soften it. What must be must be, and yet was ever a woman's pride so humbled!"

She grew inarticulate, stood awhile with one hand at her throat, and then swung round and faced them.

"Gentlemen, to save a son and a kingdom I pluck my child out of the throne, and like a hen I hide him under my feathers. The secret must be kept, well kept."

They answered her together:

"Madame, it shall be. All our lives depend on it."

"Then let it be done quickly. I have spoken with the two women I have chosen; they are in my closet and can be trusted to the death."

Salisbury looked at her questioningly.

"Would it please you to see this young man—to assure yourself?"

Her face flushed.

"See him—this—this— —! Sir, are you blind to what my pride bears in suffering? Let me never set eyes on the young man."

Her voice choked in her throat, and feeling like men convicted of some great meanness, they passed out and left her.

A squire was on guard outside the King's door—a grizzled man, lame of one leg from a wound in the French wars, taciturn, with a mouth that shut like a trap.

Salisbury spoke to him, with a hand gripping his arm below the shoulder.

"There is great trust placed in you, Cavendish. Has Sir Robert Knollys made it plain?"

The squire nodded.

"I would have listened to no other man."

"Thunder, think you we play such a game as this for the joy of it? By my soul, Cavendish, we are like to lose our King, and our heads, unless we have a King with some blood in him. You have eyes and a shrewd head, and the devil's own courage. Play the game through. Is Sir Robert Knollys within?"

"He has been there this half-hour."

"Open, and let us pass."

They found Knollys standing with his back to the window, arms folded, teeth biting at his moustache, his eyes watching the King, who sat half-dressed in a gilded chair, his hair over his face, his whole body shaking. The lad might have had St. Vitus's dance by the way he twitched and fidgeted. His eyes had a scared and empty look. There was no shadow of kingliness upon him, nothing but the terror of an animal that seeks to slink into a corner.

"Sire, will you come with us to Madame, your mother?"

He stood up, fingers twitching, staring at them stupidly.

"Put a cloak about him."

Knollys took a red cloak from a stool, threw it over the King's shoulders, and wrapped it round him.

"You must cover your face, Sire. Friend Walworth, will you go before us, to see the way is clear?"

The lad stood pulling his lower lip with thumb and forefinger, his eyes looking vacantly at Salisbury's shoes. A hood was found, and put on back to front so that it served as a mask. He said nothing, but let them do with him what they pleased. Simon of Sudbury took him by the hand. Cold and moist, it clasped his with a spasmodic twitching of the fingers.

Salisbury glanced meaningly at Knollys.

"You shall see us anon, sir. Cavendish knows all that can be known."

When the King had gone to his mother's chamber to lie hidden in her bed, Knollys took a candle from a sconce, traversed a gallery, and made his way up a newel stair. The door at the top was barred on the inside. He knocked thrice, and the door was opened.

Knollys wasted no words.

"Come."

Fulk followed him, and they passed down the stairway and back to the King's chamber. Cavendish was waiting outside the door. He stared at Fulk with the air of a watch-dog half loath to let a stranger into his master's room. But one clear look at Fulk's face made him stand back with a growl of astonishment.

"S'death!"

Knollys smiled grimly.

"It was what I said, Cavendish, when I first set eyes on our man. Come in with us, for you are the councillor we need. You have seen the King in the flesh, naked and dressed, day in day out."

They went in and barred the door on the inside.

"Now for the play. Out with the clothes, Cavendish. Sit you down, Fulk Ferrers, well in the light here. Have a good look at him, Cavendish. Hum! What about a razor?"

Cavendish scanned Fulk's face, feeling his chin, and looking him in the eyes as though challenging his courage.

"A little cropping of the hair and a scrape with a razor. Too much on the upper lip, too, for a lad of fifteen. Let's hear your voice, brother."

Fulk smiled at him.

"Like you, sir, I serve the King."

"Too much trumpet in it! Softly, more softly, and it will do."

"Good Cavendish, to-morrow he has to play the hero, and heroes speak like clarions! We shall put it about the King has dreamed a most marvellous dream and come to his kingliness thereby. Now for the toilet."

Cavendish turned to and served as barber, robeman, and player. He knew all the tricks of the King's person, how he looked, spoke, wore his clothes, carried his head, and sat in a chair. He prompted Fulk all the time he was busy with him, acting the tricks and mannerisms himself, and making Fulk act them after him.

The result delighted Knollys.

"Thunder! you have quick wits and a sharp eye. The King's rings—you must wear the rings."

The business was nearly ended when they heard footsteps without and the sound of voices. Someone knocked, and Knollys went to the door.

"Who's there?"

"All's well, Knollys."

"Tarry one moment."

He let Cavendish finish with Fulk before he opened the door and suffered the two earls, Walworth, and the archbishop to enter. They paused on the threshold, and stood looking at a young man seated in the King's chair, wearing the King's clothes with an air of fine serenity.

They were astonished, and, drawing near, stood about Fulk, staring at him.

Cavendish gave a short laugh.

"Sire, here are your good councillors."

"Gentlemen, you are very welcome. What commands shall I lay upon you?"

Salisbury's eyes flashed under a frowning forehead.

"Young man, know you what you carry on your shoulders?"

"Your heads, sir—and my own."

"Aye—and more than that. Here's my sword. Swear on the cross thereof that you will keep troth with us."

Fulk swore, looking straight in Salisbury's eyes.

"Good, you are in our hands, and we in yours. Now, let us get ready for to-morrow's hazard. None of us will get much sleep to-night."

Cavendish went to stand on guard outside the door, while Fulk sat in the King's chair with five pedagogues to put him through his part. It was a long lesson that they gave him, and a merciless catechising followed the lesson, lest some small thing might betray them.

Salisbury spoke last.

"Hold aloof, proudly. We will stand about you, and keep meddlers at a distance. Remember, a King may please himself, but when you meet with these peasants, ride high in the saddle, and yet with a kind of valiant frankness. A mob should be treated as you would treat a strange dog. Never flinch, and yet be not too familiar."

They watched Fulk's face as though trying to forecast the issue of the morrow. He sat erect in the chair, mouth firm, eyes steady.

"Sirs," he said very quietly; "if I am my father's son I have the blood of mastery in me. It will be served."

CHAPTER XIX

Friday's dawn came in stealthily, with a mist that foretold heat, masking the windings of the river. The King's standard on the White Tower hung in folds against the pole, and haze covered the city, a silver fog through which the towers and steeples struck, sending their wind vanes and fleches to glitter in the sunlight.

Knollys and Walworth the Mayor were on the platform of the White Tower soon after dawn, peering down like hawks into the dark spaces outside the walls. What would the mob's temper be? What manner of sunset would follow this stealthy dawn? There was much movement down yonder. All through the night a restless murmur had risen from the streets and alleys. Seen through the haze, the square of St. Catharine looked like a stagnant pool swarming with tadpoles.

Soon after dawn hundreds of peasants came crowding to the gates and walls. They crowed like cocks, and the conceit seemed to please them.

"Cock-a-doodle-do!"

"Up, all slug-a-beds! St. George and the King!"

They took up the cry.

"Ha, for King Richard and the Commons! Send us out our King."

Other great lords joined Knollys and Walworth on the platform of the White Tower. They stood in a group, close to the drooping standard, listening to the cries of the mob. Their faces were very grave and grim.

"To-day's game is a game of chess, sirs, and it is the King's move. Knights, castles, and bishops are of no account."

"All hangs on the courage of a bastard!"

"A good hawk or I'm no judge. Let's fly him."

Salisbury struck the standard pole with his fist.

"St. George and King Richard for Merrie England! That is our cry. The lad shall serve. Let these hinds march to Mile End, and meet the King face to face. We will send our trumpeters to the outer gate. Now God in heaven alone knows what this day will bring."

It was six o'clock when trumpets sounded from the outer gate and a herald wearing the King's coat stood out against the sky line. Thousands of heads came crowding forward. The herald held up his hand for silence, and his big voice carried.

"Give heed, give heed!"

Someone bawled, "Crow, good cock!"

"St. George and King Richard for England! Ye Commons and good men all, take heed, and hear the words of the King. 'I will come forth and speak with my people, and meet them face to face. None shall stand between us. I, Richard the King, am King!' Therefore, sirs, march you to Mile End peaceably, in good order, like honest fellows. The King will ride out and bring you banners. Shout for St. George and King Richard!"

And shout they did, like madmen.

The King's company gathered in the great court, while the King heard Mass in the chapel, Simon of Sudbury serving at the altar, little thinking that it was to be his last Mass. Salisbury, Warwick, Knollys, Walworth, and Cavendish were with the bastard King. He walked in their midst down the stairway, and they held close to him when he came out from the gloom of the entry into the full June sunlight.

His banners were gathered below. Trumpets blew; the men of the guard tossed their pikes. All eyes sought the King. He was in red and white, a light gold crown set upon his velvet cap, his sword at his side, a rich collar of gold about his throat, his gloves studded with jewels. He stood there for a moment at the head of the stairway in the midst of the great lords, his face white in the sunlight, the proud face of a King.

A great silence held. Those who gazed upon him wondered. It was a King who had come out to them—not a cringing, frightened boy. The weak figure had stiffened; the eyes were furtive no longer; the mouth was straight and purposeful.

But no idle gazing was to be suffered. The great lords kept close about their King, and stood round him while he mounted his white horse. He looked at no one, spoke to none, but kept his soul for the great adventure. The trumpets blew, the banners swayed; King Richard, at the head of his lords and gentlemen, rode forward to meet the Commons.

Cavendish rode a little behind the King and on his left, a grim man with watchful eyes. Salisbury and Warwick were close at his heels. Knollys and Walworth rode with the main company, shadowing the King's half-brothers, Sir John Holland and the Earl of Kent.

There was a moment's halt under the arch of the outer gate, for one of the bars had jammed in its socket; and while the porters were tugging at it Knollys came pushing forward till his horse was close to the King's.

"Sir, a word in your ear."

He leant over.

"Sir, you have two half-brothers, you remember, apt to be hot-headed fools. I have caught them giving each other strange looks. The mob does not love them."

"Let them bide in the Tower."

"Sir, it would be better to rid ourselves of them. Take your chance, or shall I bid them save their skins?"

He beckoned to Salisbury, who edged his horse up. Knollys spoke in a whisper.

"The Hollands have scented a fox."

"Send the young hounds hunting it! The two young meddlers!"

Knollys bit his moustache.

"I carry the King's orders. A word to them—that their heads have been asked for! We will wait our chance on the way, and smuggle them into the city to hide."

"Good, very good."

One of the porters who had been peering through the grille came to them with a white face.

"Sirs, the crowd is great without."

"Tsst! they have marched to Mile End."

"Sirs, not the Kentish men."

Fulk waved him aside.

"Well, am I afraid of my own people! Open the gates. Let the trumpets blow. Now, sirs, for St. George and Richard of England!"

The gate swung back and the young King on the white horse rode out into the sea of heads and faces. For the moment a great silence held—the silence of a mistrustful crowd whose goodwill hangs upon the flash of an eye or the set of a head; but this lad with the crown rode out proudly. His eyes were steady and fearless, and he smiled at the crowd.

"Good sirs, well met."

His courage captured them. The cock of his head, the braced-back shoulders, the blue metal of his eyes, these things counted. These rough fellows from the fields shouted tumultuously and crowded about him.

"King Richard for Merrie England!"

Fulk stood in his stirrups.

"Sirs, I am Richard your King. To Mile End! Follow my banners."

The crowd made way for him, and he passed with his company of lords and gentlemen, who rode close together and scarcely looked at the crowd. The banners swept under the arch of the gate, and the men of Kent were on the move—all save a few who seemed to stare and loiter as though a King and such a company were not to be seen more than once in a lifetime. The porters were closing the gate when these loiterers gathered suddenly, rushed in a body through the barriers, hurled back the half-closed gate, and struck down the guards and porters. They stood there shouting and tossing their weapons.

The tail of the King's company was not fifty paces away, and some of the riders faltered; white faces looked back over half-turned shoulders.

"S'death—they have taken the gate behind us!"

Salisbury spoke through clenched teeth.

"Ride on, ride on, sir. Look not back."

Fulk had not faltered. He looked at the Kentish men who crowded round him, and smiled.

"Shout for King Richard, sirs."

And they cheered him gallantly.

Fulk rode on, to behold a marvel—a marvel that wiped the crowd of faces away from before his eyes. Halfway across St. Catharine's Square a wagon was standing in the thick of the press, with a swarm of brown figures clinging to it to get a view, and in the front of the wagon, like a red torch burning amid brushwood, stood Isoult of the Rose.

CHAPTER XX

They looked at each other, these two—Fulk, like a man who stares into the heart of a fire; Isoult, with eyes that showed at first no more than a tired wonder. She saw the red bridle tighten, the white horse draw in. Then the truth leapt at her out of the eyes that had flashed with a startled swiftness to hers.

Then she saw the red bridle jerked and Fulk's profile, stark and clear, as he pressed his heels into the white horse's flanks. God, how nearly he had betrayed himself when his heart had leapt in him with a cry of "Isoult, Isoult!"

All the blood in his body seemed thundering into his brain. He had to steady himself, clench his teeth, fix his eyes on the tops of the houses, ride on without so much as another side glance.

She was not dead then, but living, with red lips and raven hair. How had it happened? Was she a traitress after all, and had she but tricked Merlin to save him out of pity? Pity! He looked as though he had been struck with a whip, his face white as a frost, with tense lips and quivering nostrils. Pity!

Wrath blew through him like a winter wind. She might betray him—he who was playing the King—if he had betrayed himself to her in that one flash of the eyes! He set his teeth. And then from some more passionate memory a braver faith leapt to the challenge. What ignoble thoughts were these! She was alive, but what might life have meant to her, to a falcon with a broken wing? He seemed to see Merlin grinning at him from under his cowl—Merlin with the lean and hungry mouth and the big teeth that glistened.

His heart cried out with new passion, "Isoult, Isoult!"

He found Salisbury riding at his side and staring at him with curious eyes.

"Sir, you look grim."

Fulk twisted out a smile.

"Good sir, that may be true. I would ask for nothing better than to trample on these gentry as one tramples on corn."

"S'death, go gently. Speak them fair. Make promises. We must humour the beast till we have the twitch on his nose."

"The King makes for the King to break. My lord, I take you."

So "The King behind the King" rode on.

Isoult was still standing in the wagon, staring like a blind woman at the White Tower. The brown figures beside her had swarmed down to follow the King's banners, and the crowd had melted like mist, some hundreds of the rougher sort charging down to the gate that had been seized by Wat the Tiler and Jack Straw.

A man climbed into the wagon and touched her shoulder, and, turning sharply, she looked into the eyes of Guy the Stallion.

"Come, girl, all the fun of the fair! Am I to miss it because I am your gallant?"

She let him draw her to the tail end of the wagon, but when he sprang down and would have put his arms about her to lift her to the ground she repulsed him fiercely.

"Off, fool!"

He snarled, and showed his teeth.

"I hold the end of the leash, my falcon, and, by cock, you are too fine a bird to be lost."

She went with him, mute with scorn, yet conscious of her own helplessness and that she was at the mercy of such men as these. Moreover, she was still blinded to all other things but that vision of Fulk Ferrers, turned King, and riding a great white horse. She might have let him go by with nothing more than astonishment that two mortal creatures should be so alike, but for the way his eyes had fallen on her.

As they passed through the gate she glanced at Guy, who carried his naked sword over his shoulder, and her heart leapt in her at the thought of the bold game Fulk was playing. How had it come about? Where was the real King? Why had the great lords ventured on such a hazard? Had they set him up with his hawk's eyes and the proud throw back of his head to play a part that was beyond the courage of the stripling Richard? Would he carry it through, tame this herd of wild beasts, and turn them again into quiet oxen? And what if the trick were discovered? What of Merlin, the Grey Friar?

She heard Guy rap out an oath.

"Bones of the saints, here's blood!"

A shouting mob came pouring through one of the inner gateways. Carried in the midst, like a man in a mill-race, was Simon of Sudbury, the Archbishop, and Chancellor. His vestments had been half torn from him. His white face was splashed with blood, the mouth awry, the eyes staring.

Guy pressed Isoult back against a wall.

"S'death, they have caught Master Simon! I know that fat face of his."

Wat the Tiler broke away from the crowd, and his beard was all froth and spittle from shouting.

"Friend Guy, there are swine to be stuck in yonder. Rout them out—the Prior of St. John, and some of Lancaster's rats."

He stared hard into Isoult's eyes.

"Go and show the Red Queen a fine colour. Simon of Sudbury's head is going to dance on a pike."

When the mob had passed Guy seized her wrist and drew her on, and she went with him, mutely, as though the old Isoult were dead in her, the Isoult who could rule men with a flash of the eyes. She thought of Fulk on his white horse riding out proudly to face these boors, and she prayed fiercely that he might fool them. She was weary of this mob adventure; and, loathing these hinds with a great loathing, she believed once more in the pride of the sword, scorning the baser clay that stank of the potter's hands.

They reached the great court about the White Tower, and here Bedlam—a bloody Bedlam—had been let loose. The mob swarmed everywhere. They had driven a dozen of the King's knights into a corner and were pulling their beards and spitting in their faces. Two hacked bodies lay close to the chapel entry, the bodies of two of John of Gaunt's men who had been caught in his hated colours. From the windows of the White Tower came yells and curses. A man leant out, waving a red hand.

"Taken—taken—bully Robert Hales!"

The mob roared.

"Bring him out! Throw him down!"

A whirl of figures came down the outer steps with an old man in their midst. His fierce white beard stuck out under a grim mouth; the swineherds and scullions had not cowed him.

They dragged him this way and that, like hounds pulling at a fox.

"A horse-block! A horse-block!"

One was found and rolled forward, and Sir Robert Hales thrown across it, face upwards, his hands clutching the air.

Guy rushed forward, and jostled through.

"My stroke, sirs. Room, room! I'll do't at one swash!"

Isoult quailed, and turned away.

The door of the White Tower stood open at the head of the steps down which the men of Kent had dragged Sir Robert Hales. The steps themselves were deserted for the moment, and Isoult climbed them and fled into the cool gloom of the great tower, trying to forget the sight of the old man flung face upwards across the horse-block. A desire to escape from these wretches seized her, and she fled along passages and up stairways, knowing not where she went, but seeking for some place where she might hide.

Loud laughter and a pother of rough voices broke suddenly from a room at the top of a short flight of broad steps. Isoult heard the proud, but appealing voice of a woman and the laughter seemed to falter and die down.

The door was half open, and Isoult, gliding along the wall, climbed the steps and peered through the gap at the hinges.

It was a noble room hung with sky-blue arras dusted with silver stars, and over by the window stood a great bed covered with a canopy of purple cloth. Hutches and chests had been broken open, and rich clothes and stuffs of cloth of silver and gold had been scattered about the floor. In the bed sat the Princess, the King's mother, white as her own night gear. Three women cowered in a corner. A dozen or more peasants were crowded round, snapping their fingers in the Princess's face, jeering, and threatening to pull the clothes from her, and thrusting the points of their pikes into the bed.

"Men of Kent, have you forgotten Edward the Black Prince?"

She faced them fearlessly, in spite of deathly fear, and the white pride of her face was like a white flame, keeping the men back. They were awed and, a little ashamed, faltered, grinned at each other, and then slunk back towards the door.

Isoult hid herself in a dark recess in the thickness of the wall, and they went crowding down the stairs past her.

"I've seen the King's mother a'bed, Jock!"

"That be some'at to remember!"

Isoult was still in hiding when one of the Princess's women came to the door and ran down the flight of steps. She looked this way and that like a frightened deer, and then, putting her hands to her mouth, called up the great stairway.

"Eustace! Geoffrey!"

She stood listening, her face strained and expectant. Down the stairway came two men, descending step by step, the one in front craning his head forward to see that the way was clear.

"Quick, for the love of Our Lady. The wretches have been here!"

They disappeared with the woman into the Princess's room.

Some instinct kept Isoult hidden in the dark recess. She heard voices, eager, conspiring voices that spoke in hurrying undertones. Then, footsteps approached. The door creaked; there was the sound of heavy breathing. A woman came out and went gliding down the stairs to see that they were clear. She called back, "Come."

Isoult saw the Princess carried out on a mattress laid upon the frame of a pallet bed. The men were at the head and foot, a woman at each side. A purple quilt covered the Princess, who lay with a veil thrown over her head.

They disappeared round a bend of the stairs, and curiosity made Isoult follow them, shadowing them round each corner and along each gallery as they went down and down into the deeps of the tower. She nearly betrayed herself at the end of a long, dim passage where a door had to be opened and the Princess's bed forced through.

Then an oblong patch of daylight shone out abruptly. A flight of steps went up towards it, and Isoult saw the bed-bearers struggling up towards the light.

Near the top of the steps one of the men missed his footing and slipped sideways against the wall. The bed tilted. There was a cry. One of the women clutched the Princess, but Isoult saw a lad's head and shoulders jerked out from under the quilt.

There was a moment's agony. The bed was righted; the lad thrust back under the quilt. One of the women who had crept on ahead came back, waving them forward. The knot of figures struggled out into the daylight and disappeared from Isoult's view.

She ran up the steps, and her eyes came level with the flagstones of a small courtyard. The men and women had carried the bed across it, and were disappearing through a doorway in the opposite wall. One of the women glanced back anxiously over her shoulder, for she could hear men coming down a long slope that led into the courtyard. She did not see Isoult.

Then they vanished through the doorway, and Isoult climbed the last steps, and running across the court, laid her cheek to the doorpost, and peered round. A sloping passage went down under a vaulted roof, and at the end of it she saw water swishing to and fro, and the legs of a man standing beside the black snout of a barge.

All of a sudden she understood. Richard the King was hidden in that bed, and they were smuggling him out of the Tower lest this bold trick should be betrayed.

She heard voices behind her, and starting back into the courtyard, found herself looking into the eyes of Guy the Stallion. He carried a bloody sword over his shoulder, and some of the lowest curs from out of the city were at his heels.

"Hullo, my wench, what tricks have you been playing?"

He caught her by the bosom, and she humoured him, knowing Fulk's peril and her own.

"Playing at hide and seek with the Knight of the Bloody Sword, O brave Sir Guy!"

She laughed in his face.

"Come. I hear the Princess is above. I have a desire to look on a Princess."

"By cock, you shall. We'll show her a comelier woman than herself."

CHAPTER XXI

At Mile End Fulk Ferrers sat on his white horse, a little apart from his lords and gentlemen, who held together like desperate men expecting treachery. With the rich colours of their clothes and the glint of their harness they looked like some noble pile of plunder heaped up in the midst of a ploughed field, for the brown men of the soil in their thousands closed them in on every side.

Fulk had ridden forward thirty paces ahead of his company. He sat there on his white horse, with the peasants crowding round with their solemn, hairy faces. Imperturbable, stung to a tense audacity, he looked down at them with fearless eyes; sometimes he smiled; he knew himself their King.

"Sirs, here are we together, King Richard and his Commons. Speak out. Am I afraid to listen to your desires?"

They surged round him, looking up into his face, held by his blue eyes and the mouth that did not falter. He had left over yonder the lords whom they hated, and had ridden into their midst, a King who was not afraid.

They cheered him.

"Long live King Richard."

He held up a fist.

"Long life to myself, say I, my friends. But to your business. I am your King. I am here. I listen. Let no one come between us."

A hundred voices shouted for all manner of changes, but since their cries smothered each other, they grew more silent, and pushed some of their leaders and spokesmen to the front. Wat the Tiler, Jack Straw, and John Ball had remained behind with those who had seized the Tower, but Merlin stood hidden in the crowd, whispering to his neighbours and prompting them in their demands.

"Sir, noble sir, land at fourpence an acre."

"We will be serfs no longer."

"Down with the market tolls."

"No more grinding at the lord's mill."

"No heriot, and no dues, and no fleecing of a poor man when his wench marries."

For an hour or more Fulk sat there in their midst, listening to the babel of their desires, patiently, proudly, knowing behind his pride that for the moment the kingdom was at their mercy. The great brown mob palpitated about him. He was a rock in the midst of the sea, a solitary oak on a wind-blown heath.

His hand went up for a great silence, and it came—after much wrangling and shouting.

"Sirs, it seems to me good that men should be free. I, Richard the King, grant you your desires."

They surged round him, shouting like madmen.

"King Richard! King Richard!"

"The King's word carries!"

"We knew we would have justice if we had the ear of the King."

"St. George for Merrie England!"

"Yes, yes; and let the clerks put it all in writing."

Fulk turned his horse and made a sign to Cavendish to approach.

"Let my banners advance. Room, sirs, room for my banners."

Yet to one man in the crowd the game was going too smoothly, and that man was Father Merlin. This lad on the white horse seemed likely to carry the people away with him, and Merlin stood biting his nails and watching Fulk malevolently from under his hood. This young King on the white horse held the grey friar at a disadvantage. The one was lifted up valiantly before all men; the other lurked in the crowd, fearing to thrust to the front because of his grey frock.

"Fools, fools, to be cozened!"

A snarl of rage broke from him when the crowd honoured the King's banners. Each county was to have its banner, and the men of each county were to march back with the King's banner to their homes. Clerks were to be set that night to make out the charters, and two men from each county were to tarry behind their fellows to carry the charters into the countryside.

A voice trumpeted its scorn.

"Fools, you are being tricked, sent home like sheep!"

Fulk heard the cry. His face seemed to glow like white metal. He stood in his stirrups, high above the crowd.

"Who is it that challenges the word of the King? Let him stand out."

He had the crowd with him, and angry shouts went up.

"Bring the rat out."

"Who calls the King a liar?"

"Smite the churl on the mouth."

Merlin pulled his cowl down, pushed through, and slunk away.

"*Pax, pax,*" he said; "it was not I who challenged the King."

But his red mouth looked fierce, and his eyes formidable, under his cowl.

In another hour this great crowd had been tamed and won, the men of each county standing massed about the King's banners. A clerk sat on an overturned tub beside Fulk's horse, dipping his quill into the ink-horn at his girdle, making a rough draft of the King's charter to the Commons. And the men who were to tarry behind stood and looked over the clerk's shoulders, knowing nothing of letters, but seeing in them symbols of strange power.

Fulk sent a trumpeter to start the men upon their march. They circled round him with their banners, like a huge wheel with the figure on the white horse for the hub. The King's lords and gentlemen thanked God and the saints for a marvel.

"To your homes, sirs."

Fulk returned to his lords, and saw that a dusty, grey-faced man was standing beside Salisbury's horse. Walworth and Knollys were whispering together, their heads almost touching.

"To the Tower, my lords."

Salisbury covered his mouth with his gloved hand.

"Listen. The Tower is ours no longer."

He pushed his horse close to Fulk's.

"Wat and his ruffians broke in. Simon of Sudbury is dead, his head hacked off on Tower Hill. Others are dead with him. By God, we are on the edge of hell. Keep a brave face."

Fulk's eyes flashed.

"Have I faltered? Have I not poured out lies without flinching?"

"Sir, you have saved the kingdom. But he—the other— —"

"What! have they taken him?"

"Our Lady be thanked, no. We had news. Something was carried out in the Princess's bed, put aboard a boat, and smuggled to the Wardrobe in Carter Street."

Fulk's lips came together in a hard line.

"By the Cross, the ice is thin. We have got rid of these good sheep, but should we be betrayed——"

"We shall be, with Simon of Sudbury. Wat and John Ball have their thousands still—beasts who have tasted blood."

"Then whither go we, since the Tower is ours no longer?"

"To the Wardrobe, sir, to comfort the Princess."

The trumpets sounded, and the King's company unwound itself into a trail of steel and colour. Fulk rode forward on his white horse, Salisbury beside him, Cavendish close on his other flank.

"King Richard! King Richard!"

Fulk's eyes glittered. He spoke to Salisbury under his breath.

"Sir, my tongue burns in my mouth. The promises I have made these poor fools!"

"You have put the twitch on the beast's nose. Who rules, the herd or the herdsman?"

"Give me Wat and his bloody rogues, and that grey friar—I'll speak fire to them, and show them the sword."

They re-entered the city, and were stared at by people whose eyes were sullen and threatening, men whose blood was ripe for violence, men who thought of the plunder and the wine and the bodies of women surrendered to their desires. Here Merlin came by his own again. The sheep were pattering back to their fields, but the wolves remained.

Fulk met the eyes of these lust-hungry men. His face grew more bleak, his eyes full of a hard, cold light.

"Sir, this pleases me better."

"These curs that snarl?"

"By my troth, yes. Have we no swords, no good men to read these scullions a lesson?"

"Gently, by God, gently. Fifty thousand men are not to be whipped by five hundred."

"Fifty thousand!"

"The scum of the city is with them. Who does not love plundering a rich man's house?"

They came to the Walbrook and the bridge was narrow and the press great. Fulk had to rein in; the great company behind him swayed like a dragon with painted scales.

Fulk's eyes fell into a sudden stare.

On the parapet of the bridge sat Isoult with Guy the Stallion standing beside her. She was so close to him that Fulk could have touched her with the point of a sword.

Their eyes met, and held. Fulk saw that she knew him, and into Isoult's face the blood crept like fire.

She held her head high so that her throat showed.

"Long live King Richard, long live the King!"

Fulk's eyes stared into hers, and they were the eyes of a strong man and not the eyes of a boy.

The crowd gave back, and he rode on with a voice crying within him, "Isoult—ah, Isoult!"

The woman on the parapet found a man gripping her wrist. She glanced down and met the red eyes of Guy the Stallion.

"God's death, wench, I see light."

She did not falter.

"And all heaven opened, Sir Guy!"

"That was no King!"

"His ghost then!"

"It is that bastard of the forest, Fulk Ferrers, and you know it."

She laughed in his face.

"Friend Guy, you have drunk too much wine."

CHAPTER XXII

The Inn of The Painted Lady stood near the river, a gaudy, cut-throat, bold-faced house, the plaster between its beams daubed a hard, bright red, the barge-boards of its gables painted blue. The "Painted Lady" herself on her sign wore scarlet and blue, and her round eyes ogled the passers-by.

The inn door was barred that night, the windows shuttered. Nothing but chinks of light came from it, furtive gleams that lost themselves quickly in the darkness. The lane in front of it was rough and dirty and full of holes, and from the lane a narrow passage went down between two houses to the river.

Hither came Guy, holding Isoult fast by the wrist. And he found Merlin in "The Painted Lady," and though it was June, sitting on a stool before the fire, his cowl thrown back, his gaunt face glistening, the nails of his right hand bitten to the quick.

Isoult was bidden up the ladder stairs into an attic, and Guy sidled up to Merlin and touched him on the shoulder.

"Prettily fooled, by cock, and by no King!"

Merlin turned on him savagely.

"No King, say you? Too much of a King!"

Then Guy bent to him and whispered, and Merlin started and straightened like a man stabbed in the back.

"Thunder!"

"Ask the wench. It was the bastard, or I'm no man."

"*Mea culpa!*" He struck his chin with his fist. "Fool priest, blind ape! And I never scented the fox!"

He sprang up.

"That Sussex hawk—that love child of a Prince! Hallo, listen."

Men were coming down the lane with a rattle of arms. Someone knocked at the door.

"Who's there?"

"Wat and John Ball."

Merlin nodded Guy towards the door. He dropped the bar, and they came crowding in—men whose hands were bloody and whose throats were dry.

"Why bitest thou thy beard, St. Francis?"

"Saints, is the man hungry? Here is good Father John who has not touched a crust."

Merlin caught Wat by the shoulder.

"I'm in no mood for your clowning when the lords have made fools of us all."

"Good sir, I think not."

"Bah! a few old men butchered! Come, hear news!"

He dragged Wat to the far end of the long room where the fire burnt on the hearth. Jack Straw and John Ball joined them, and the rest of the men were for crowding up. Merlin flapped his long arms at them.

"Back! We want no gossips here."

They shouted for the innkeeper.

"What has befallen old Pot Harry?"

"He has fled."

"But left his cellar behind him! Down, brothers, down among the hogsheads."

They crowded, shouting, into a narrow passage, leaving Merlin, Wat the Tiler, Jack Straw, and John Ball alone. Guy tramped to and fro, twisting his moustaches.

The voices by the fire grew angry and querulous.

"What! A stuffed King?"

"He had fettle enough to fool us of forty thousand men. They went, at his bidding, bleating like sheep."

"This is a fool's tale. I'd not give a groat for it."

"The wench, Isoult, knows whether it be the truth or a lie."

"Where is the woman?"

"Above, in the attic."

"Have her down. We'll make her speak."

Merlin turned to Guy.

"Bid her come."

Guy climbed the ladder stair, and forced up the trap-door with one hand. His head disappeared through the opening.

"Isoult, Father Merlin has need of you."

He climbed down, and stood looking up with a grin on his face. There was no light but the light of the fire and the flare of a torch burning in a cresset. Isoult's red dress showed on the stairs. She descended them slowly, gathering her skirt up with one hand.

The men by the fire stared at her. Their faces looked gaunt and shadowy. Merlin was licking his lips.

"My sister, the truth lies with you. Friend Guy has used his eyes. Speak!"

She stood before them in all her comeliness.

"What truth, Merlin?"

"Tsst! You know well. The King they sent out to us is no King."

She looked at him, and shrugged her shoulders.

"Is Guy never thirsty?"

"No fencing. Speak out. Was it Fulk Ferrers you saw on the white horse?"

He went near, stooping, and staring her in the face.

"Fulk Ferrers?"

"Yes—Fulk Ferrers."

She spread her hands.

"Are my eyes quicker than yours? You should know."

"A woman's eyes look deep."

"Mine saw a King."

He snarled impatiently.

"That will not serve. Answer me. Was it Fulk Ferrers?"

She answered him calmly.

"No."

Merlin flung out his arms, and his mouth worked.

"A lie—by the Book, a lie!"

"The father knoweth his children. I have answered you."

Jack Straw sidled up, drawing a knife from its sheath.

"Persuasion—a touch of persuasion! Hold her."

Guy caught her arms from behind. She stood rigid, staring at the fire.

"The blade of a knife under a thumb nail, hey?"

Isoult did not resist, did not move, but set her teeth and kept her lips shut.

Wat the Tiler sprang up, knocking his stool over.

"Let be. This is a coward's game. Answer me, Isoult. Was it Richard the King on the white horse?"

"It was the King—as I know him."

Merlin clutched at her, but Wat thrust him aside.

"Out! You have an answer. Isoult, I am a friend."

She met his sinister eyes.

"Yes and no. I have spoken."

Merlin flung back towards the fire in a rage.

"Go, and get you above. Close the trap on her, Guy. This bird may serve as a lure."

Blood was dripping from Isoult's hand; she did not heed it, but turned and walked towards the stairs. Guy tried to whisper to her, but she would not listen.

They gathered about the fire, hunching themselves on their stools and putting their heads together. John Ball had been in a stupor of prayer, and he was still kneeling with his face in the shadow. Merlin and Wat were the two who talked. Their voices rose and fell like a wind blowing fitfully through a hole in the wall.

As for Isoult, she found some straw and a horse-cloth in the attic, and spreading them over the trap-door, made her bed there, so that no one could steal in on her in the night.

CHAPTER XXIII

In the Princess's chamber at the Wardrobe the real King sat on an oak hutch, kicking his heels against a panel upon which some craftsman had carved the Pelican in her Piety. The lad looked sulky and silent, or as though some inward pain were gnawing in him, the ache of his own shame.

Suddenly he started up, and went towards the door; but his mother, who had been kneeling at her *prie-dieu*, rose and put herself in his way.

"What would you, sweet son?"

There was less petulance and more manhood in his frown.

"Let me pass. I am the King. I'll not suffer this upstart."

"Son, he has done nobly."

A furtive malice came into his eyes.

"I shall remember it—and him. Let me pass, mother. I go out to claim my own."

This new spirit in him filled her with a secret exultation, but she kept her place by the door and would not let him come to it.

"No, sweet son, no. It cannot be, this day—or even to-morrow. This Fulk Ferrers has kept faith with us. Were we to break troth with him it would be giving him death."

Richard's eyes glittered as though a new thought had come to him. He pulled at his lower lip with finger and thumb.

"Two Kings cannot live in one kingdom."

He gave a queer, sinister laugh.

"Yes, I will remember Master Fulk Ferrers. I shall be in his debt, mother. I will find my way of paying that debt."

He returned to the hutch, perched himself and sat thinking, his eyes staring at the opposite wall. His mother drew a stool near to the door, and taking up a "Book of the Hours," watched him, while pretending to read.

She saw a secret, gloating smile steal over his face. He still pulled at his lower lip with his thumb and forefinger, and the smile on his face was not pleasant to behold.

"What is in thy heart, Richard?"

"Honours, madam, for my brother King. He shall not complain of me, neither shall his tongue be in danger of telling the truth. I shall so work with him that his lips shall be sealed."

"Gratitude, even secret gratitude, becomes a King, Richard."

"Mother, I am grateful; I shall not forget."

Such were the words spoken in the chamber of the Princess, but in the King's chamber stranger words were passing between strong men.

"I have done your work, sirs; now leave me to mine."

Fulk was walking to and fro, driven by his own desires. Yet three men baulked him—Salisbury, Knollys, and Cavendish the squire, standing with their backs to the door while he paced up and down.

"We have not uncrowned you yet, Fulk Ferrers."

"What if I uncrown myself?"

Salisbury's eyes were grim.

"By my faith, we will call it treason. Listen to me, my master; the danger is with us still—aye, greater danger, because some men are desperate. You are ours till it is past."

Fulk faced him, head in air.

"Treason, my lord! Speak not big words to me. What I choose I choose."

"Big words are in other mouths. Cavendish—here, speak up, good Cavendish."

"I keep a dagger, sir, not a tongue."

Fulk flashed round on him.

"Ha, cut-throat—Master Knife-in-the-back!"

"True for you, Fulk Ferrers. I serve. I keep mum. But I am your comrade to the death if you keep troth."

"Play fair, lad, play fair."

"Fair! Am I to be fair to you all and false to my own self?"

He turned, and, walking to the window, drummed with his fingers on the sill. Knollys had not spoken, but had watched and listened. He came forward now, and spoke in Salisbury's ear.

"Love fires the blood, sir. There is a man's heart in his words. Leave me alone with him."

They went out, Cavendish remaining on guard outside the door.

Knollys walked to the window and laid a hand on Fulk's shoulder.

"Lad, speak out; it is a woman."

Fulk did not stir.

"True, a woman. I thought her dead. I saw her—living—to-day."

"Isoult—Isoult of the Rose? She who——?"

"Isoult—aye, Isoult. In the hands of these scullions! God—I'll not suffer it! She could have betrayed me to-day—you, all of us—but her heart kept troth. Knollys, I must out, beat the city——"

Knollys' hand gripped his shoulder.

"Fulk, son Fulk, patience. What could you do, alone, lost in the first alley? Leave it to me. I have spies. They shall go and search."

"But to stand here kicking my toes against the wall!"

"Swear troth to us for one more day. By God, lad, I love the fettle in you. You are my hawk. I flew you. Never a royal bird flew better. Comrade in arms——!"

They gripped hands of a sudden.

"Knollys, I'll do it. Troth—for another day, though my heart is out yonder."

"Trust me, lad. I'll send out beaters and prickers. The rose shall not be worn on a churl's coat."

Yet Fulk slept but little that night, for the thought of Isoult was like fire in him—Isoult, who had come from death to life, with her red lips and her coal-black hair. He thought of Merlin and the Stallion and those beasts of the field, and the hot youth in him grew mad and furious. Was this rich rose to be torn and crushed by such hands?

Dawn came, and Fulk, restless, hot-eyed, and impatient, stood at the window and looked out towards the sunrise. Roofs, towers, and pinnacles were black against the yellow east, and although it was but daybreak the dark web of the city seemed to tremble with hidden life. From somewhere came a murmur of voices. In more than one black tower bells were ringing.

The door of the King's chamber opened, and Cavendish stood there with the look of a man out to meet foul weather.

"What news, Cavendish?"

"Sleet and wind, sir. The day may be rougher than yesterday. My Lords Salisbury and Warwick, and Walworth the Mayor have never seen their beds."

"And our good friends—the Commons?"

"There is the peril, sir. Those screech owls, John Ball and Jack Straw, have been flying through the city. Many of those who marched off yesterday have marched back again. Our spies have been out since sunset. Wat spoke at Paul's Cross at midnight—bloody words, I promise you. They say the King's charters are not to be trusted."

He laughed grimly, ironically.

"If the fools knew! We have been gathering what power we can. Knollys has several hundred men hidden round about his quarters. Perducas d'Albreth has his free companions. Walworth promises to do what he can with the city bands."

"And the day's business? By my sword, Cavendish, I am ready to stretch my wings."

"We play the game boldly, sir. Clerks have been scribbling charters all night, and it is our wisdom to put a bold face on it. We ride to Westminster to hear Mass."

Fulk's eyes shone.

"What of Knollys? Is he here?"

"Knollys bides with his men, ready to make a sally, should it come to blows."

"He sent me no message?"

"Not a word."

That Saturday morning Fulk rode to Westminster at the head of no more than sixty souls. No one came out to see them; no one shouted "God save the King!" The highway was empty, the houses shuttered and dumb; but within the walls the city hummed like a hive, for Wat and Merlin had heard that the King had ridden out.

Fulk heard Mass, but his thoughts were all of Isoult. The candles on the high altar were a yellow blur; the sacring bell made a mere tinkling sound a long way off. He knelt, but the sacred bread found no prayer between his lips; the "Deo gratias" was all he listened for, because of the restless love in him, and the lust for action.

On the homeward ride a white-faced messenger met them, a man with fear in his eyes.

"Sir, sir, turn back. The mob is at Smithfield, and mad as a mad dog."

Fulk reined in.

"Say you so, my friend? Let us see whether the King's touch cannot cure this madness."

Walworth and Cavendish drew close to him, after questioning the messenger.

"It is playing with fire! And yet— —"

"If we fly the fire the wind will blow it after us. And fire can be quenched."

They looked in his eyes, and saw the indomitable spirit of the sire in the eyes of the son.

"Nothing venture, nothing have."

"Lead on, sirs. Now, for the great hazard!"

Before they had ridden another furlong, outlying scuds of the thundercloud came drifting towards them. Ragged knots of men streamed up with bows and bills in their hand, gathering before and behind the King's company. Some walked close to his horse, and shouted at him insolently.

"Sir King, Wat our captain would speak with you."

"What of the charters?"

"The charters—the charters!"

"Down with all lords and gentlemen."

Then Smithfield opened before them, and those who rode in the King's company saw the space black with a waiting multitude. It was a mute, formidable crowd; but when the white horse came into view, a slow, swelling roar went up, a sound like the rush of a flood-wake when a dam has broken.

Fulk's lips grew thin, his nostrils dilated.

A knot of figures stood out some twenty paces in front of the main mass grouped behind Wat the Tiler, who was mounted on a black horse, and carried a naked sword over his shoulder. Behind him were John Ball, Jack Straw, and the rebel leaders, and with them Merlin, the grey friar, in a brown smock and a green hood and leggings of leather.

Fulk's eyes were on Wat the Tiler, measuring the man with his bull's throat and insolent eyes. Of a sudden there was a movement among the figures behind the man on the black horse. Someone was being pushed forward into the open.

It was Isoult, dressed in a russet cloak and a red hood. Fulk saw her, and for the moment his heart seemed to stand still within him. A man held her by the wrist and was pointing towards the King on the white horse, and the man was Father Merlin.

CHAPTER XXIV

Fulk's eyes were two blue stones set in a face of granite. He sat his horse, alert yet motionless, watching Isoult and the man behind her. It was Merlin. Fulk knew him in spite of his peasant's clothes. Merlin, with his chin thrust forward and his yellow teeth gleaming.

He was speaking to Isoult.

"The truth—out with it! That is no King, but a bastard called Fulk Ferrers."

He drove his nails into her wrist, but her lips remained closed.

Fulk saw and understood.

There was the secret glitter of a knife in Merlin's fist. He held it behind Isoult's left shoulder, and spoke in her ear.

"Speak, jade, speak."

"It is the King."

"You lie!"

She closed her eyes, and stood rigid.

"Strike and have done. I'll utter no word."

"You jade!"

"Strike, and have done."

Wat's eyes were on them. He turned his horse and cursed Merlin.

"Hold, fool!"

"The jade will not speak."

"By God's eyes, I like her for it. Put up that knife, curse you, and leave the bastard to me. I have a voice that will scare the kingliness out of him."

He shouted to the mob behind him.

"Brothers, I go to win our kingdom. Stand fast till I brandish my sword. Then rush on them and slay all—all save the lad on the white horse."

He rode out towards Fulk, who was waiting at the head of his knights and gentlemen. Wat made his black horse prance and cut capers, to show these lords that he was something of a horseman. His eyes were fixed insolently on Fulk, as though to cow his courage.

"King, seest thou all these men? They have sworn to do whatsoever I shall tell them."

Fulk kept his eyes on Wat's.

"My friend, do not boast of it—too soon."

"What of the charters, King?"

"They will be ready by noon."

Wat stared at him meaningly.

"All clerks and lawyers are liars, and they serve the King."

Cavendish and Walworth had ridden up close to Fulk, and Wat saw in Cavendish an old enemy who had once given him a thrashing.

"God's eyes, here is the cur Cavendish! Give me thy dagger, Cavendish; I shall have need of it."

Cavendish's grim face darkened.

"Not I. To the bottomless pit with you, son of a whelp."

"To the point of a pike with your head, bully Cavendish. I'll see to it. What have you there—the King's sword?"

"The King's sword."

The Tiler leant forward in the saddle, and his eyes were dangerous.

"By Jesus! the King's sword! This fellow here on the white horse has no right to it. Give me the King's sword."

"I'll see thee in hell first."

Wat clapped his hand on his own sword.

"Am I a fool, ye noble knaves? What, this is no King, but a Prince's bastard. I know thee, Fulk Ferrers."

He glared in Fulk's eyes, not noticing Walworth, who was spurring his horse forward.

Fulk spoke but two words.

"Kill, kill!"

The chest of Walworth's horse struck Wat's on the flank. A sword flashed, and smote the Tiler across the face. He reeled, toppled out of the saddle, and lay sprawling before the hoofs of Fulk's white horse.

"Kill!"

Cavendish was out of the saddle and on him like a hound on a fox. Wat tried to rise, but Cavendish's dagger went home, once in the throat and twice in the chest. Wat's body twisted, relaxed, lay still.

A great silence held, like the hush in a forest between two gusts of a gathering storm. The mob was mute, staring at the dead body and the King on the white horse.

Then a great bellow of rage went up.

"They have slain our captain! Kill—kill!"

CHAPTER XXV

A flare of light leapt into Fulk's eyes. His figure seemed to dilate, to tower higher on his white horse. He was lifted up, the god of a great moment.

The peasants were bending their bows. Bills, pikes, scythes, and clubs waved in the air. Their shouts were like the cries of wild beasts.

Fulk drove the spurs into his horse and rode forward.

"Sirs, what would you? Listen to me—your King."

They faltered and stood still, staring upon him, their bows half bent, their weapons wavering.

Out before them all leapt a fanatic figure, a figure in a brown smock and green hood, a figure that tossed its arms and foamed at the mouth. It was Merlin, inarticulate for the moment, smothered by his own frenzy.

"A lie, a lie! Hear, men of the fields!"

A second figure sprang forward, waving a red kerchief. It was Isoult.

Fulk saw the crest of the wave about to break on him and his company. Merlin's mouth was a red circle, open to shout the truth. Then a closed hand swept up and round, and opened its fingers within a foot of its face. Never had simpler stuff served more nobly. Merlin's mouth and eyes were full of red pepper.

He choked, ground his knuckles into his eyes, tried to speak, but was bent double with anguish.

Isoult stood forward, laughing, and waving her kerchief.

"A jest, a noble jest! The King, the King!"

His voice carried.

"Sirs, the King—our King! Hear him!"

Fulk turned in the saddle, and spoke to Cavendish, who had followed him.

"Cavendish, as you love honour, look to that woman yonder. Guard her for me with your life. Bring Wat's horse to me. Speed!"

He spurred his horse, and rode forward to the very edge of the crowd, looking on these men of the fields with masterful eyes and holding up a hand for silence.

"Sirs, sirs, I am your King. We have slain a traitor—a traitor who dared to lay a hand upon his sword. Follow me. I—King Richard—will be your captain."

Some cheered, others looked at him sullenly. He rode his white horse to and fro in front of them, and then drew rein beside Isoult.

"A horse—a horse!"

Cavendish came leading dead Wat's black horse. Fulk looked at Isoult, and she at him, and in that glance all their valour and passion met and mingled.

"Sirs, I am King Richard. Behold the Queen of the Commons. Behold your Queen!"

Isoult understood. Cavendish gave her his hand and knee, and she was on the black horse's back, facing the crowd and smiling.

Fulk saluted her; eyes and heart were in that homage.

"Men of England, behold the Queen of the Commons. I am Richard, your captain. Now, by the splendour of God, I charge you follow me."

He had won them. They cheered, surged round him, waving their caps and hoods on the points of their bows and bills. Merlin, a coughing, sneezing, impotently raging thing, was smothered in the eddies of the crowd. Fulk stretched out a hand for Isoult's. He spoke to her, looking in her eyes.

"My desire, I had thought you dead."

"I am alive, to soar with you, brave falcon."

She gazed at him with strange, passionate pride.

"Ah, King of the Burning Heart!"

"I am the green leaf of the rose. By my soul, I know that you dared death."

He kissed her hand before them all, and the mob shouted.

"Long live King Richard and the Queen of the Commons."

When they would give him silence he shouted, "Sirs, follow me."

And they followed him like sheep into the open fields about Islington.

Isoult's eyes were on Fulk as they rode, but now and again she glanced back at the crowding faces of the mob.

"What will you do with them?"

"Bide my time. Men are coming who will not fail us."

He did not trust in vain. Fulk had drawn rein, and the mob had spread out over a stretch of grass land, trampling the uncut hay under their feet when a cloud of dust arose between them and the city. Spear points and pennons caught the sunlight, and across the fields Robert Knollys came riding at the head of a thousand men. They bulked bigger than their number, thundering in close order, trumpets screaming, spears bristling, with a clash and jingle of steel. Behind them came Walworth the Mayor, at the head of certain city bands, bows strung, and brown bills flashing.

"Come."

Fulk seized the bridle of Isoult's horse, clapped in the spurs, and rode to meet Knollys' great company. They opened and let him through. He drew rein before the forest of spears, and halted them with upraised arm.

Knollys rode forward.

"Sir, by the splendour of God, let our trumpets sound, and let us trample these wretches into the grass."

"No, by God; for they have trusted me. They shall go unharmed. Send Walworth to me. He shall speak to them."

The mob hung there, wavering, and making a discordant and querulous clamour. They were without leaders, and cowed and dumbfounded by Knollys' spears.

Walworth came riding up, and Fulk spoke with him.

"Walworth, good friend, down on your knees. This shall be remembered."

He knighted him, smiling as he bent to touch him with his sword.

"My hand is as good as another's. Now, Sir Mayor, ride to those men yonder, demand my banners, say that I am merciful, that I have held back those who would have slaughtered them. Bid them depart—each man to his own home."

Walworth rode forward and spoke to them, and then Fulk and his fellows beheld a wonderful, strange sight. It was as though the bank of a pool had given way, and the brown wash of that multitude of heads and faces broke and flowed away on every side. They surrendered the banners and fled, swarming over the fields in ragged masses, some flying towards the city, others into the open country. This revolt was repulsed, broken, scattered.

Fulk sat on his horse and watched them, and a strange light came into his eyes. He heard Knollys speaking.

"Now are they like sheep that but an hour ago were very wolves. And one man has conquered them."

Fulk turned to him.

"No, by God; but for a woman's wit we should have been beaten into the dust."

His eyes sought Isoult.

"Now have we soared together, you and I, into the blue."

CHAPTER XXVI

It was night, and the Princess knelt at her *prie-dieu* in her chamber at the Wardrobe, and offered up thanks for the passing of this great peril. And being a noble lady, and a woman of heart, she prayed for Fulk Ferrers as well as for her son.

Fulk had been brought to her, and she had looked him in the eyes, marvelling, and trying to put the bitterness out of her heart.

"Sir, we are your very great debtors."

Fulk, though a young man, had felt her pride, her beauty, and her shame, and had kissed her hands.

"Madame, if I have served, I have served. Let no man speak of it hereafter, for I shall not."

She had gazed at him questioningly.

"Can a man, and a young man, step down and forget so generously?"

"I shall keep faith," and he had smiled; "but I may crave to rule a company of 'spears' instead of a herd of deer."

The Princess had given him the words of a great lady; but in the King's chamber the real King sat sullenly in his chair, frowning and biting his thumbnail. With him were my Lords Salisbury and Warwick, and Sir Robert Knollys—men who looked at the lad with stark scorn, because of the paltry temper he was showing now that the peril was past. Shame had bitten deep into him and left a poison in the wound. His heart was too meagre to be magnanimous—a little, peevish, cunning heart that could not humble itself and so be healed.

He started up suddenly, petulant, and full of spite.

"I'll not see this fellow, this bastard. Let him keep out of my sight."

Salisbury towered near him like an oak.

"Sir, this bastard, as you call him, has your sire's blood in him. And he has saved your kingdom."

The lad was in a wild-cat mood, which served him for a sort of mannerless courage.

"Old fool, am I to have this ruffler held up before me like the image of a saint? Silence, I say I am King. I will play the King—aye, and better than he has played it."

They eyed him with disrelish.

"Let no man dare to speak his name to me or I will dub him traitor."

"Never was there a more honourable traitor, sir, than this."

"Am I the King? Am I to be obeyed? I will deal with this swashbuckler."

Knollys' heel was beating the ground.

"Sir King, have a care."

"Sir, do you threaten?"

Knollys' wrath and scorn burst like a thundercloud.

"Boy, I served your sire, who was a noble prince and a great captain. Threaten! Let the truth threaten. This young man is your half-brother, and, by my soul, he is ten times more the prince than you are!"

Richard's rage was the rage of an ape.

"Treason, sir, you speak treason!"

"Treason! Who shall charge Knollys with treason? You—a thing that cowered under its mother's bed-quilt? By the splendour of God, all Christendom shall know the truth if you seek to deal treacherously with the man who has served you."

Richard glanced at the faces of the two lords, but in their eyes he saw the same words shining unspoken. Their eyes cowed him, and he began to whimper.

"Sirs, will you drive me witless with shame?"

Knollys softened.

"Son of a great prince, follow your sire and all this shall be buried. Let this shame be trodden under your feet. Play the King, and all men shall hail you King and son of your father."

Richard was cunning behind his cowering.

"But this Fulk Ferrers, what shall be done with him?"

Knollys' wrath revived.

"Done with him? If there is a heart in you, sir, you will do deeds that are noble. Fulk Ferrers can keep faith. Let him be honoured—in good season. Let him have a coffer full of gold, knighthood, a company of spears at his back, a pennon to carry. He will not cumber this kingship of yours. The falcon flies where the quarry is to be stooped at."

"What mean you, sir?"

"Are there not wars and great adventures in France and Spain? Are not great knights and captains welcomed? This son of a prince will not wilt on a doorstep."

They left him alone in his chamber to think over their words, and went below to a room that was used as a council chamber, and gathered the King's Council about the board. Other lords and knights, good men and honourable, had been told the truth, swearing on the Cross to keep it hidden. It was midnight, and they debated together, while Cavendish slept across the door.

"What is to be done, sirs? This hawk cannot fly as he pleases."

Walworth had a plan to offer, and he was as shrewd as any man in London.

"Gentlemen, suffer me. This young man has dealt valiantly with us; let us deal valiantly with him. By the Lord Christ, I, for one, am ready to dip into my coffers. Let him have arms and horses, and treasure—good men, and a good ship. Let him sail into Spain or Portugal. Let us make him a King of Adventure."

The rest applauded. Salisbury took up the talking.

"You are a wise man, Walworth, and a generous, but the moment is urgent. Two Kings in one house—tsst, it is too perilous! We must hide him somewhere till the wind has fallen—he and this love of his, Isoult of the Rose."

"Whence comes she?"

"God knows. Half Breton, half English, I have heard it whispered."

Knollys caught Walworth's eyes.

"Walworth has a plan. Let him speak."

"Sirs, in Surrey, there is the King's Manor of the Black Mere—the house set on an island in the midst of a goodly sheet of water, very solitary and very safe. Let him go thither, riding by night, and lie hidden there with a few men who can be trusted."

"Aye, and let him grow a beard. It will cover up the kingliness."

"There is much in a beard—a good lusty beard!"

"Then, when 'tis safe, we will launch this good falcon and his mate into the Spanish skies."

Knollys put in a last word.

"I and ten of my men will ride with them to the Black Mere. Can you give us a guide, Sir Mayor?"

"Aye, one to be trusted."

Knollys took a light and went above to a little room under the tiles, where Fulk was lodged now that Richard the King was King again. Isoult slept with the Princess's women.

Knollys had to hammer lustily on the door, before Fulk, wrapped in his surcoat, let him in.

"You sleep as well as you face a mob, my son. Shut the door. I have much to say."

"More rebels to fool?"

"No, a much grimmer business. The King's Council has most solemnly decreed that you shall grow a beard."

CHAPTER XXVII

It was a grey dawn, because of the mist on the river, with a promise of heat and of a cloudless sky. On London Bridge the houses looked as though they were smothered in white smoke, and the river went gliding stealthily with hardly a ripple against the piers. A great, straw-coloured sun hung blurred in the east, and when some bell tolled the sound was heavy and distant.

Grey, too, was the friar who sat on a wooden bench against the wall of a house and waited for the gate of the bridge to open. The friar's cowl was drawn down over his face; his beads hung in a brown loop, and his hands played with them restlessly—hands with big knuckles, and black hair spreading from the wrists.

Sometimes he threw his head back and looked at the battlements of the Bridge Gate. There were two heads up yonder, stuck upon spikes, and Merlin had seen them outlined against the sky when the dawn was breaking—two round, black shapes, sinister and stiff. And now that the day had dawned, he looked up at the two heads, with their ragged necks, the heads of John Ball and of Jack Straw.

Merlin's eyes were red, but not with weeping. A ferocious, grinning scorn betrayed itself as he stared at the head of the Priest of Kent. He had not loved John Ball, because John Ball had been too much loved by the people.

He began to talk to the head ironically, yet with arrogance.

"Come, good Jack, what dreams dreamest thou up yonder? That tongue of thine will turn to leather, and thy head grow brown like a rotten apple. And thou hast never loved a woman! What hast thou to boast of? What hast thou enjoyed? They deserted thee and ran—thy brave children, thou friend of the poor, thou father of rats! The poor!"

He struck his chest with his fist.

"We have been fooled, but Merlin's head is on his shoulders. I have a game to play. They would have stuck my head up yonder had I not gone about boldly and not slunk in a cellar. The grey frock serves."

He stared at Jack Straw.

"Prithee, Jack, didst thou not desire Isoult? Fool, where is thy body now? But Merlin lives; he will strike and he will love. Courage! It is good to lie in a great lord's pocket. Put no faith in the poor."

The city began to stir itself. A lad driving an ass with panniers piled with vegetables came up the street to the gate. A cart laden with charcoal lumbered up, followed by more carts full of sacks and hay. Heads poked out of windows; a child squalled; doors opened. An old woman who sold hot pies came and set up a board close to Father Merlin, and asked him for a blessing.

He blessed her and her pies, and his long jowl looked hungry.

"Good father, is it a fast day?"

"No, goodwife; I will eat—and thou shalt be paid in heaven."

She gave him half a pie on a dock leaf, and Merlin made a meal.

The gate had opened, and the carts rolled over London Bridge. Merlin followed them, drawing his cowl down and walking like one deep in holy meditation, his hands muffled in his sleeves. Merlin passed little companies of men pushing over the bridge—men with cowed and sullen faces, who were slinking back to the villages whence they had marched with such noise and tumult. The city itself still owned an air of emptiness and of fear. Companies of men-at-arms were riding through the streets, seeing that no crowd rallied, and whenever he heard the clatter of hoofs Merlin drew aside into a passage or doorway.

It was still very early when he came to Carter Street and sat down on the horse-block outside the gate of the Wardrobe. The gate had not opened yet; the street was empty.

Merlin told his beads. He was in a white sweat of fear, for this audacity of his meant that his neck was stretched out under the edge of an axe. His eyes were red and restless under his grey cowl. So much hung on the temper of a groom or a servant.

He heard chains fall and bars withdrawn. The gate opened. A fat, red-headed porter came and stood in the entry, straddling wide with his feet, his thumbs tucked into his belt. He sighted the grey friar and stared.

Merlin rose and went to the gate.

"My son, I have watched all the night, for my need is urgent. Life and death hang on it. I must see the King."

The porter eyed him apprisingly.

"The King is abed, Master Friar."

Merlin pulled out his crucifix and held it towards the man.

"My friend, would you win the King's thanks? I have words that are for the King's ear, and for his alone. I know what I know. See—I kiss the Cross; now let your lips touch it."

The porter obeyed him.

"My son, I will make thee serve God, St. Francis, and the King. I will put fifty gold pieces into thy pocket, for the King will give thee whatsoever I shall ask. Take me to the King's chamber. Let no one meddle. Thou canst search me if thou thinkest me a fool with a knife."

The porter led him into his lodge, and searched him from top to toe.

"Now, speed thee; let no lords and busybodies meddle; my words are for the King alone."

This fat fellow did not guess that Merlin's skin was like the skin of a goose, all cold prickles, and yet ready to sweat. So much hung on the chances of the moment. The King's chamber was Heaven, the courtyard and passages and stairs that led to it part of a hazardous Valley of Death. One shrewd glance from some loitering gentleman, and Merlin's head might join the heads of John Ball and Jack Straw.

Luck was with him. A sleepy squire, not the grim Cavendish, was yawning on a bench outside the door of the King's chamber. Words passed between the porter and the squire, and the porter was thinking of possible favours, for what harm could there be in chancing that this friar would do what he said?

The squire consented to waken the King. Merlin won through. The squire returned, yawning behind his hand.

"Come, Grey Brother, the King will speak with you."

The shutters had been thrown open, and through the traceried windows a patterning of sunlight poured down upon the oak floor. Richard was abed, blinking and stretching his arms. He rolled over and looked at Merlin with sleepy eyes.

Merlin made the sign of the cross.

"*Pax Dei*, O King!"

"What would you, good father?"

"Sir, I am a humble friar, but one who wishes the King well. In these troublous times all men do not speak the truth."

His eyes had scanned the lad's face with a veiled but fierce eagerness, and a sudden exultation leapt in him. He had tempted Death, but Death and Fulk Ferrers were not in the bed—nothing but the real King, a King who had lain hidden through the roughest hours of the storm. For two days Merlin had been asking himself questions, and his subtlety had unravelled the riddle.

He approached the bed.

"Sir, I would speak with you alone."

Richard looked at him suspiciously.

"Why should I listen to you, friar?"

"Because, sir, I shall speak of a traitor and of a bastard thing that is dangerous to you."

Richard rose on one elbow, his face sharpening.

"Ah! I will hear you. Miles, out of the room; but guard the door. Let no one enter unless I call."

The squire left Merlin standing there with folded hands, hiding exultation with humility.

"Now, Master Friar."

"Sir, I, a son of St. Francis, walking the ways of this wicked world, have heard many strange things, learnt many strange secrets. I came to London with the rebels."

Richard sat up in bed, and his eyes were mistrustful.

"The rebels, say you?"

Merlin held up his crucifix.

"My son, have no fear. I was with them, to serve at a crisis. I spoke to them of peace and goodwill, but sometimes God bids us hate when hatred is just and good. Hear me."

He leant forward and began to speak in whispers, his libidinous lips moving quickly under the shadow of his cowl. The lad in bed seemed bewitched; he did not move or utter a word, but his eyes were full of sinister lights. Merlin watched him. Hate was beckoning to an unconfessed hate, bidding it show itself and come out into the open. He had guessed cunningly, and he had guessed well.

Merlin saw a curious tremor pass through the King's body. One hand crumpled up the quilt.

"Good father, my heart burns in me. Have they not caused me to hate and to distrust?"

It was he who spoke now—Merlin who listened.

"I was sick in soul, and these lords stormed at me. It was a cunning plot. I see it now. And you—you charge these noble uncles of mine with treason?"

Merlin spread his hands.

"Whom does Fulk Ferrers serve? In whose forest has he been hidden all these years? The Duke of Lancaster should know the why and the wherefore."

"Traitor that he is! And Thomas of Woodstock—what of Thomas of Woodstock?"

"Why has he hidden himself in Wales? To wait—and to watch. This woman, Isoult of the Rose, is his spy."

Richard sat rigid, white to the lips.

"Good father, whom can a King trust?"

"My hate, sir, is your hatred."

"This Fulk Ferrers?"

"Can two Kings live? No peace will be yours while schemers have this puppet to play with."

Their eyes met, and a kind of leering hatred showed in them. Merlin drew his stool closer to the bed. He began to speak in eager whispers, and Richard listened and smiled.

"Enough! You shall serve."

He began to whisper in turn.

"These Lords of the Council have told me their plan. This Fulk Ferrers and the woman are to be hidden. Now I may guess the why and the wherefore."

"Speak, sir."

"They ride to-night."

"Whither?"

"In Surrey I have a manor called the Manor of the Black Mere, a very secret place. The fellow is to grow a beard, and therefore he takes the woman with him that she may watch it grow."

He laughed, but Merlin's eyes blazed.

"Sir, God shall deal out justice."

"And I will deal out favour. Take this ring."

He slipped a ring off his finger, a gold circle set with diamonds and rubies, and with a signet attached—two "R's" intertwined.

"The white and red. This shall be your pledge and proof. I am the King. I will deal with traitors as I please."

Merlin rose up and crossed himself.

"Sir, there shall be silence. All lips shall be sealed."

CHAPTER XXVIII

London was asleep, a mere confusion of black roofs and spires without a lantern or a rushlight shining to mimic the stars; but at the Wardrobe torches were burning in the narrow courtyard within the gate. Five horses and a pad were waiting, and four archers stood in the shadow of the wall, leaning on their bows. Cavendish had mounted one of the horses. The porter was ready to unbar the gate.

Then Knollys, in light harness, came down into the courtyard, and with him a tall man in black armour, the vizor of whose basinet was closed. Three men-at-arms followed them. No one spoke. They mounted their horses. The porter was unbarring the gate.

The horse of the man in black armour grew restless, striking the stones with one fore-hoof.

Knollys laughed.

"Like master, like horse! Where is that page of yours, friend Godamar?"

The voice that answered was muffled by the helmet.

"I wait, sir, I wait."

A door opened somewhere, and a figure came out into the torchlight—the figure of a slim lad wrapped in a green cloak. He wore a steel cap, with a hood of chain mail, and the scabbard of a sword knocked against his neat legs.

"Late, ever late, Master Bertrand!"

The page ran to the pad, mounted lightly, and put himself beside the man in the black armour.

"Pardon, lording, pardon."

"Boy, did I not chasten you the very first day we met!"

They rode out through the gate and were met at the barrier by a man wrapped up in a black cloak and hood. A second figure stood at a little distance, a figure that leant upon a quarter-staff.

Knollys bent low in the saddle.

"Walworth?"

"Walworth it is."

"Good."

"I come with you to Ludgate, and yonder is your guide."

They filed along the silent streets, Walworth walking beside Knollys' horse, the black knight and his page riding together, Cavendish, the men-at-arms, and the archers following. The guide, a bearded fellow in a brown smock and rough woollen stockings and cow-hide shoes, tramped along with his staff over his shoulder.

There was no parleying at Ludgate. Walworth went forward, and the gate opened instantly to let them through. As they passed under the arch they saw Walworth standing in the doorway of the guardroom, but he did not speak or move.

Some fifty yards beyond the gate Knollys called the guide and an archer to him.

"Lead the way, Jack. We follow."

The archer had had his order, and walked with his bow strung and an arrow ready.

Knollys held back, letting the black knight and the page go forward. He waited for Cavendish, and spoke to him behind his hand.

"Friend, we shall be thanked for knowing that we are not wanted. Let them talk—let them talk."

It was a still night, with hundreds of stars shining, silver points in sable velvet. The man in black and the page rode side by side, the archer and the guide some twenty paces ahead of them, Knollys and Cavendish the same distance behind.

The man in black was the first to speak.

"Isoult, it was not I who planned this mummery."

She held up a warning hand.

"Ssst, lording, am I not Bertrand, your page, and we ride to take ship for France?"

"No, by God, you are she who——"

"Be careful, be careful!"

He brought his horse close to hers, so that they rode knee to knee.

"I'll put my visor up. There's no danger for the moment."

"Speak low, Fulk."

"The horse's hoofs will smother it. Isoult, did they threaten you?"

"Threaten?"

"These lords, the King's Councillors."

"No, by my heart, they were very courteous. I came by my own will."

She could see his eyes shining. A hand came out and gripped her wrist.

"Isoult—heart of my desire!"

She did not look at him, but spoke very softly.

"Wait! you do not know who—or where—or whence."

His grip tightened.

"Who am I that I should ask? Whence came I, who am I, whither do I go? A captain of free-lances, a man of adventure, a sworder in foreign lands—that shall I be."

"Does your pride quarrel with such a lot?"

"Perhaps—no."

"Neither does mine, for you will be a great captain, a king of many adventures."

He was silent awhile.

"Isoult, I'll not go alone. By all the blood in my body——!"

She turned to him sharply, and he saw her face white, and passionate, and earnest.

"Listen. Who am I? The child of a Breton gentleman, of a good man who fell into the Devil's lap. I was desired, and I fled; but he who desired me was strong and cunning. Yet he did not prevail. I—a knight's daughter, fled, dressed as a common singing-girl, to the English, and Thomas of Woodstock, the King's uncle, looked on me with the eyes of a calf. He spoke fair words, swore I should be his lady, and, since I feared that other lover, I sailed with Thomas of Woodstock into England. He gave me a fair manor house in the west to live in, still spoke fair words, and hid what was in his heart. It was Merlin who betrayed Thomas of Woodstock to me, and in those days I did not know the colour of Father Merlin's soul. I swore a feud against all lords and nobles, went wandering, and pitied the poor. My bitterness made a fool of me, for I joined myself to John Ball and his dreams, called myself 'Queen of the Outlaws,' and sang wild songs to all who were discontented. That is my tale, Friend Fulk. I have told it you. But never has any man called me his."

His grip on her wrist did not relax.

"Brave heart, well flown."

She turned her face, and he caught the shine of her eyes.

"Ah, but am I tamed—I, the Breton falcon?"

"Who would see you tamed? Not I, by my sword! Who would mate with a white pigeon?"

She laughed softly.

"Enough, hot-headed one. Those men are listening."

He would not let her hand go for the moment.

"Isoult, by the shine in your eyes I will have none but you."

"So many men have said; but—I—I will think on it."

So they rode on into the night; while Father Merlin sat before the fire at "The Painted Lady," and the men who were his creatures stood in a half-circle watching him like dogs. Here were Guy the Stallion and the Polecat, Jack o' the Knife, Peter of Alton, Will Sunburst, and several more, all rank rogues and thieves. And they stood and grumbled together, and watched the grey friar.

Then Guy had a fit of courage.

"Master Merlin, no man quarrels with cutting throats for a good purse; but, by cock, I'll not walk out into the dark with my eyes shut. There's blood!"

The rest applauded him.

"Guy has a tongue."

"Let's see the inside of the gentleman's fist."

Merlin swung round on his stool and faced them, and his face was not pleasant to behold.

"Fools and jays, come, look. Bring a torch."

They gathered round, and he held out his hand with something that glittered on the third finger. Their heads came together over it, the light of the torch flickering on their faces.

Then Guy straightened with a good, wholesome oath.

"Son of Satan, the King's signet!"

Merlin's lips curled.

"Is it a good pledge, sirs?"

"We serve the King!"

"Fetch me a grindstone, neighbours; I will put me a double edge on my knife."

A head came poking in at the door.

"Father Merlin, the boat is at the steps."

"Come, good rogues, come."

They picked up sundry bundles and swarmed after him down the narrow way between the houses to the river. A boat was waiting at the steps, a man squatting in the bow and holding the chain.

Merlin climbed in and the rest followed.

"Up stream, up stream, my brothers. Let London town sing, 'Nunc dimittis.'?"

CHAPTER XXIX

When they had breasted the chalk hills with their beech woods, great yews, and wild junipers, and saw the lush valley country below them, Cavendish rode on ahead to speak with the King's reeve, who kept the Manor of the Black Mere. Cavendish had hunted in these parts, and knew the ways and the lie of the land. They saw him ford a stream that ran at the foot of the hills, splashing through the shallows, the water crackling into white foam under his horse's hoofs.

Knollys and Fulk rode together, the mock page following on her pad. She made a comely youth with her ripe lips, and her dark eyes, and that daring and imperious chin of hers in the air. The hood of chain mail hid her hair, that was fastened up in a silver net. Her long-lipped mouth had an elusive and mischievous look, and sometimes she smiled as she watched Fulk in his black harness masterful even in the saddle.

Knollys was in a playful mood.

"It is not generous of us to set her to watch your beard grow, my son, yet she chose to come in that short cloak and her green hose. I can see petticoats in that big wallet strapped to the pad's saddle. Sir Tristram and his lady! And no loving-cup needed!"

Fulk was a little in the air, and had too much passion in him to be playful.

"We owe her these heads on our shoulders."

"Tsst, lad! The girl is splendid. I would change with you, if I could. To start again on adventures in strange lands with such a mate to keep your blood afire! Ha! the French wars, the Breton moors, the fine, lusty, galloping life! And the black eyes and the wines of Spain! If I were young again—if I were young."

Fulk's thoughts were back in that Sussex forest, turning towards that cold woman, his mother, and the silent man who had reared him as a son. Ever since he had caught Isoult by moonlight, hunting the duke's deer, the world had been turned topsy-turvy, and the old life had vanished. He knew that he could never go back and guard deer in a Sussex forest. Isoult had come sailing like a splendid falcon out of the blue, challenging him to soar with her in quest of great adventures.

"Knollys, the King will keep faith?"

"We shall see to it, my son."

"I must have good men, a good ship, and good money. My pride has had a bold flight. It will not come back to perch so easily."

"Would you change with your half-brother?"

"Yes—and no. But I keep faith, and I shall not let it be forgotten."

Knollys laughed.

"No, in faith, you would be dangerous—to forget. We have pledged our faith to you. No prince of the blood shall set out more royally. Even the good Walworth is ready to pay you for his knighthood! A man may send in a big bill for saving a kingdom. I will ride down hither before many days are passed, and bring you news."

They rode through but one village, and saw nothing but women, old men, and children. Sullen faces looked at them from behind half-closed doors. The men who had slunk home from London did not show themselves, mistrusting anything that rode upon a horse. The fields were still deserted, though here and there they saw a man swinging a scythe. The people were cowed, afraid of their own violence, profoundly discouraged by the deaths of their leaders. The lords and the lawyers would be out for vengeance, and the mob that had threatened a kingdom had scattered in a panic, and was ready to cringe.

The country grew wilder, rolling woods meeting heather-covered hills that were purpling against the blue of the summer sky. It was an empty landscape where deer might range and the hawk hover without sighting such a thing as man.

At Beggars Thorn they reined in, for here Knollys and his men were to turn back.

"There is no more kick in Master Adam. You will not be troubled. Cavendish will see you housed."

He slung Fulk a fat wallet.

"Wine and dainties, my son. God speed you."

He drew close and these two embraced, for comrade's love—man's love—had sprung up between them.

"Grace to you, Master Bertrand."

He looked at Isoult, and smiled.

"The knave of a boy! How could you cock your chin at me. Farewell, farewell!"

He left them the guide and turned back with his men for London town.

It was evening—a still, June evening—when they came towards the Black Mere. Heathlands sloped to a deep valley, where woods of birch and of beech threw light and heavy shadows. The track followed a long, winding strip of grassland knee deep with grass and flowers, and into it opened the woodland ways, tunnels of mystery.

Then the Black Mere lay before them, a great black pool in the hollows of green park-like slopes. Willows grew on the banks, trailing thin, grey foliage in the water among the flags and rushes. Here and there a tongue of woodland came down to the edge of the pool, throwing a long black shadow upon water that already looked black. No wind blew; not a ripple showed. The evening sunlight, streaming through the trees, made circles and bands of polished gold upon the water.

In the centre of the pool lay an island, and on this island stood the manor house of the Black Mere, its black timber and white plaster built into quaint squares and lozenges. Little windows were sunk deep in the thatch—heather thatch, the colour of the water in the pool. The upper storey overhung the lower, carried on great oak posts and brackets. At one end of the island was an orchard shut in by a palisade. Willows grew on the banks, making a grey, misty screen.

The place looked solitary and deserted. No smoke rose from it, and the flat-bottomed boat was lying chained to the island landing stage.

They found Cavendish's horse tethered to a tree, and a pile of clothes on the grass near it.

The guide looked puzzled.

"An empty nest, lording."

Someone hailed them, and a half-naked man with a piece of sacking tied round him came down to the landing-stage. It was Cavendish.

"Coming, coming!"

He climbed into the boat, unmoored it, and taking the pole, brought the boat across the water.

"Reeve Roger has had a fright. Not a soul on the island. The old rogue was afraid of having his throat cut by the rebels; he is safe in Farnham, Guildford, or Windsor."

He threw the chain to the guide, sprang out, and going behind a willow tree, slipped into his clothes, and as he dressed he talked.

"I had to swim over. Not a soul has been there. You will find mead and wine in the buttery, flour and salt meat in the kitchen, herbs and green stuff in the garden, fowls and eggs in the yard and stables. If you must fast you can fish in the pool. How does it please you, Sir Godamar? Can your page cook?"

The page answered for himself.

"I can cook, squire, as well as I can say my prayers."

"Noble child! A merry jest to you. Shall I take Master Numskull back with me?"

Fulk laughed, glancing at Isoult.

"Yes, take him, friend Cavendish."

"If I am brisk I shall make Guildford before it is too dark to see. How many miles, Jock?"

"Nine, lording."

"We shall do it, and have time to help with the horses. Jock is a wonder on his legs."

There were two poles in the boat, and Cavendish and the guide served as ferrymen. Fulk's horse, who behaved like a fine gentleman, was taken across first, and then Isoult and her pad, and the pad pretended to be restive. They stabled the beasts and found them oats, water, and straw.

Fulk went across with them to bring back the boat.

"Good luck to you, Cavendish. Tell Knollys that we are hermits."

"May your beard grow, sir. And have a care how you play with that pole in your harness. Not God Almighty could fish you out of the mud if you tumbled overboard in all that gear!"

Cavendish mounted his horse, and Jock shouldered his quarter-staff, and Fulk watched them disappear up the narrow meadow that lost itself in the gloom of the woods.

Then he picked up the pole to ferry back to Isoult.

CHAPTER XXX

She was not there when Fulk turned the boat; the little landing-stage was deserted. Isoult had gone into the house.

He dropped the pole lazily into the shallows, and heard the water prattling at the prow, and as the boat moved over towards the island a surge of emotion rose in him, a sudden wonder, something akin to awe. The long slants of sunlight made blurs of gold about him on the water. The woods seemed fringed with fire. The evening was very strange and very still.

The boat had glided within ten yards of the island when Fulk saw Isoult come out of the timber porch and down through a rose and herb garden to the landing-stage. She had thrown off her cloak and her steel cap and hood, and changed swiftly into a woman—a woman in a grey-blue tunic slashed and edged with green. It left her throat and her forearms bare, and was crossed by a girdle of green leather, where it fitted like a sheath about her hips. Her hair was held in a silver net, falling low over the nape of her neck and over her ears.

Fulk stood motionless, the pole trailing in the water and the boat sliding slowly and more slowly towards the bank. He was wondering, mute. The witchery of it all possessed him: the still sun-steeped beauty of this lonely pool, the flaming woods, the woman who stood there looking down at him with mysterious eyes. His tongue had nothing to utter; his manhood seemed mute.

The boat stopped within half a pole's length of the stage, Fulk standing with the pole held slantwise, water dripping from it on to the still surface of the pool.

Isoult laughed, and her soft, mysterious laughter went over the water.

"Lording, will you not set foot on the solid earth?"

Fulk drew in his breath deeply, dropped the end of the pole into the water, and brought the boat to the stage. Half mechanically, he threw out the chain, and Isoult slipped the ring over the mooring post.

"Lording, let me serve!"

She stretched out a hand to help him in his armour, and Fulk paused with one foot on the gunwale, looking at her intently from under the raised vizor of his bassinet.

"Isoult!"

Her eyes seemed to grow full of light, full of a mystery of things unspoken.

"Come; I will unarm you, I will play the page."

He stepped ashore, still holding her hand and looking at her with a kind of wonder. His lips hardly moved when he uttered her name, "Isoult."

A path from the water's edge to the house led up through the garden where herbs and roses grew. Here were marjoram, thyme, rue, lavender, sage, and mint, with low hedges of trimmed box. The rose bushes were the height of a man, and covered with red and white roses, and their scent lay heavy on the still June air. In the midst of the garden was a circle of turf, with a sun-dial set upon an octagonal stone pillar.

Isoult looked at the dial, and smiled.

"Time flies, my friend!"

He answered her:

"Time stands still."

She paused by the dial.

"Time is in ourselves, and the hours are so many beats of the heart. Sit you down here on the grass, and I will help you out of your harness."

He unbuckled his sword and dagger, and sat down with his back to the stone pillar, as though he were turning his back on Time. Isoult knelt and unfastened the laces of his helmet, and when she had unhelmed him she touched his chin with her fingers and laughed.

"How long will it be, lording, how long?"

"I shall have a ruffian's chin."

"And then a fine black peak of a beard that will cock itself in the air and frighten your enemies."

He laughed with her, and she began to unbuckle his harness, and her nearness cast a spell. She seemed part of the sun-glitter on the water, part of the green of the willows, part of the smell of the roses. And there was a mystery in her eyes.

"My lord is hungry, and athirst."

He looked at her as she knelt.

"I am athirst, Isoult, yet will I not touch the cup—for honour's sake."

"Proud and steadfast as ever!"

He reached out and caught her hands.

"Isoult, would you mock me—because— —"

She let herself bend nearer, her face overhanging his.

"Because?"

"I serve one whose pride is as a new-forged sword."

Her eyes flashed at him, and grew full of tremulous, strange light.

"If I desire and am desired, yet can I honour the man who is lord of his own love."

"Isoult— —"

"Dear heart, I know what I know."

She freed her hands, took his sword, drew it out of the scabbard, and touched the blade with her lips.

"Good sword, no shame shall ever come to thee. I—Isoult—swear it."

He took the sword from her, and held it pommel upwards.

"On the Cross I answer to that! Isoult—to the death!"

She bent suddenly and kissed him on the mouth, and, rising, stretched out her arms to the sunset.

"Oh, life—oh, joy! Come, heart of mine, let us be children."

Fulk fastened his belt over his green cote-hardie, and sprang up, his eyes alight.

"What a mate for a man!"

"A mate who can find him supper! Come, gather up your harness or the dew will rust it, and I, your page, shall have the cleaning of it!"

She picked up his helmet, leaving him the rest of the war-gear. The hall, with its dark beams and high timber roof, was filling with shadows. Slants of sunlight came stealthily in at the windows. The rushes on the floor still looked fresh and green.

Fulk laid his sword and armour on the daïs table, while Isoult climbed the stairs ascending to the solar. She passed through the narrow doorway and disappeared.

In a minute or so she was back again with a leather wallet in one hand a lute in the other.

"These good people had sense. There is a bed up yonder, and I found the lute in a press. The wallet is my own."

"Knollys left me wine and sweetmeats!"

"Ah, the fine gentleman! Run, find them. See, here— —"

She showed him a manchet of white bread in the wallet.

"To-morrow you shall fire the oven and I will bake bread. Now, for the kitchen. Where shall we sup—out yonder among the roses?"

"What could be better?"

"Then take a saddle-cloth and spread it on the grass. I will follow."

She came out to him there with a great pewter dish on which were wooden platters, a knife, the manchet of bread, a jar of honey, and two cups of maplewood. Fulk had the wine that Knollys had given him.

"This will serve—for a night."

"Wine and honey and white bread. And yet I have no hunger in me, Isoult."

She smiled in his eyes.

"Go, fetch the lute, while I lay the board."

He went, like a man dreaming, and returned to find her cutting the manchet into slices and spreading them with honey.

"To-morrow you shall see how I can cook. White meat and broth and bread, and wine-cakes and honey-manna! I bid you be hungry, or my hands will be grieved."

They made their meal there, while the sun sank to the horizon, its level rays pouring over the woods and fringing the tree-tops with fire. The red roses glowed with a transparent brilliance, like precious stones. The grassland track between the woods had become a gulf of gloom. The water under the farther bank lay black as ink, but the willows above it were dusted with gold.

Fulk poured wine into the maplewood cups. He watched Isoult drink, her white throat showing.

"A pledge, Isoult, a pledge."

They touched cups, looking into each other's eyes.

"To my dear lady."

"To my dear lord."

Dusk drew on. The west was all gold, the trees black as ebony, the water in the pool still as glass.

Isoult took the lute and touched the strings.

"Sing, my desire, sing!"

"What shall I sing to you?"

"I care not, so that I hear your voice."

So Isoult sang to him—first, an old Breton lay of love and enchantment and old forests and great deeds of arms. The dusk deepened, and she sat mute for a moment, her fingers striking an occasional note from the strings. Her face seemed to grow whiter, her hair more black, and her eyes had a deeper mystery.

Then she began to sing, a song out of her own heart.

"Hear now the wind through the aspens,
And the swallows calling;
And into my heart they come,
The whispering of the aspen leaves
And the sound of the swallows calling,
Listen—listen.
A strange joy steals over.
There is a breath on my lips,
And into my eyes flashes the faith of a sword.
Dear lord, is thy blood as red
As the blood in my heart?
Whither shall we go?
Out into strange lands, into the south,
Under the same stars?
And I will hold thee,
And thy honour as mine.
Listen—listen!
The swallows are calling,
And I hear the great rivers
Running to the sea."

The dusk deepened. They clasped hands, and sat looking into each other's eyes, and at the dark waters of the mere. The glow died out of the west; night came like the dew.

A moon was climbing when they rose and went up through the garden to the house.

"Isoult, I am your watchman to-night."

"I shall sleep and not fear."

Fulk had left flint and steel, tinder, and two torches ready on a bench in the hall. He struck a light, kindled the torches, thrust one into a cresset on the wall, and bore the other.

"My lady goes to her chamber."

He passed up the stairs before her to the solar, thrust the door open, and stood aside for her to enter.

"Sleep, Isoult, and have no fear."

Her eyes looked into his.

"Dear heart, I will pray for you."

He gave her the torch, and she passed in, and Fulk closed the door after her. He brought up a bundle of straw and a dorser from the hall, made himself a bed there, and lay before her door that night, his naked sword beside him.

CHAPTER XXXI

Dawn came and Fulk awoke, to see through the arch of the doorway where the steps went down into the hall, the rays of light striking in through the narrow windows. Everything was very still. He arose noiselessly, and going down into the hall, went out through the great doorway into the garden.

A curtain of mist covered the mere, though the tops of the willows were glimmering in the sunlight. The roses were laden with dew, and the grass about the sun-dial was a carpet of silver grey.

The delight of the dawn stirred in his blood, the still, stealthy freshness of it all, the mystery, the moist perfumes. He went down to the mere's edge, where the water lay black and still under the mist. The lure of the still water drew him. He stripped, hanging his clothes on a willow, and climbing into the stern of the barge, took his plunge thence, and came up in the thick of a ring of ripples.

Isoult had heard Fulk stirring. She dressed, and came out with her hair hanging about her, to find his sword lying beside the bed he had made himself outside her door. She picked it up, and pressed the blade to her lips.

"Keep troth—ever."

She, too, passed out into the garden, and saw the waters of the mere troubled by some strong thing that delighted in its strength. Fulk had circled the island thrice, and a beam of sunlight broke through the mist and shone on his head and shoulders as he came swimming round the willows.

Isoult stood there, holding his sword, her black hair hanging about her like smoke. And as he came near she began to sing.

"Wine and bread and honey sweet;

Sticks for the bakehouse, spits for the meat,

Spices and cakes and cups of gold,

And good ypocrasse to keep out the cold!"

He turned on one flank, and saw her in the thick of the white mist.

"Isoult!"

"My hawk can swim as well as fly! I, too, can swim—perhaps as fast as you, friend Fulk."

"Perhaps faster. How didst sleep?"

"With good dreams. And now I am thinking that my lord will have a hunger."

"As big as my love."

"I must see to it."

She returned to the house, and Fulk climbed out, dried himself by rubbing his limbs and body with his hands, and put on his clothes. He heard Isoult singing.

> "I took my man a cup of wine,
>
> For he is gay, and he is mine,
>
> Sing, birds, sing;
>
> The dawn is in,
>
> With dew upon the heather."

Her voice stirred the deeps in him, and he stood motionless by the water's edge, watching the mist-blurred sun heaving up over the edge of the world.

They were boy and girl together that day, playing at life with laughter holding the hands of love. There was bread to be baked, a fat fowl to be chased and caught in the yard, herbs to be gathered, a fire to be lit under the great brick bake-oven. Fulk carried in faggots and lit a fire, both under the oven and under the black pot that hung on the chain in the cook's chimney. He left Isoult dabbling her hands in flour, and went to water and feed the horses, turning them out afterwards into the orchard where the hoar apple trees wriggled their boughs against the blue. In a loft over the stable he found a couple of bows and a sheaf of arrows, and he took them back with him into the kitchen.

Isoult was putting her bread into the oven, handling the long iron shovel that bakers use.

"Woodman, more faggots. I will teach you to shoot—when I have shown you how to bake."

He laughed, and thrust in more wood.

"I caught you once with a bow, Isoult!"

"Ah! I have not had vengeance for that! I can ride with you, swim with you, shoot with you. Not too high in the stirrups, my friend."

"I will shoot you a match for love."

"The boy with the bow is blind!"

Fulk went across in the boat that afternoon and set up an old smock he had found in the stable, on a stake thrust into the bank. He and Isoult stood by the sun-dial, and shot at the mark in turn. Isoult's first arrow flew over and stuck in the grass. Fulk's struck the stake and broke.

She turned and laughed.

"Now your head is in the air! I will shoot the smock off the stake before you will."

He watched her bend her bow, her face intent, her eyes steady. The bow string sang. He saw the arrow strike the smock and jerk it off the stake as though a hand had snatched it away.

Her dark eyes teased him.

"That was a brave shot."

He laughed with her and for her, his pride of love mounting.

"What a mate for a man! When we go adventuring you shall carry the bow."

Towards evening they put out in the boat, Isoult with her lute, Fulk sitting in the prow and handling the pole. He let the boat drift, giving an occasional thrust with the pole, so that they moved from the willow shadows into the sunlight, and from the sunlight into the shadows. Sometimes Isoult sang, but more often they were silent, knowing that their eyes could say all that their lips could have uttered.

Neither of them saw a grey thing crawling through the long grass towards one of the thickets that touched the very edge of the mere. The crawling figure reached the tangle of hazels and hollies, wriggled through, and, rising on its knees, peered cautiously over the water.

The boat had drifted close to the willows that grew on the farther bank. Fulk was leaning forward over the pole, Isoult touching the strings of the lute. The evening sunlight played upon the water, dappling it with gold between the network of shadows.

Merlin's hand went to the knife at his girdle.

"Fools, have you forgotten me?"

He knelt there among the hazels, biting his nails, black jealousy in his blood.

"I bide my time, Master Fulk; I bide my time."

And that night Fulk again slept across Isoult's door, his naked sword beside him. But no one crossed the water. The moon shone on it, and there was not a ripple.

CHAPTER XXXII

Fulk slept heavily that night, so heavily that when the day had come he did not hear the opening of Isoult's door. Stepping over him as he lay, she stood for a moment, looking down at him and at the naked sword by his side.

"Had it been an enemy, something would have warned thee, Fulk. They would not have caught thee sleeping."

She bent over him dearly, her hair almost brushing against his face.

"Sleep on, dear lad. Were I to kiss thee thou wouldst wake."

She passed down the stairway into the hall, and noiselessly unbarring the door, went out into the garden. It was very early and very still, and, like yesterday, a morning of white mist and stealthy sunlight. The trees, the rose bushes, and the grass were grey with dew, and the willows drooped over water that was smooth as glass.

Isoult was barefooted, her hair hanging about her, and, barefooted, she walked down the path to the grass bank by the willows. The boat lay moored close by, its black timber reflected in the water.

Isoult threw off her blue tunic and hung it on the nearest willow; the white shift followed the blue tunic. She stepped into the boat, and, standing on the seat in the stern, looked down at herself in the water. Her hair hung round her like a black mantle, her shoulders gleaming through. She gathered it up, and fastened it into a net that she had brought with her, and all the white beauty of her body stood displayed, as pure and miraculous a thing as human eyes could look upon. For a minute she stood there, her whiteness mirrored in the water, smiling to herself, and moving her arms with a sinuous and swaying indolence. She knew herself to be part of the enchantment of the hour, part of its secret and innocent wonder. The morning's eyes were grey and soft and misty, and Isoult's eyes were as soft and as mysterious as the eyes of the morning.

But there were other eyes that looked at her over the water—carnal eyes that gloated over her beauty and coveted it. She suspected no peril, thinking herself alone with the mist and the grey willows.

Raising her arms above her head, she stood poised for a moment on the gunwale, and then took her plunge, going in clean as an arrow. Coming up, she turned on her side and struck out for the deep water, swimming with an overhand stroke, one white flank showing now and again.

Fulk awoke just as Isoult gave herself to the water. He sat up, saw the open door, and was on his feet, holding his sword.

"Isoult!"

There was no answer.

He looked into her room, with a lover's shyness, saw the empty bed, and a cloak lying on a stool.

Then he laughed, remembering something she had said to him the night before.

The door of the hall stood open. Fulk left his sword and dagger lying on the daïs table, and went to search for her in the garden, but no one answered when he called. He had reached the dial on its pedestal when he caught sight of the blue tunic and the white shift hanging on the willow tree, and he saw, too, that the mere was troubled, and that ripples were moving, although there was no wind.

Fulk stepped into the boat, and through the mist that still hung thinly over the water saw Isoult swimming in the mere. She had circled the island, and was keeping towards the farther bank, and her face, turned towards him, seemed to float upon the water.

"Isoult."

Her laughter came over the mere.

"What, awake at last, sluggard!"

She lifted a white arm.

"I can ride with you, and shoot with you, and I would match you in the water. There's a challenge!"

His man's laughter, deep and quiet, crossed over to meet hers.

"Perhaps I should be beaten!"

"Faint heart. I dare you to race me."

She reached the shallows on the farther side, and putting up her hands, unfastened the net that held her hair, and as she rose she let her hair fall in black masses, covering her like a veil. The water lay in a grey circle about her waist. She raised her arms and held them out to him, half mockingly.

"Come. Am I to dare you again? If you can catch me—I am yours."

Fulk had bent down and was unfastening his shoes when he heard a rustling in the brushwood on the other side of the mere. Isoult's back was turned towards the farther bank, where the thicket that had hidden Merlin came close to the water's edge. It was not ten paces from where Isoult stood, and as Fulk raised his head he saw two men spring out from among the hazels and dash into the shallows towards Isoult.

He stood up, shouting.

"Swim! swim!"

Fulk saw her throw herself forward and dive like a waterfowl under the water. But her long hair that she had loosened proved her undoing. It floated long enough for one of the fellows to snatch at it and to draw her back.

Then Fulk saw her, struggling, naked, trying to break away from the men who held her.

"Fulk—Fulk!"

For the first time he heard fear in her voice, and his love was like wine poured upon fire.

"Dogs, off—off!"

A scoffing voice answered him across the mere.

"Who catches—holds."

Merlin came out from behind the hazels, and stood watching the men struggling with Isoult. Her hair fell all about her as they half carried and half dragged her up the bank to where Merlin stood. Three more men came out of the thicket. An old cloak was thrown about Isoult, and the men closed round her, hiding her from Fulk's view.

Merlin looked over the water.

"If the stag follows the doe, he shall give up his antlers."

CHAPTER XXXIII

Fulk ran back into the great hall, caught up his sword from the table, but did not tarry to think of shield or helmet.

His rage blew like a north wind, and his face met it, bleak and grim.

"God!"

He saw nothing but Isoult, naked and afraid, struggling in the hands of those two men.

And Merlin! The devil in Fulk was a silent devil, with hard eyes and a cruel mouth.

The group over the water was making away towards the beech woods. Fulk unchained the boat, sprang in, and laying his sword on one of the seats, took the pole and sent the boat surging over. The prow ran well up the bank, and stuck fast among the flags and sedges. He had scarcely set foot on the grass when two men dashed at him out of the thicket.

That sword of his looked a slim thing to tackle a brown bill and stout oak cudgel, but Fulk was as cool as the steel, though a devil's temper raged in him. He was too quick and too fierce for these clumsy slashers. One had the point in his throat, the other was cut to the left ear. Fulk left them lying, and ran on.

Merlin and the rest had reached the beech woods, and a trampled track through the long grass showed the way they had gone. Fulk was not concerned with the possible odds. He was the male robbed of his mate, ready to rush at death, take wounds and not feel them. His sword felt like metal at white heat. It was thirsty. His face was not pleasant to behold, the grim white face of a man whose eyes see blood.

The track through the grass went into the beech wood where the trees stood at a little distance from each other with chequered stretches of brown leaves and short, sweet turf. Fulk glimpsed something ahead down one of the woodland ways. His nostrils expanded; his lips were nothing but a thin, hard line.

He ran on between the great smooth boles of the beeches and under boughs that swept within a bow's length of the ground, his feet making the dead leaves crackle, or going noiselessly over the patches of grass. He could see figures moving ahead of him, a grey shape, pausing ever and again, a white face looking back, a man half hidden by some tree-trunk and handling a bow. Once he heard a half-smothered cry, and something leapt in him, a fury of tenderness that stung him like fire.

A sudden glade opened in the beech wood, and he saw all that he desired to see, someone to be rescued, someone to be spoken to with the sword. They had thrown an old red cloak about Isoult, and two men were holding her, one with a brown fist half hidden in her hair. Three more fellows were waiting like dogs at Merlin's heel—Merlin who had faced about and was pointing towards Fulk with the knife that he had drawn from his girdle.

One man put a horn to his lips and blew a blast that whimpered into the distant woodlands. The others were handling their bows. Fulk gave them no leisure to shoot at him as they pleased. He ran in to give them cold steel.

Two arrows went past him. He saw Merlin leap aside, shouting to his men.

"Kill—kill!"

Fulk had an arrow through his sleeve before he marked out his first man. Maybe he had the mastery of these fellows before a blow was struck, for he came at them like a white-faced devil out of hell, and his eyes were as terrible as his sword. He slashed at one man's bow, and the hand fell with it, the wretch staring stupidly at a bleeding stump. A little fat rascal with a poleaxe had the point under his ribs. A tall, raw-boned horse-thief stabbed at Fulk with a short sword, but not getting home with the blow, had his throat slashed as a judgment. One of the men who guarded Isoult had run forward to join in the tussle, but thought better of it and hung back.

Fulk heard Isoult utter a warning cry.

"Your back—guard your back!"

As he struck the fourth man down he had a vision of Isoult struggling and breaking free. She ran towards him.

"Behind you, behind you!"

Merlin had crept up like a shadow, knife raised. And as Fulk half turned, Isoult ran between them, striking at Merlin's knife with her arm, and was stabbed between the wrist and elbow for her courage.

Fulk swung a hasty blow at Merlin and knocked him flat. But the blade had not bitten. A long, red bruise showed across the friar's forehead. His wits had been rattled like dice in a dice-box.

"Run, run!"

She caught Fulk's wrist, and he saw her arm all red where Merlin's knife had smitten her.

"Let me settle with this damned priest!"

"You are blood mad—run! There are more to come, I tell you. Hear them giving tongue."

True enough, they heard men running through the beech wood, shouting as they ran. Fulk shouldered his sword and gripped Isoult's hand. It was to be a race to the mere; the feet that rustled the dead leaves in the wood came on like a March wind.

"Art faint, Isoult?"

He looked in her eyes as they ran side by side.

"It was nothing—a mere bodkin prick through the flesh."

He lifted her arm and pressed his lips to it, even where the blood reddened it.

"My desire, twice have you given me of your blood."

"Do I grudge it?"

"Not yet have I matched it with mine."

They reached the grassland and saw the mere all silver with the slant of the morning sunlight, and the boat lying by the bank. Fulk fell behind Isoult now that they were in the open, letting her hand go. A glance over the shoulder showed him Merlin's pack in full cry through the beech wood.

"Why are you behind me?"

"Keep your breath—and run."

He was covering her, remembering how that chance arrow had struck her down that night when they had made a dash to escape from Merlin and his Sussex rebels.

They reached the mere. Isoult sprang into the boat, and Fulk followed, throwing his sword into the stern and picking up the pole. He had thrust the boat off as he climbed in.

"Down, Isoult, lie down."

An arrow struck the gunwale and stood quivering there when they were half across the mere. A second hissed into the water close to the boat; another struck the pole and snapped in two.

The boat touched the landing-stage. Fulk dropped the pole and caught Isoult under the shoulders.

"Up; keep behind me."

"I'll not hide behind you."

"Love is a shield."

He half lifted her out of the boat, bent for an instant to throw the ring of the chain over the post and to snatch up his sword.

"Now!"

They made their dash for the house, and reached the porch untouched.

Fulk caught Isoult's face between his hands and kissed her on the lips.

CHAPTER XXXIV

They were breathless, both of them, and exultant, though Death in a grey friar's frock raged to and fro beyond the water. Fulk closed the heavy, nail-studded door of the hall, and, standing on a stool, took a look at the enemy through one of the narrow windows.

There were about twenty men on the farther bank, thorough rapscallions and cut-throats, all of them, whom Guy the Stallion and the Polecat had got together. Merlin was walking up and down like a grey wolf behind the bars of a cage. Fulk saw Guy the Stallion to the front as usual, cocking his red beard fiercely, with that hacked old sword of his over his shoulder.

They seemed undecided and ready to argue among themselves, while Merlin cursed them because they were not savage enough to suit his temper. He kept showing them his right hand, a gesture that puzzled Fulk, and pointing them across the water, but these rats would not or could not swim.

Fulk stepped down from the stool.

"Watch Merlin for me while I play the surgeon."

She took his place on the stool, while Fulk ransacked the solar for clean linen and brought a bowl of water and a cup of wine from the kitchen. He set the bowl of water and the linen on a second stool, and handed Isoult the wine cup.

"Drink, my desire."

"The dogs yonder will not take to the water, though Merlin lashes them with his tongue."

"Have a care. If they see a face they will let fly at the window."

He bathed her wounded forearm as gently as a falconer imps the wing of a hawk. It was a clean stab, and the blood had ceased to ooze; so Fulk left well alone, and pouring in a little sweet oil from a phial he had found in a cupboard, set to bandage the arm with strips of linen.

"Say if I hurt, Isoult."

"Am I a child? And you are very gentle."

She laughed softly.

"I must have my shift and tunic."

"I will bring them in."

"And be shot for your pains!"

"I shall put on my harness. It is stout stuff. They can shoot till they have emptied their quivers."

He knotted the bandage, kissed her fingers.

"Isoult!"

She turned to him, stooping a little, her eyes all a-kindle.

"Six men could not say you nay!"

"Because of one woman!"

"Ah—ah!"

She kissed him, with passion, her eyes half closed.

"Brave heart, I did not call in vain. What care I so long as we are together?"

She drew her hand across his cheek.

"Fetch your harness. I will help you to arm, and I can keep watch."

He brought his armour, bassinet, gorget, breast and back pieces, shoulder-plates, arm guards, gauntlets, cuishes, genouillères, greaves, and solerets. Isoult was as good as any squire. She climbed on the stool every half minute to keep Merlin and his lousels under view.

When she had fastened the laces of his bassinet she asked him, "What will you do now, great captain?"

"Rescue your clothes, dear lady."

"And then?"

"Start a few planks and sink the boat, and bring the horses under cover."

"And then?"

"Bolt all the shutters, barricade the door that leads from the kitchen into the yard."

"And then?"

"Eat."

She laughed.

"We are well victualled; we can stand a siege."

Fulk buckled on his dagger, dropped the vizor of his bassinet, took his shield and sword, and marched out into the garden. Through the grid of his vizor he saw Merlin waving his long arms, and his men handling their bows. Fulk went down to the water's edge as though Merlin and his footpads were not there, and taking Isoult's blue tunic and white shift from the willow tree, laid them over the blade of his sword.

Arrows came with a vengeance, testing his harness. He slung his shield over his back and walked back in leisurely fashion to the house, re-entered the hall, and held out the clothes to Isoult.

She laughed, coloured as she took them, and fled away up the stairs to the solar.

Fulk made a second sally, and keeping to the far side of the island, managed to bring the horses in without being discovered. He found an axe in the wood-lodge, just the tool for starting some of the boat planks, but had he tarried much longer there would have been no boat for him to deal with. A mop head floated within ten yards of it.

The swimmer turned and struck out for the open water, while a scattering of arrows and curses showed the temper of Merlin's men at seeing their fellow balked. Fulk paid no heed. He started two planks with the back of the axe; water welled in and the boat settled slowly, the stern sinking first, the bow remaining level with the surface, being held there by the chain.

The men had given over shooting, and were watching their comrade, who had been swimming to and fro in the open water as though to show them that he was as good as any water-dog. He turned at last to swim in, and, getting on his feet in the shallows, started to wade the last few yards. Fulk was watching him, guessing that this was the only fellow among them who could swim, and thinking that if he had had a bow in his hand he would have cut short this gentleman's possible adventures. He had hardly thought the thought when he saw something strike the wading man between his naked shoulders. The white flight feathers of an arrow showed as the fellow threw up his arms and pitched forward into the shallow water.

Those on the bank jumped down to drag him out, though it was but to save a dead man from drowning! Merlin stood scanning the windows of the manor house, and calling to his gentry to mark them and shoot at anything that showed. And then a second arrow came flying and stuck in Merlin's grey frock.

The barb rasped his skin, nothing more; but it had flown near enough to chasten his courage. He shook his fist at the house, and took cover in the nearest thicket, having the wit to know that Isoult owed him no mercy.

Fulk went in and found her in the loft over the kitchen, where a window overlooked the mere. She was standing well back in the room, an arrow ready on the string, her hair cast back and knotted over her neck.

"What a woman for tempting death!"

He drew her aside to where no arrow flying in at the window could touch her.

"I gave Merlin a fright. And there was the man who swam for the boat, and another after Merlin had jumped into the bushes. That makes two to my own bow."

He held her close, looking down at her from under his raised vizor.

"God, what a mate for a man! But no more playing with death. I'll take a bow and drive these gentry to cover."

CHAPTER XXXV

Fulk went down to bar and barricade the door that opened from the passage leading to the kitchen quarters from the yard. He dragged all the lumber he could find in the kitchen and offices, tables, casks, flour bins, stools, and benches, and piled them in the passage way. All this gear, jammed together behind the door, would give Merlin's men some trouble if they tried to break in on that side. Fulk remembered that he had seen a ladder hanging on brackets under the stable eaves. He went out by the hall door, and with an axe broke the ladder in pieces.

Then he thought of victuals and water. The well was round behind the wood lodge, and Fulk drew several buckets, carried them in, and filled every empty jug and crock that he could find. He caught a couple of fowls, wrung their necks, and hung them in the larder. Nor were faggots forgotten; there was a stack of them behind the house, and Fulk made sure of having fuel for the baking of their bread.

When he climbed the ladder into the loft he found that Isoult had discovered an old hauberk and a rusty helmet with a face guard and had armed herself to mighty good purpose. She was at the window, with an arrow ready on the string.

"I have brought down another bird."

He chided her.

"Heart of mine, can you never leave death alone?"

He dropped his vizor, and, drawing her aside, took her place at the window. Merlin's men were scattered along the further bank, watching for something tangible to shoot at.

Fulk counted them.

"Seventeen trailbastons left. We have settled eight between us this morning."

Even as he spoke, an arrow flew in at the window and stuck in the opposite wall.

"They have marked us down. If we keep to this one window their arrows will fly in like wasps."

They returned to the hall, and Fulk dragged the daïs table against the wall. It was a good length, and made a platform from which he could command two out of the six lancet windows.

"I'll take toll while I can."

He went into the kitchen and came back with a broomstick, a loaf, and an old piece of dark sacking, and sticking the loaf on the end of the broomstick, fastened the cloth to it with a couple of skewers.

"Nothing like a good use of one's wits. Show that at the other windows, and bob it to and fro. I wager it will fool them."

Fulk had laid his arrows ready against the wall, and that battle of the bows began and lasted no more than thirteen minutes. The loaf on the broomstick was slain three times over. Fulk brought down two men and winged another, till Merlin's men lost heart and took cover in the thickets. They had shot off nearly all their arrows, and had no more than six left between them.

Fulk stood there, waiting for a chance shot.

"Seventeen less three leaves fourteen, without counting Master Merlin."

He mused, leaning one shoulder against the wall.

"Can you read me this riddle, Isoult? Who has set these dogs on us?"

She had taken off her helmet, and stood looking up at him.

"Who can tell?"

His face had grown grim, though she could not see it.

"Treachery somewhere! Or was it chance? I would trust Knollys and Cavendish to the death. No; chance has it. Some underling has blabbed on the road and Merlin got wind of it. They have a blood debt against us, Isoult. But for us these scullions might be lording it in London."

He half raised his bow, but dropped it again.

"I thought I had a shot. When night comes the game will begin."

"They will have to cross the water."

"Merlin has wit enough. They will cut down trees and float over. We shall have to hold the house against them."

The day brought no further adventures, and Fulk and Isoult made ready against a probable siege. They fastened the shutters of all the lower windows, and carried a store of food and water up into the solar, Fulk foreseeing that he might have to make his last stand there if Merlin's men broke in. The gentry across the water kept close in the thickets. Fulk saw the smoke of a fire rising and guessed that they would lie hidden till night came.

About sunset they heard the sound of men felling timber in the wood nearest the mere. Fulk and Isoult were supping at the daïs table, and they looked at each other meaningly.

"Axes! Merlin is getting ready."

Dusk fell, and they went to their stations, Isoult taking a window in the short passage leading from the stairs to the solar, Fulk going to the loft window over the kitchen. Over the tree tops he could see streaks of yellow sky banded by purple clouds. A blue gloom seemed to rise in the woods like water and flow out over the valley. Axes were still at work in the wood, but Merlin's men did not show themselves, having come by a wholesome respect for the shooting of the two in the house over the water.

Before long the moon would be up in a clear summer sky, and Fulk guessed that Merlin would seize the darkness between sunset and moonrise to get his timber float dragged down to the water. Sure enough, as the dusk deepened, he saw figures appear on the edge of the wood—dim, busy figures that hacked at the undergrowth and hauled at ropes made of girdles knotted together. It was a long carry to the edge of the wood, and the chances of a hit so vague that Fulk husbanded his arrows and left the men alone.

The darkness increased. Fulk went down into the hall, lit a torch, and set three more ready in the brackets. Then he joined Isoult at her window in the passage leading to the solar.

"We shall have Merlin knocking at the door before midnight."

"Listen!"

They heard an occasional shout, the crackling of brushwood, and then a confused sound as of men labouring to draw some heavy thing over the grass.

"Hurry, moon, hurry."

They waited, standing close together, Isoult's hair touching Fulk's helmet as they watched the eastern sky.

"Look. It is rising."

A faint, silvery radiance showed above the trees, spread, and brightened till the yellow rim of the moon shone like the top of a great dome. They watched it rise, solemn and huge and tawny, making the blackness of the woods seem more black.

Shouts came from the edge of the mere. Isoult gripped Fulk's hands.

"They are there."

Dim shapes were moving over yonder; ropes creaked and strained. They heard men splashing in the shallows where the shadows of the woods still lay upon the water.

Ripples appeared, breaking the still surface of the mere where the moon shone upon it. There was more splashing, and the sound of some heavy thing slithering down the bank.

Fulk took his bow.

"We may get a shot at them as they ferry over."

"See, there—over the willows!"

A rough raft made of young tree-trunks lashed together with withes was moving out into the moonlight. The figures of men were dotted over it, men who paddled with paddles made of oak boughs. All about this clumsy ferry-boat the water broke into gobbets and spurts of silver.

Fulk aimed and let fly, stepping aside for Isoult to take her shot. A shrill yell went up. They heard men cursing. Then the raft moved behind the willows and was screened from view.

Fulk caught Isoult to him.

"Isoult!"

She threw her arms about him.

"Dear heart, I shall go down and make a first fight of it in the hall. Bide here. If they press me too hard I shall take to the stairs."

A sudden solemnity seized them, a sense of peril, and of the nearness of desperate ends. They had laughed while they had shot their arrows across the mere, but now this scum of outlaws and broken men had floated over, and both Fulk and Isoult knew that Merlin would show no mercy.

She pressed her body against his harness.

"Man, man, whatever befalls we face it together."

"They shall come at you only over my body."

"Ah, ah—if death takes you shall I tarry behind? I carry a knife."

"By God, it shall not be so. Stand here with your bow and succour me if the chance offers. I go to light the torches."

He hastened down the stairs, and taking a torch that had half burned itself out, he kindled three other torches that were ready in the brackets. Merlin's men were in the porch. He could hear a scuffling sound like the sound of a pack of dogs sniffing and pawing at a door.

A harsh voice shouted a summons.

"Fulk Ferrers, Fulk Ferrers, the badger is to be drawn out of his earth!"

Fulk rested his two hands on the pommel of his sword.

"I am here, Merlin; but you shall lose your dogs in the hunting."

A discordant laugh answered him.

"What! Are you still on the high horse? Think not, Fulk Ferrers, that the great ones have need of you any longer. Nay, it is otherwise. I have been sent to shrive a mock King and to bury him."

"You lie."

"Tell me, then, what did the King and his Council promise Knollys if he would trap you here? And how is it that I, Merlin, carry the King's ring on my finger?"

"Merlin, you lie."

"Believe what you choose, fool. We are here to make an end."

Fulk's face grew more sharp and grim behind his vizor, for it flashed on him that Merlin's sneers might be near the truth. It was strange, now that he came to think of it, that they should have found the house of the Black Mere empty. It was still more strange that Merlin should have known whither to lead his thieves and cut-throats. And yet it went bitterly against the grain with him to think Knollys guilty of treachery.

Then they struck the first blow upon the door, and the timbers creaked, and the bar strained in its sockets. They were using a tree-trunk as a ram, six men swinging it, while the rest stood ready.

Fulk's blood was up. He thought of Isoult, and his heart grew great and fierce within him. If this pack of wolves had been set on them to make an end—well, by God, he would cheat them and their masters.

He tossed his shield to Isoult, who stood at the head of the stairs, drew his dagger, and took his stand about four paces behind the great door. A second blow had started the planking. A third split the door from top to bottom, though the iron hinge straps held the two halves together. The end of the tree trunk burst through and stood a yard beyond the broken door. The men worked it to and fro till the hinge bolts snapped one by one. The gap widened, showing wild and shadowy faces, the blade of a sword, and a hand holding an axe.

Someone knocked the bar up; the two halves of the door fell apart. Those behind pushed on those in front. A tangle of bodies, heads, arms, and weapons jammed themselves in the doorway.

Fulk seized his chance. The first man in went down with a broken skull. The second stumbled as he swung a blow at Fulk with a poleaxe, and had the dagger in his face. Then the whole pack broke through, and Fulk sprang back, knowing that their numbers would smother him if he let them close.

He covered the stairway leading to the solar, and for the moment Merlin's men held back. A voice cursed them from the porch.

"At him, dogs, drag the fool down."

Guy the Stallion was the first man to leap forward, but death took him before he could strike a blow. Isoult had loosed an arrow at him from the head of the stairs. Its white feathers showed under the red tuft of Guy's beard.

He faltered, and sprawled, his sword flying from his hand. The rest charged over his body. Fulk backed up the stairs like a stag at bay, and paused halfway up to make his stand.

CHAPTER XXXVI

Then began as mad a fight as any fire-eater could have desired.

The stairway was not more than three feet broad; there was no handrail to it, and it went up steeply, yet Merlin's men tried to rush it in a body, only to cumber each other and help the man with the sword. Isoult had passed Fulk his shield, and he held it slantwise before him, and used the sword-point under it, knowing that such thrusts were more deadly than any slashing.

One fellow fell full length, run through the body, and those who were crowded together behind him tried to thrust at Fulk with their pikes or hack at him with axe or sword. There was no room for so many weapons at once, and Fulk's shield was a pent-house that was not to be beaten down. He stabbed at the men from under it, giving swift, fierce thrusts that they could not parry. Two more went down, one rolling over the edge of the stairs; those in front, pressed by Fulk's sword, fell back on those behind, till the crowd upon the stairs lost its foothold and went tumbling down in confusion.

But these footpads, horse-thieves, and deer-stealers were no sheep; their blood was up, and the devil roused in them. The dead men were taken by the heels, and dragged down the stairs out of the way. They hurled stools at Fulk, benches, fire-irons, the halves of the broken door, even crockery, and iron pots that they brought from the kitchen. It was as though all the cooks and scullions in a king's castle had gone mad. Three of them seized the daïs table and dragged it up beside the stairway, and so made a kind of fighting platform to take Fulk in the flank. The first who climbed it had an arrow through his throat, for Isoult was ready with her bow. Fulk stabbed the second as he reached up and tried to seize his ankle. The third fellow jumped down again, and two more dead men were lying amid the pile of wreckage on the stairs.

Merlin's men held back. Two had been slain at the door, three on the stairs; two more were wounded; in all there were but nine of them left standing. They had drawn away to the far end of the hall, where Merlin gnashed his teeth at them and cursed them for cowards.

One of them bethought him of his bow and of the last of the arrows that he had left in the porch. He ran for it, pushed to the front, but was slain by Isoult as he bent his bow. The arrow shot up into the roof of the hall, struck a beam, turned, and dropped back upon the floor.

Fulk glanced anxiously at the torches, for they were burning low. The fools had not thought to put out the lights and to attack in the dark, but Merlin thought of it at that moment.

"Out with the torches."

Then Fulk did a rash thing. He leapt on to the daïs table, and from it to the floor, and charged the men at the end of the hall. They stared at him stupidly, and then, turning like sheep before a sheep-dog, tumbled out of the great doorway with Merlin at their heels.

Fulk had left three spare torches in the solar. He called to Isoult, bidding her throw them down, and as he waited he could hear Merlin cursing his men outside the porch.

"What, eight to one, and no fight left in you!"

They answered sullenly.

"The man is a devil."

"And that harness of his is too good."

"As for the woman—hell take her!—she shoots like Robin of Sherwood."

Fulk kindled fresh torches and set them in the brackets, and, returning to the stairway, climbed over the wreckage and the dead men, and sat down on the topmost step.

"Well fought! well fought!"

She came and knelt behind him, her bow laid ready.

"Those arrows of yours saved us. By Heaven, I am thirsty."

She went into the solar, found a piece of clean linen, and, soaking it in wine, took it to him so that he might quench his thirst.

"They are accursedly quiet out yonder. Merlin is dangerous when he is quiet."

"I would have put an arrow through him, but he kept behind his men."

Silence held, yet it was a silence that was not absolute, but rather a cautious suppression of sound that hinted at movement going on out yonder in the darkness. The two on the stairs strained their ears, knowing well that some fresh mischief was brewing.

Isoult held up a hand.

"Did you hear that?"

"This helmet muffles things."

"It was like the sound of dry sticks breaking."

Fulk started up.

"Faggots! There is a big pile behind the house."

As he stood listening something flew from the porch across the hall, struck one of the torches, and knocked it out of the bracket. It was a cunning hand that had thrown the stick—a hand that had knocked over many a pheasant roosting low down on a tree on a windy night. A second stick brought down the other torch. One flared on the floor; the other went out instantly. Luckily, it was a stone-paved floor, or the house would have been alight. They still had a torch burning outside the doorway of the solar.

Then they heard Merlin's voice. He stood in the porch, just screened by the door-post from one of Isoult's arrows.

"Fulk Ferrers, a word with you and with the woman."

"Stand forward like a man."

Merlin laughed.

"I take no risks, since this business must be ended. Fulk Ferrers, you are dead already. We shall use cunning, my friend; we shall not rush like fools on your sword. Since you must die, I come to speak with you and with Isoult."

"Say your say."

"The doom has gone out against you, Fulk Ferrers, but not against this woman. Let her choose, or choose you for her. Shall she die or live? For if she bides with you, by all the saints, she shall not be spared."

Fulk felt Isoult's hand upon his arm.

"It is my right to answer Merlin. Merlin—you lean cur out of hell, hear me. I bide here, if it be for death; nor shall death be your gift to me."

He did not answer immediately.

"Good, so be it. But before dawn I will ask you the same question. Think well of death, Isoult. Look in his cold eyes, and think of the worms and the clay."

The torch on the floor spluttered and went out, and the great hall sank into sudden darkness, for the closed shutters kept out the moonlight. Fulk knew that Isoult was very close to him.

"Heart of mine, we will face it out together."

"They shall not have thee, Isoult, I swear it. Now that the lights are out we may have these heroes crawling up to take us unawares."

"There are two oak hutches in the solar. We can pile them one on the other, at the top of the stairs."

"Well thought of."

"Hallo, our last torch in there is out."

They had to grope their way into the solar, feel for the oak chests, and carry them out into the gallery. They set one upon the other, jamming them slantwise across the entry at the head of the stairs.

Fulk went to the window of the solar, guided by chinks of light. It had a central mullion, and two shutters, and there was a drop of about fifteen feet to the ground. He opened one of the shutters noiselessly, and looked down over the window ledge. Something black showed below, three or four faggots laid across two casks that had been set on end. He heard two men whispering in this pent-house, where they were safe from arrows shot from above.

Merlin had had this bolt-hole guarded, and Fulk closed the shutter and went back into the gallery, where Isoult kept watch behind the two oak chests.

CHAPTER XXXVII

They brought a settle out from the solar, and setting it against the wall, made ready for a night's vigil. Since the last torch had gone out the place was in utter darkness save for one patch of moonlight at the far end of the hall.

Fulk pulled off his right gauntlet, and felt for Isoult's hand.

"Try to sleep. Why should two keep watch?"

"Then it is you who should sleep."

"By my love, do you think that I could sleep to-night? There will be some devil's work to be baffled."

They sat close together like two children, listening for any sound, for the night had grown strangely silent, and silence told them nothing, save that there was danger near.

An hour passed before Fulk and Isoult heard a sound of stirring in the darkness. Voices spoke in undertones, and there was the crackling of brittle wood. There was movement down yonder in the hall, a kind of groping movement that came nearer and nearer. Fulk stood ready behind the barricade made of chests, thinking that Merlin's men were crawling up the stairway, but it was a subtler attack that they were preparing.

A faggot was thrown down with a crash at the foot of the stairs. They heard men running. More faggots were carried in and piled in a heap that covered the dead men and the wrecked furniture. The darkness hid them at their work, though there was just one patch of moonlight where the doorway of the hall opened, and Fulk could see nothing more than the suggestion of shadows coming and going across this patch of moonlight.

He found Isoult beside him, and her very nearness quickened his consciousness of their danger.

"Are we to be smoked out?"

"Burnt like rats. The house is all timber and thatch."

"What's to be done?"

"Isoult, there is but one thing to be done. Help me to lift this chest aside."

She put her hands to it, and between them they carried it back into the solar.

"Isoult!"

He caught her and held her almost roughly, for the love in him had come to desperate ends.

"Let us fight rather than burn."

"That's the cry. I will give these dogs cold steel in the dark. It is a chance, and nothing more. If I can but clear the hall of them, we can throw faggots across the doorway and hold it. And we can open the shutters and get out of this black pit."

He held her a moment longer.

"Isoult, bide here, but come to me if I call. It will mean that I have won the fight. If I do not call, you will know how things have sped. Unbuckle these greaves and thigh-pieces; they are too heavy for such a game as hide-and-seek."

She knelt down and plucked at the buckles, and her fingers trembled a little.

"Fulk, fight through, fight through."

He touched her hair with his hand.

"There is life for us yet."

Fulk climbed over the oak chest and went step by step down the stairs, stooping with one hand stretched out to feel what lay before him. He had laid aside his gauntlets, and stuck his dagger into its sheath, meaning to trust solely to his sword and to quick wits and quick feet. Six steps from the bottom his hand touched the faggots, and feeling about him cautiously he found that he could step down on to the daïs table. As he crouched there, faggot after faggot was carried in and thrown upon the pile. Moving along the daïs table to the end wall of the hall, he came upon a gap that had been left, and through it he was able to slip to the ground.

Fulk groped his way round by the wall till he came to the wooden screen across the far end of the hall and was able to see the outline of the great doorway filled with pale moonlight. A man appeared in it, carrying a faggot, but he vanished directly he gained the inside of the hall.

Fulk saw his chance and took it. He could not tell how many men were in the hall, but he judged that he would have to deal with no more than two or three at a time, since they were strung out in their coming and going between the woodstack and the door of the hall. Holding his sword pointed ready, he moved along the screen and reached the borderland where darkness and moonlight met just as another figure appeared in the porch with a couple of faggots on its back.

Fulk struck so hard and so swiftly that the man went down without a cry, the faggots falling on top of him. Fulk kept in the shadow as running footsteps came down the hall. A second figure appeared, bending over the fallen man, not grasping what had happened. Fulk laid him beside his comrade, only to be struck in turn by some invisible enemy. A blow on his helmet made his ears ring.

He thrust in the direction from which the blow had come, struck nothing in the darkness, but heard a quick shuffle of footsteps go up the hall. He gave chase, following the footsteps, drawing his dagger as he ran. The footsteps stopped abruptly, and Fulk halted in response, probing the darkness about him with his sword. He thought that he heard the sound of someone breathing close on his left, and he let out a deep thrust towards the sound, and touched something solid.

The unseen gave a snarl of pain. A body blundered against Fulk, staggered, and gripped him with desperate arms. Fulk could not use his sword, and the man who had closed with him crooked one knee round his, and tried to throw him on his back. They swayed and tottered across the hall, Fulk stiffening every muscle and sinew. His dagger cut that tangle. The man made a sobbing sound in his throat; his arms relaxed; Fulk felt him sink away into the darkness. He used his sword again to make sure of the business, and, turning towards the doorway, reached it as two other figures appeared with faggots on their shoulders. The long sword shot out into the moonlight; the first man fell on his face; the other dropped his faggots and ran.

Fulk called to Isoult, and he heard the crackling of wood as she climbed over the faggots, and for a moment he listened anxiously, wondering whether he had left any live thing lurking in the darkness.

"Here—here, by the doorway."

He stepped forward into the moonlight, and she joined him there, her bow in her hand, her arrow ready in her girdle.

"Not hurt?"

"Not a scratch. Stand here with your bow. I will give them something to climb over."

He picked up the fallen faggots and threw them across the doorway, on top of the dead men who lay there. Several more from the stack against the solar stairway made a breastwork four feet high, sufficient to stop a rush.

"Keep in the shadow."

As he spoke he saw her raise her bow and take a snapping shot at something that had showed outside the porch. A man yelped like a dog struck with a stone. Voices muttered together—voices that moved slowly away from the porch.

Fulk and Isoult stood listening.

"I slew four here: three by the door and one in yonder. That leaves but five."

Isoult's eyes never left the panel of light framed by the heap of faggots and the arch of the doorway.

"All the windows are shuttered."

"They may try to fire the house from the outside—thrust a torch into the thatch."

"Let them try it. There is God's air outside for us. Your bow and my sword can tackle five men."

"Listen!"

She touched his arm, and he heard what she had heard—the splashing of water down by the mere.

"Are more coming over?"

"No, no; it is on this side."

There was no doubt as to the sound; it was the noise made by the men's rough paddles striking the water. They had taken to the raft of tree trunks, and were ferrying back across the mere, for the sound went away towards the farther bank.

Fulk dropped his sword, caught Isoult, and held her.

"Isoult, Isoult, death goes over the water."

"Ah—and life comes in!"

A great silence descended over the Black Mere—a silence that was strangely soft and kindly after that half silence that had hidden the stealthy movements of men. For a while they stood listening, hardly believing that they were alone. But the stillness was unbroken; the peril that had threatened them had melted into the night.

Fulk threw the faggots aside and went out into the moonlight. He was cautious at first, half suspecting some trick, and he looked sharply to right and left as he walked down through the garden to the mere. All ripples had died away; the water lay still and untroubled.

Isoult had followed him, and they held hands and looked over the mere.

"What of to-morrow, Isoult, what of to-morrow?"

"I would rather be beyond the sea, where Merlin is not."

"Is Merlin still to be feared?"

"He is a lustful hound who has hunted for many masters. Who knows whom he serves?"

They made their way back to the house, but it seemed full of a horror of darkness and of dead men lying in their blood. Isoult would not enter it.

"That darkness would choke me. I would rather lie out under the moon."

Fulk remembered the horses, and went round to the stables to see if the beasts were safe. The door was still shut as he had left it, and he blessed the good luck that had left them the horses, for they might need them on the morrow.

He found a truss of hay, and, carrying it into the garden, broke the bands, and spread it under an old yew tree about ten paces from the house.

"Lie down and sleep. I will keep watch."

"We will take turns at watching."

"Sleep first, then."

"Promise that you will wake me."

"I promise."

She lay down, being dead weary, and conscious of her weariness now that the stress of their peril had passed. Fulk sat down beside her under the yew, and very soon she was asleep; nor had he the heart to wake her that night, though he could hardly keep his own eyes open. So he watched the night out and the dawn in, listening to Isoult's breathing, and loving her as he listened. The grey half-light grew in the east; the birds woke; a soft wind came out of the west and stirred the willows.

A sudden restlessness seized on Fulk as he looked at Isoult sleeping, and thought of the dead men in yonder. He rose, and went towards the porch, telling himself that he would carry out wine and food, so that the horror of the place should not hurt her.

Dead men and faggots were lying in a tangle by the door. Fulk stepped over them, his nostrils narrowing, his eyes looking at them askance. He threw open several of the shutters, and let daylight into the hall, and it was then that he saw something that made him turn sharply and stand staring at a grey figure that lay in the middle of the hall close to the round hearth.

The grey cowl had slipped back, and a line of grinning teeth and a gaunt, stark chin showed. One arm was half bent and standing up rigidly in the air, the fingers and hand turned over like a shepherd's crook. It was Merlin, the man who had wrestled with Fulk in the dark and been stabbed for his pains.

Fulk went and stood over him, staring. Then he bent nearer, his eyes fixed upon Merlin's upraised hand. It was as though the dead man were holding it up for him to see—Richard's ring, the very ring that Fulk had worn when he had played the King behind the King.

He turned sharply and ran out of the hall, to find Isoult awake and sitting up under the yew. She had unlaced his helmet for him before she had fallen asleep, and Fulk's face was as grim as a cold winter dawn.

"Merlin is in yonder."

"Merlin?"

"Dead. He is one of those whom I slew in the dark. I know now whom he served."

"Ah!"

"He has the King's ring upon his finger."

CHAPTER XXXVIII

Fulk's eyes were cold as a frost, and a great and bitter scorn possessed him. He had kept faith with the King and his lords, and now that they no longer needed him they had gone about to be rid of so dangerous a friend by setting bravos to murder him.

Fulk had a sullen face when they sat down under the yew tree to make their morning meal, nor did Isoult vex him with much talking. Her own scorn was up in arms. She thought of Knollys and Cavendish, and of the way they had brought them down to the Black Mere and left them to be set upon and butchered by ruffians and outlaws in charge of an arch-rebel. And somehow she could not believe it—could not believe that Knollys knew.

"Are you sure it is the King's ring?"

He answered her grimly:

"I wore it on my own finger."

"Yet I could swear that Knollys knows nothing of it."

"You think that? It would be strange if he did not!"

His voice was sharp with scorn.

"Knollys planned the adventure. Knollys brought us here—in secret. Pah! it makes my gorge rise!"

"Have faith in a friend. Might not I be the traitress?"

He flashed a look at her.

"Isoult, if I sneer and am savage, bear with me. This—has hurt—more than wounds."

Instantly she was kneeling before him, her hands on his shoulders.

"I know, I know. Such treachery bites deep. But there are other lands than this, and you and I will seek them."

He caught her and held her fast.

"Dear heart, heal me. We will ride out together, this very morning, and take ship for France. The shipmen will want money, and, by God, I feel minded to turn robber for a day and empty some rich fool's purse. We must have money."

"Sell the horses."

"Then as to the ports. Southampton and the great ones will be watched. The King's doom is on us."

She laughed softly.

"Am I not something of a wanderer, and yet know nothing of the ways? We have no need of ports and shipmen. A fishing-boat will serve. I have money for that."

She showed him where she had ten gold pieces sewn up in her tunic.

"Isoult, you are a wonder of a woman."

Yet his face and eyes looked sad.

"We shall go out like beggars. And it was in my heart to make you a great lady, with a ship to carry us, and 'spears' in our pay."

"Then make me a great lady. Who will be prouder than Isoult when your sword wins that which it deserves? A stout heart is better than a full purse."

He kissed her, and her fresh breath mingled with his, and for a while she lay in his arms, loving him dearly, and the dead men and the King's ring were forgotten.

Then Fulk gave a sudden cry. She looked up and saw his eyes flashing at something over the water.

"Merlin's men?"

"No. A pennon and spears."

She drew away and sprang up, shading her eyes with her hand, the hot colour out of her face.

"It is Knollys! Surely it is Knollys!"

Fulk stood in the shade of the yew.

"Yes, it is Knollys. How many men can you count? Thirty, if there is one. He has come to bury us, perhaps, or to do Merlin's work if Merlin should have failed."

"Fulk, I'll not believe it."

"We shall know the truth soon enough. Stay here."

He took his sword, and, walking down to the water's edge, posted himself there like a sentinel, the point of his sword grounded, his hands resting on the pommel. Knollys and his men came riding down towards the mere, the sunlight flashing on their harness, for the gentry rode armed through the months that followed the rising.

Knollys tossed his spear, but Fulk did not move. He mistrusted all men that morning.

"Hail, hail!"

They reined in on the farther bank, not knowing that dead men had been dragged by the heels into the thickets. But Merlin's raft of tree trunks lay in the shallows and Knollys eyed it and looked puzzled.

They could see Isoult under the yew tree, and Fulk standing in his harness by the water's edge, and looking more like an enemy than a friend. Knollys' face darkened. He spoke sharply to Cavendish, who set his horse beside him.

"Somehow, I smell blood here. And I see no boat."

He looked across at Fulk, who had not moved, but waited there as though ready to fight any man who should seek to land.

Knollys dismounted, and, climbing down the bank, stepped on to Merlin's craft that lay among the flags and sedges. It was solid enough, and the rough paddles were there just as the men had left them, but Knollys stepped ashore again and called Cavendish to him.

"Something has flown askew here. Unbuckle this harness of mine. I am going over on this noble ship and may have to swim for it. The lad over yonder looks as though he were in a white rage and ready to fight all Christendom."

He left his sword and armour with Cavendish, put on his cote-hardie, and, calling two unarmed servants down to the water, bade them take the paddles and ferry him over. It was a slow and a devious passage, the raft doing its best to spin in a circle, for the paddles were clumsy tools. Knollys stood with his feet well apart on the tree-trunks, watching Fulk with increasing curiosity.

"Hold there! Sir Robert Knollys, let those fellows of yours keep their places. I will speak with you—alone."

His hands were on the hilt of his sword, his head held high, his eyes dangerous.

Knollys sprang ashore.

"What game is this that you are playing, my friend?"

"If you had come armed you would not have set foot here. Tell those fellows to keep their places."

"Come, come, lad."

"Knollys, there is a devil in me. Beware! I have looked murder and treachery in the eyes. I trust no man this morning."

"These are strange words."

"Are they, by God! If you would see dead men—come hither."

He turned sharply, and strode off towards the house, Knollys following him with a face that was growing grim. In the porch dead men and faggots were still jumbled together, and the stones were crusted with blood.

Knollys stared.

"Whose men are these?"

"You shall see."

He led him into the hall where Merlin lay, and stood pointing with his sword.

"Dost know that hound, Knollys?"

"No, by my God!"

"Look closer. Whose ring is that—there, on the crooked hand?"

Knollys stooped, and then straightened, as though dumbfounded.

"The King's ring!"

"Even so—the King's ring. And these were the King's men, these footpads and brothel-sweepings led by that damned priest. We fought and beat them, and they tried to burn the house about us. And this grey hound carried the King's ring. Strange happenings, Knollys! Stranger still, who was it that betrayed us?"

Knollys started round with a face like thunder.

"Fulk Ferrers, you speak as though you charged me with this."

"I charge the whole world—till I know the truth. Who brought us here? How was it the place was empty? Who betrayed the secret to Merlin? Who gave Merlin the King's ring?"

Knollys opened his mouth to speak, but no words came. He turned, and began to stamp up and down the hall, glancing at Merlin every time he passed.

"Thunder!"

He wheeled round and faced Fulk.

"By God, lad, such words take some swallowing! And this black treachery! The boy knew! He gave the ring! He has spat upon our honour!"

His eyes were like the eyes of a man leading a charge of horse.

"Shall I, Robert Knollys, have to pledge myself on the Cross? Where is Isoult?"

"Out yonder."

"Bring her in to me. Let her hear."

Fulk went out into the garden and brought her into the hall, where Knollys was pacing up and down. He paused in his stride, swung round, and saw Isoult's bandaged arm.

"Wounded?"

"She turned a knife aside from me, Knollys."

"Isoult, a woman can look into a man's eyes and read his honour. Fulk here looks at me askance, as though I, Robert Knollys, were a false and bloody dog fit to hunt with that dead hound yonder. By the Cross of Christ, I knew nothing of this treachery."

Isoult was ready with her answer.

"I believe it."

But Knollys looked at Fulk.

"Let him speak, for I was his father's comrade in arms."

Something gave way in Fulk's mistrust. The blood rushed to his face; his eyes grew generous. He stood forward, holding out a hand.

"Knollys, God pardon me. I have had a devil in me since I saw the ring on that friar's hand."

"And, by heaven, lad, I too have a devil in me. Richard is at Windsor; I would put this ring in the false boy's nose."

He went to where Merlin lay, and, taking the ring from the dead hand, slipped it on his own little finger.

"Madame Isoult, trust your man to me. I will leave Cavendish and a guard here. They shall clear out these shambles. And to-morrow you shall see our faces again."

She looked Knollys steadily in the eyes.

"Yes, I trust you. But this man of mine has not slept."

Fulk laughed.

"What is a night without a bed to a forester? Knollys, I am with you. Our horses are in the stable."

"You shall take Cavendish's. It will save time, and we can get fresh mounts on the road. I blow like a north wind when my blood is up. Come."

He took Isoult's hand, lifted it to his lips, and then turned towards the door.

"Take her in your arms, lad. A brave woman is worth all the good wine in the world."

CHAPTER XXXIX

It was late in the afternoon when they saw William of Wykeham's tower rising above the trees like a casket of rose-red marble. The track ran near the river, and a long curve of placid water ended in the great castle set upon its hill. It was lush country, and very green, and pleasant to behold, and in some of the meadows men were making hay.

Fulk had donned his helmet before leaving the Black Mere. He had said but little during the ride, and his heart was still bitter in him. He looked at the great round tower rising against the sky, and muttered to himself, "That the King of such a castle should be a liar and a coward!"

The royal banner drifted in the wind, and as they rode up the narrow street a company of men-at-arms clattered down with a knight in green armour at their head. Knollys beckoned him aside; and they drew apart and spoke together while the men-at-arms rode on. And Fulk looked at them longingly; he would not grumble if he had five hundred such fellows at his back.

Knollys rejoined him.

"Richard is out with his hawks, but will be back before nightfall. The Princess is in the castle, and so are Salisbury and Warwick."

They rode up to the gate, and the guard passed them when they saw Knollys' face. In the first court they dismounted, leaving their horses with the grooms. A page came forward. Knollys asked for my Lord of Salisbury, and the lad answered that Salisbury was at chess in the garden with the Princess. Knollys bade him lead on.

He spoke to Fulk as they followed the page.

"Keep your vizor down; say nothing; leave all to me."

They came into the garden, a green space surrounded by a great yew hedge. Two peacocks strutted about, spreading their tails. In the centre was a stone basin in which goldfish swam to and fro. The Princess had set up her chess-table in the shade of a little stone pavilion that was covered with climbing roses, and on a bench sat three of her ladies, two reading together out of a book, the third busy with gold orfrey work. A page stood behind Salisbury's chair. The chessmen were of ivory, white and red, and at Knollys' coming the Princess was conning the board, one hand poised tentatively over her queen.

Knollys and Fulk paused some paces away; Salisbury was bending forward in his chair and frowning a little. The Princess made her move, not having heard the footsteps on the grass.

"Madame, here is Sir Robert Knollys."

She turned slowly, smiling, though her eyes were sad.

"Sir Robert, our very good friend."

Knollys walked forward, but Fulk kept apart.

"Madame, I break your game. I ask you to pardon me. I have ridden twenty miles that you may help me to heal my honour."

"Is a Knollys' honour ever in need of healing?"

"Madame, it has suffered in serving another."

He glanced meaningly at the gentlewomen and at Salisbury's page. The Princess understood.

"Ladies, I would be alone."

They rose, bowed to her, and moved away over the grass. Salisbury spoke to his page.

"Get you gone, child."

He too rose, but Knollys motioned him to remain.

"My lord, your honour is in like case with mine. We need you here with us."

The Princess glanced at Fulk, who stood some ten paces away in the shadow of the yew hedge.

"Who is that man who comes to us in harness—with his vizor down?"

"Madame, you shall hear. Of your courtesy I would ask you to look at this ring."

He gave her the ring that he had taken from Merlin's hand, and she held it in her palm, her eyes growing suddenly troubled.

"It is my son's ring."

She looked steadily at Knollys.

"Sir, I charge you—tell me, has anything evil befallen my son?"

"Madame, my news does not run that way. No harm has come to the King through this ring, save the harm that he has done to his own soul and to my honour. I pray you, let my Lord of Salisbury see it."

She passed it to Salisbury, her pride rising.

"How came you by this ring, Sir Robert?"

"I took it this day from the hand of a dead man—a man who had been sent out to murder, but had been slain by him whom he was to murder."

"What mean you?"

"Madame, I will tell you why my honour is sorely wounded, as is the honour of my Lord Salisbury and all those who counselled the King. Was it not but yesterday that a certain young man saved this kingdom? Did he not keep faith with us, and did not we pledge ourselves to keep faith with him?"

Her eyes darkened as she heard him.

"Sir Robert Knollys, I judge that I am no coward. If some shameful thing has happened, let us have the truth, and that quickly."

"Madame, when the Devil gets to work, the wrath in a man is apt to rage. Need I tell you how Fulk Ferrers and Isoult of the Rose were sent secretly to the Black Mere? The King knew it. Whether another tempted him I cannot say, but a certain Franciscan led some thirty rogues thither. Wit and bold fighting saved Fulk Ferrers. The friar was slain in the fight, and on his finger was the King's ring."

She sat stiffly in her chair, bleak-faced and horror-stricken.

"Is this possible?"

Her eyes wandered towards Fulk, and Knollys understood the look.

"Madame, it is he. Forgive him if he is bitter against his own half-brother."

For some moments the Princess sat rigid, staring at nothing. Then she spoke in a slow, toneless voice.

"Let him draw near."

When Fulk Ferrers looked on the Princess's face a sudden great and chivalrous pity stirred in him. The look in her eyes slew the bitterness in him.

"Fulk Ferrers, let me see your face."

He put his vizor up, and, going on one knee, bent his head to her.

"Madame, it seems that I have brought you evil when I would have brought you good."

Her eyes flashed.

"Look up. Ah, how strange! Should I not hate you, Fulk Ferrers, with all the strength of the woman in me?"

He answered her simply.

"Hate me, Madame, if it eases your heart. For, somehow, you have put all anger out of me."

She looked at him intently.

"Why has God given you what my son has not? Had not his father courage? Am I a coward? Oh, it is bitter!"

She strove with herself, and her face grew beautiful as her calm pride won the day.

"Sir Robert Knollys, and you, my Lord of Salisbury, I swear that no dishonour shall live when I can drive it forth. I will go through with this to the end. Who knows but that out of deep shame honour may rise re-born and valiant?"

She rose from her chair.

"Come with me to the King's chamber to-night. Let Fulk Ferrers be ready without the door. I will see this great wrong righted."

They stood with bowed heads as she left them there in the garden.

CHAPTER XL

The King had supped and was playing at "tables" with one of his gentlemen. The room was hung with blue arras, covered with lions rampant in gold. The sun had long set, and a soft, blue-black sky showed through the open window, with here and there a star showing. Candles burnt in sconces on the walls, and the floor was littered with rushes and sweet herbs.

A page came in, a child with flaxen hair.

"Sire, Madame the Princess would see you. She is in the great gallery, and coming hither."

Richard was not pleased.

"Bid her come, little fool. Sit you still, Falconbridge; we play on."

They were intent on the game when the Princess entered, and Richard did not raise his eyes to see that Knollys and Salisbury were with her. Knollys had closed the door, and they stood gazing at the King.

"Richard!"

There was such a whipping sharpness in her voice that the King looked up startled, and saw Salisbury and Knollys. Nor did their grim faces please him.

"Ah, my Lord of Salisbury!"

"Falconbridge, leave us."

"Madame—mother, the game is not done."

She stepped forward, swept the pieces off the board, her face like stone. Falconbridge rose incontinently and went out, pushing past Fulk, who was standing in the passage.

"What means all this?"

"Son, there are words to be spoken between us, words that I for one would gladly not hear."

He looked at her uneasily.

"What spoil-sport business is this?"

She stretched out a closed hand, and, opening her fingers suddenly, showed the ring lying in her palm.

"Richard, this was lost to you. Take back your own."

They were watching him, and they saw his lower lip loosen, his eyes grow shallow with a kind of fear.

"That ring of mine! I had mislaid it."

He was lying, and his flaccid face betrayed him.

"Mislaid! That is a word to use! Mislaid! Soul of my God, it is your honour that you have mislaid!"

He tried to bluster.

"What foolery is this? I lose a ring, and strange words come back with it."

"Tell me, son, how did you lose the ring to the grey friar? How came it that a certain man was betrayed? How was it that your ring wrought murder?"

He was white to the lips now.

"It is false."

She saw him shrink and falter, and a bitter, scornful cry escaped from her.

"Son, son, you shame me to the death; but by the fear of God that is in me I will bring you down into the dust. For out of the dust you must rise. Let Fulk Ferrers come to us."

Knollys went to the door, and Richard's eyes followed him—eyes that seemed to expect a ghost. He saw Fulk enter—Fulk the young man in his own likeness, bareheaded, calm, with a steadfast look about his eyes. And he sat back in his chair, shrinking, moistening his lips.

"Son, behold your brother! He is alive, not dead. Give God thanks for it."

A moment's silence prevailed. It was as though no words were great enough to sound the deeps of that silence.

Then Fulk was inspired. He crossed the room and stood before Richard's chair.

"Brother, why should hate live between us? Let us take hands and swear comradeship. Then I will go and trouble you and this land no longer."

Richard rose slowly, falteringly, his eyes on Fulk's. The other's manhood seemed to flow into him. His lips grew firmer, his bearing more steady.

"Brother!"

He bowed his head suddenly, caught at Fulk's hands, and burst into tears.

Again there was silence, save for the sound of his weeping. They let him weep. Presently he raised his head, and his face had a new nobility.

"I, Richard of England, stand here in my shame. Mother, look on me with pity."

"Son, there is a new heart in you."

His wet eyes flashed.

"Fulk Ferrers, God forgive me my littleness and my coward thoughts. And of you, Sir Robert Knollys, and of you, my Lord of Salisbury, I ask pardon. Tell me, sirs, what can be done?"

Knollys drew his sword out of its scabbard.

"Knighthood helps in the wars."

Richard looked questioningly at Fulk.

"Will you take it at my hands?"

"They are a King's hands."

"Then kneel, brother, kneel."

Fulk knelt, and Knollys' sword served to give the stroke on the shoulder.

"Rise, Sir Fulk Ferrers. If thou art minded to leave this English land, by this shame of mine, thou shalt go as the son of a prince should go."

"Let him have men and money, sir."

Fulk rose, and Richard gave him Knollys' sword.

"Keep it, brother. Knollys shall be recompensed. And I am thinking that thou art leaving something of thyself behind with me. My Lord of Salisbury, let all things be done nobly. It is the King's will."

CHAPTER XLI

They rode back to the Black Mere next morning, and a buxom old gentleman on a white palfrey rode with them, even Father Hilarius, whom Knollys had chartered and sworn to secrecy and discretion. Father Hilarius was a merry soul. He cracked jests by the way, and the sly good humour oozed out of him like honey out of a broken comb. Nothing pleased him better than a marriage. He liked the cup of wine at the end of it, and the sententious benignity of his own words concerning love and the begetting of children.

Fulk took the quips in good part. Father Hilarius's wit blew like a blithe west wind; it harmed nobody on a hot day in summer.

At the Black Mere they had refloated the barge, buried the dead in defiance of all crowners, and cleansed the hall. Some lover-sense had made blunt Cavendish order the place to be strewn with fresh herbs and flowers, and Isoult had smiled when she had seen these men of the sword at their labours.

So Fulk, Knollys, and Father Hilarius were ferried over, and Isoult met them at the water's edge. She was a splendour that morning, and the shine of her lit a light in men's eyes.

Knollys was a little boisterous and exultant.

"Madame Isoult, we have brought back knighthood and a shipload of fine plunder, not to speak of that very great saint and cenobite, Father Hilarius."

Father Hilarius bobbed and looked sly.

"Daughter, I am the most timid of men. Sir Robert here is a terrible fellow! I was his chaplain in France. Ahem! I will say no more."

They left Fulk and Isoult together, and that togetherness of theirs ended in the orchard, where Knollys, Cavendish, and Father Hilarius set the seal to a great adventure. The priest smacked his lips over it, and was ready to wink at a man who was married with his head in an iron pot.

Knollys made a feast for them in the hall, and when they had feasted Isoult brought her lute and sang them songs. And Father Hilarius extended his toes in an ecstasy, and drank more wine.

"Surely never was such a voice heard in heaven! My son, you will grow into an angel."

Knollys chuckled.

"A devil of an angel with a coal-black beard! Isoult, would it please you to be married to an angel?"

She laughed and looked at Fulk.

"I would sooner have the man."

Which saying Father Hilarius took to be a most excellent and subtle jest, for he spread himself and exulted.